WITHOUT MERCY

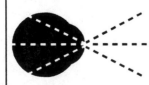

This Large Print Book carries the
Seal of Approval of N.A.V.H.

A "WHERE ARE THEY NOW?" MYSTERY

WITHOUT MERCY

TONI L. P. KELNER

WHEELER PUBLISHING
A part of Gale, Cengage Learning

GALE
CENGAGE Learning

Detroit • New York • San Francisco • New Haven, Conn • Waterville, Maine • London

GALE
CENGAGE Learning

Copyright © 2008 by Toni L. P. Kelner.
Wheeler Publishing, a part of Gale, Cengage Learning.

ALL RIGHTS RESERVED

Wheeler Publishing Large Print Softcover.
The text of this Large Print edition is unabridged.
Other aspects of the book may vary from the original edition.
Set in 16 pt. Plantin.
Printed on permanent paper.

LIBRARY OF CONGRESS CATALOGING-IN-PUBLICATION DATA

Kelner, Toni L. P.
    Without mercy : a "where are they now?" mystery / by Toni L.P. Kelner.
      p. cm.
    ISBN-13: 978-1-59722-847-3 (softcover : alk. paper)
    ISBN-10: 1-59722-847-8 (softcover : alk. paper)
    1. Reporters and reporting—Fiction. 2. Television comedies—Fiction. 3. Murder—Fiction. 4. Large type books.
I. Title.
PS3561.E39734W58 2008b

                                          2008035507

Published in 2008 by arrangement with Tekno Books and Ed Gorman.

Printed in the United States of America
1 2 3 4 5 6 7 12 11 10 09 08

To two incredibly generous writers,
who never gave up on me:
Dana Cameron
Charlaine Harris

ACKNOWLEDGMENTS

I want to thank:

Joan Brandt, my most patient agent, who always goes above and beyond the call of duty.

Christian F. Cooper for his colorful descriptions of the life behind magazine covers.

Judy Copek for explaining what a real computer maven can do.

The marvelous folks from DorothyL and the Mystery Writers of America for prompt, detailed answers to my random questions, from funerals on Sundays to lag times for autopsies.

Margery Flax, for her insider's knowledge of Manhattan.

Judith W. Kelner for dressing my characters so much better than I could have.

Joni Langevoort, who donated actual money to charity so I would name a character for her charming and talented daughter. (Clearly, Joni's daughter takes after her.)

Sally Powers, for her insight into casting and how the entertainment industry works.

My daughters, Maggie and Valerie, who put up with it all, and give me hugs too.

My husband, Stephen P. Kelner Jr., for applying encouragement and editing whenever needed. Which was often.

CHAPTER 1

"More than any other sitcom of the late seventies, *Kissing Cousins* polarizes those who remember it. Just as music fans categorize themselves by their favorite Beatle, television viewers of a certain age reveal much about themselves by their favorite Cousin."

—"Curse of the *Kissing Cousins*" by Tilda Harper, *Entertain Me!*

"Starsky or Hutch?" Cooper asked. "The TV show, not the movie."

"Starsky," Shannon said. "I loved that sweater he wore."

"Not the car?"

"Oh, absolutely the car. I wanted a car like that so bad — I was dying to lose my virginity in that car — but my parents wouldn't buy me one. Then I found out about a guy at my school who painted his Torino just like Starsky's, and I thought I had it made."

"And? Did you go out with him?" Cooper prompted.

She wrinkled her nose. "No. It turned out he looked like Huggy Bear."

"Ouch." Cooper turned back to his computer screen. "Jon or Ponch from *CHiPs?*"

"Ponch," Shannon said decisively. "Never could resist the tan or the teeth." Shannon's own teeth and tan were nothing to sneer at, and owed just as much to nature as the average actor's.

Cooper entered the answer. "Roy DeSoto or John Gage?"

"Who?"

"The guys on *Emergency!*"

"Oh, yeah." Shannon thought for a minute. "Can I pick that dark-haired doctor at the hospital instead? He was hot."

"Sorry, he's not on the list. DeSoto or Gage."

"Gage."

"Peter or Greg Brady?"

"Peter," Shannon said decisively.

"No way! Greg was the cute one," objected Nicole, who was waiting to play guinea pig for the pop psychology quiz Cooper was vetting for the next issue of *Entertain Me!*

"Peter was cuter," Shannon insisted.

"I liked Bobby," Cooper said dreamily.

"You pervert!" Shannon said. "Bobby was a baby."

"Not in the revival series," he said. "You remember, when he became a race car driver? He was a cuddly bear then. Then he wrecked and ended up in a wheelchair. I like a man who's vulnerable."

"You mean you like a man who can't run away," Nicole quipped.

"Bitch," he replied cheerfully. "Okay, David Cassidy or Shaun Cassidy?"

"Please! David, of course."

"Brad or Damon?" Tilda put in. Up until then, she'd just been listening to the conversation as she went over her notes for the phone interview she had scheduled for that afternoon.

"From *Kissing Cousins*?" Cooper asked.

Tilda nodded. "Brad was the jock, and Damon was the freak."

"Brad," Shannon replied, just as Nicole answered, "Damon." Then the two women looked at each other and said, "Ewwww!"

"What about you?" Cooper asked Tilda.

Cooper was a good enough friend to know that Tilda would have despised Brad, so she considered picking the clean-cut jock just to throw him. Instead she answered honestly. "Mercy."

"Since when did you swing that way?" Nicole asked.

"I didn't want to bed her," Tilda said. "I just liked her." And wanted to be like her, she thought, a fact she had no inclination to share with Nicole.

"But Mercy was so strange," Shannon said. "Nobody I know liked Mercy. We all liked Sherri."

Tilda refrained from pointing out that blonde, buxom Shannon could have been Sherri, the perky cheerleader without enough synapses to snap. Instead she said, "These days, Mercy is the popular one, especially among Goths."

"Goths," Nicole said, rolling her eyes. "They were in style for what, ten minutes?"

Tilda gave Nicole the same look she'd given the hairdresser at Supercuts who suggested that she bleach her hair blonde. She'd been more than a little Goth herself a couple of years ago, and Nicole knew it.

The office's front door slammed open, and when they heard the raised voices in the lobby, Cooper, Shannon, and Nicole quickly posed themselves as busy worker-bees. Tilda didn't bother — what was the point of being a freelancer if not to avoid that kind of playacting?

As it turned out, the staff members could

have been demonstrating the lambada for all the attention they got. When Jillian and Bryce, respectively editor in chief and managing editor of *Entertain Me!* stormed in, the only thing on their minds was continuing their discussion.

"Fuck you!" Jillian said.

"No, fuck you!" Bryce replied.

"No, fuck you!"

"No, fuck you!"

Tilda would have noted the irony of such an argument between two people who were supposedly devoted to publishing clever articles and essays, but she suspected that ironic detachment was no longer in style. She'd have to check with Nicole.

Jillian stomped to her desk as loudly as she could in stiletto heels, and threw her Versace purse onto her desk. Then she glared across the room as Bryce slid into the chair behind his own desk. Tilda had once wondered why Jillian and Bryce didn't have private offices, but she'd eventually decided that they preferred being able to watch each other in order to gather ammunition for their "discussions." So they'd placed their desks facing each other across the long, narrow room. Windows lined one side of the room, and framed covers from past issues of *Entertain Me!* hung on the other.

Jillian and Bryce also liked to keep a close eye on their employees. There were two lines of four desks each arranged between the editors. Three belonged to the furiously typing copy editor, Cooper, and staff editors, Shannon and Nicole. Of the other desks, two belonged to the production editor and the art director, who were never there because they were downstairs getting their hands dirty, and one belonged to the ad manager, who was never there because he was scratching up business. The one where Tilda was sitting was a spare, left open for her and other freelancers as needed.

"Bryce, you are such an asshole," Jillian said.

"Go fuck yourself!" he replied.

"You'd pay to see that, wouldn't you?"

"Hell, no — I'd pay to not have to see it."

"Fuck you!"

"No, fuck you."

Bryce's phone rang, and he picked it up with a smirk for having gotten in the last riposte. The long-standing rule was that their discussions ended once the phone rang.

Jillian, steamed by Bryce's temporary reprieve, looked around for somebody else to scream at. "What are you doing here?" she asked Tilda.

"Phone interview with Billy Clift," Tilda answered.

"Who?"

"Elizabeth Montgomery's hairdresser."

"Right, the witch piece."

Tilda's work-in-progress, "TV Witches: Good, Bad, and Hot!", was slated for the Halloween issue of *Entertain Me!* She could have made the long-distance call from home and billed the magazine for the charges, but it was easier on their paperwork and her cash flow to call from the office. "I've already got quotes from Melissa Joan Hart from *Sabrina, the Teenage Witch,* three witches from *Charmed,* and Alyson Hannigan from *Buffy the Vampire Slayer.*"

Nicole, feigning innocence, said, "You're not just doing old shows again, are you?"

"No," Tilda said as patiently as she could manage. Jillian had already approved the story and the list of shows she'd be including, but it wouldn't have been the first time Nicole had tried to change Jillian's mind. "I also interviewed some people from Alan Ball's new HBO series." Strictly speaking, the protagonist was a telepath, not a witch, but she figured Nicole wouldn't know that.

"So that's four old shows, and only one

current one?"

"All four of those shows are still going strong in syndication and the DVDs sell like hotcakes," Tilda said.

Nicole shrugged, as if wondering why they were wasting space on "old shows." Tilda knew that the redhead was really wondering why they were wasting space on Tilda's prose, when Nicole herself wanted every byline she could wrangle.

"*Bewitched* is a classic, *Buffy* and *Charmed* are still hot, and kids like *Sabrina,*" Jillian said, which settled the question. She was the final arbiter of what was in and what was out — even Bryce deferred to her opinions in that realm. Nicole went back to what she'd been doing with a pinched look on her face.

Tilda checked her Jack Skellington watch. She had five more minutes before it was time to call Billy Clift, and she wondered if Nicole was going to make any more attempts to spike her story, or even to take it from her. Then she too was saved by the bell as her cell phone trilled the opening bars of the theme from *The Addams Family,* and she picked it up.

"Tilda," she said.

"Tilda, it's Vincent," a choked-up voice said. "Have you heard?"

"Heard about what?"

"It's Sherri. She's dead!"

CHAPTER 2

"fan n. An ardent devotee; an enthusiast. [Short for fanatic.]"
— *The American Heritage Dictionary of the English Language: Fourth Edition*

"Sherri who?" Tilda asked.

Vincent made a sound of disbelief. "Sherri from *Kissing Cousins*! I mean the actress who played Sherri. Holly Kendricks. She's dead, just like Brad and Damon. I mean the actors who played them." He paused, trying to sort out the actors from the roles they had played, a task some fans never did master. "Anyway, Sherri — Holly's been murdered."

"Murdered? Are you shitting me?" Tilda realized the others in the *Entertain Me!* office had stopped pretending to work so they could listen in.

"It's true! I just got IM'ed from someone I know who lives in Connecticut, one town

18

over from Sherri's. He said she was just found dead. You know what this means, don't you? Mercy is next!"

"You've lost me."

"It's just like you said in your article, the Cousins are cursed."

"I said no such thing, and there's no such thing as curses."

"No, but there is such a thing as a serial killer, and this one is going in order. Brad was the oldest, then Damon, Sherri, Mercy, Elbert, and Felicia. The first three are already dead, so Mercy has to be next. You've got to find her, Tilda, you've got to find her and warn her!"

Tilda looked at her watch again. She had to make the call to Elizabeth Montgomery's hairdresser soon, or miss her chance. Vincent, on the other hand, would be in a turmoil for days, so she'd have plenty of other chances with him. "Vincent, I know you're upset, but I can't talk right now."

"Wait, I've figured out the pattern. There were two months between Brad's and Damon's deaths, and one between Damon's and Sherri's. That means there's only two weeks before Mercy dies. You can't afford to wait!"

Tilda didn't know where to begin, so she didn't even try. "I'll e-mail you later, okay?

I've got to go."

"But Tilda . . ."

"Damn it, I'm losing your signal. Gotta go!" She disconnected.

Nicole had materialized next to her. "Is there something wrong, Tilda? Do you need me to handle your interview?"

"No, it's fine," Tilda said pleasantly, and started dialing the hairdresser's phone number.

"But I heard you say somebody you know was murdered."

"It wasn't somebody I know," Tilda said, "it was an actress from —" She saw the hungry look on Nicole's face and stopped. If Sherri really was dead, she damned well wasn't going to let Nicole get the story out from under her. "I've got to make this call," she said, turning away to finish dialing. She wondered if Nicole was going to stay there, eavesdropping through the whole interview, but those Manolo Blahnik shoes must have been as uncomfortable as they looked, because Nicole went back to her own desk.

Tilda got focused and spent nearly an hour talking with the hairdresser, who really did have some great trivia about working with Elizabeth Montgomery while she starred in *Bewitched,* even if she did have to wade through the wonders of meditation and rebirthing to get to it. Not to mention having to make sure she knew which quotations came from before the actress's death and which ones came after.

Once Clift had hung up, Tilda kept her headset in place to keep Nicole from pouncing. She'd been using her laptop to take notes, so it was easy enough to go online see if anything about Sherri had hit the Web. There was nothing she could find. Then she checked e-mail, receiving the expected cascade of messages from Vincent, each detailing more and more about the investigation. She had no idea how he'd tracked down the information so quickly — the man had contacts in the strangest places, and played the Web like Jimi Hendrix played the guitar. Though she didn't know the whole story, thanks to Vincent she had enough information to pitch an article. The trick would be making sure her byline was on the piece, and not Nicole's.

Tilda hung onto the phone until she saw that Jillian was momentarily unoccupied, then quickly got up to talk to her.

"Jillian, I might have a story for you."

"Impress me," Jillian said.

"You remember that piece you ran a couple of weeks ago about *Kissing Cousins* and how two of the cast members had recently died?"

"You mean 'Curse of the *Kissing Cousins*'? We got a lot of reader response on that one. Great title. Really grabbed people's attention."

The title had been Jillian's idea — Tilda hated it. She'd written about how teen actors had a hard time making it in the real world, but that title had made it sound as if King Tut's mummy was taking out the cast members, one by one. Then again, King Tut's mummy might figure into Vincent's next theory.

"One of the other cast members was found dead today," Tilda said. "Murdered, apparently. I thought I could do a down-and-dirty for the next issue, and then something more in-depth for later this month, following up on the original story."

Suddenly Nicole was there at her elbow. Tilda was less than surprised.

"Obits are done in-house," Nicole said, which meant that she herself wrote them, and if she stretched it out enough and dug up some decent art, sometimes she could talk Jillian into giving her a byline for a by-the-numbers career wrap-up. Tilda pictured Nicole's future tombstone with date of birth, date of death, and number of bylines.

"Obits, yes, but this is more of a news

piece," Tilda said.

"We're a magazine, not a newspaper," Nicole countered.

"I wrote the original story."

"Oh, yes, I remember that piece." Nicole couldn't say anything against the article since Jillian had just talked it up, but she could sneer as long as Jillian wasn't watching. Jillian wasn't watching.

Instead the editor was looking at the latest version of the table of contents for the next issue. Though feature articles were planned well in advance, a weekly like *Entertain Me!* had to allow leeway for late-breaking celebrity news. She made a notation on the page with her red pen, and announced, "Nicole, you do the obit. Tilda, you can have the in-depth, as long as you still get me the witch piece on time."

"No sweat." With studied casualness, Tilda added, "Maybe I'll be able to track down that last cast member. You remember? The one I couldn't find for the last article?"

"Sure, whatever."

Tilda was more than willing to take that as permission. "What about my deadline? I was thinking a month."

"Two weeks."

"That won't give me enough time for much more than a rehash of the last piece."

Jillian eyed her. "Three weeks, and it's your job to make sure it doesn't read like a rehash."

"Expenses?"

"Reasonable expenses, sure. Don't go crazy."

"It'll be like buying designer at Filene's Basement."

"Make it Target."

"Done," Tilda said, but Jillian had already moved on to something else. By the time she herself turned around, Nicole was already sitting where she'd been working, peering at the screen of her laptop. Fortunately Tilda had shut down before she went to see Jillian.

"What have you got on this death?" Nicole asked.

"Just that she was found dead," Tilda lied blandly. "I couldn't get any details because I had to do that interview."

"Where did she live? Where was the body found?"

Tilda just shrugged her shoulders. If Nicole wanted the story, she could damn well track down the nitty-gritty for herself.

"Then give me your friend's name. What's his connection to the dead woman?"

"Oh, he doesn't have any connection. He's just a fan who heard an Internet rumor.

Gosh, I hope it's true. I'd hate for you to waste time on it if it's not."

Nicole's eyes narrowed. "What was the actress's name?"

"Her character's name was Sherri. The actress's name?" Tilda tapped her chin with one finger in a purposely unconvincing act. "Gee, it's on the tip of my tongue. . . . Tell you what. It's in the article I did, so you can find it in the archives. Or check IMDb .com."

Nicole grimaced — she was notorious for hating to do her own basic research. "Don't you have a copy of the article on your hard disk?"

"Sorry. I always offload the files for finished projects." It wasn't true, but it was true that Nicole could find the article herself in about two minutes in the online archives. The woman was lazy, and it wouldn't be supportive to enable her. Tilda reached around Nicole to pack her laptop and papers into the black messenger bag that served as a combination pocketbook and briefcase. Nicole glared at her for a minute, then went back to her own desk and started pounding away at her keyboard.

To the room at large Tilda announced, "Later!" and headed for the door. Cooper, who disliked Nicole almost as much as Tilda did, looked up from the story he was proofing long enough to give her a discreet thumbs up.

Tilda smiled back. Not only did she have a new assignment, but she had another chance to track down her all-time favorite TV actress. This time, she wasn't going to hand in her article without Mercy.

CHAPTER 3

"Episode 5: Felicia's Bureau of Investigation
Felicia joins the Junior FBI and starts spying on the family, looking for subversive elements. The tables are turned when Elbert discovers her dossiers, prepares a similar report on her, and threatens to send it to Junior FBI Headquarters. Pops then explains to her the importance of respecting others' privacy."
— Fanboy's Online *Kissing Cousins* Episode Guide, by Vincent Peters

When Tilda stepped out onto the busy sidewalk, she was willing to admit to herself that the Boston weather was decent for a change. Sunny and bright, with a light breeze and low humidity. She'd have to remember to mark it on the calendar when she got home. She had a bet going with a friend in Albany that the weather was worse in Boston than it was there, and she was honor-bound to track those few occasions when it wasn't raining, snowing, overly hot, sticky, foggy, or some combination of the above.

She hated having to go down into the depths of the Hynes / ICA T Station to catch the subway, but she hadn't wanted to risk driving into town. Jillian insisted that *Entertain Me!* needed the prestige of a Newbury Street address. So what if there was no nearby parking to be had for love or money, and so what if Tilda was regularly short on both?

At least rush hour wasn't in full swing yet, which meant that she got a seat so she could relax while she started thinking about how to find Mercy.

Tilda had written several articles about *Kissing Cousins,* including one of her signature "Where Are They Now?" pieces for *Entertain Me!* Despite the puerile title, "Curse of the *Kissing Cousins,*" she'd been happy with the story in all respects but one: she hadn't been able to find the actress who'd played Mercy. Despite putting in extra hours and pushing her deadline until it squealed, she'd gotten nowhere. While the failure hadn't exactly haunted her, it had certainly irritated her. After all, she'd located Peter Brady's first girlfriend, the man who whistled the theme song to *The Andy Griffith Show,* and three seasons' worth of Captain James T. Kirk's bed partners. Why was it so hard to find an obscure actress from an obscure seventies TV show?

It wasn't as though *Kissing Cousins* had been a big hit, or even all that good a show. It had started out with a contrived setup right out of Sitcoms 101 — a crotchety grandfather with a heart of gold raising his two daughters' six children. The "normal" kids — Brad the jock, Sherri the cheerleader, and a Goody Two-shoes named Felicia — had lost their mother, and their father was off bravely serving his country in some never-named foreign land. The mother of the weirdoes — a vaguely drugged-out biker named Damon, Mercy the proto-Goth, and science geek Elbert — was a divorcée who'd abandoned her children while she went to find herself.

From her own interviews with Irv Munch, the show's creator and executive producer, Tilda knew that the original plan had been for the straight kids to gradually lead the weirdos away from the Dark Side of the Force, while everybody gained heartwarmingly sincere appreciation for one another's personalities and talents. Fortunately for the viewers, it was soon realized that the original concept provided as many yucks as herpes jokes. Instead, the show evolved into a kind of family feud, with each week bringing a new conflict between the sets of Cousins while the oblivious grandfather dispensed hokey wisdom and morals.

Kissing Cousins never developed much of a following — what success it had was because it came on right before *The Love Boat.* When the schedule changed, the show's audience quickly dwindled. Despite a last-ditch effort to up the cuteness quotient by adding two more Cousins, a set of twins whose parentage was never adequately established, the show died after the third season. Without syndication, it would have been completely forgotten, but these days it was shown on enough stations that a new generation had discovered the show and a cult of fans had developed.

Thanks to years of practice, Tilda noted that the trolley had arrived at Park Street even though she was deep in thought. She got off, wishing the smell of Dunkin' Donuts coffee wasn't overwhelmed by the odor of unwashed winos, and walked down the tunnel to Downtown Crossing so she could switch to the Orange Line train to Malden. Rush hour was starting to heat up, but she managed to slide into a seat just in front of a man dressed in Brooks Brothers from head to toe, and when he glared at her, gave him the blank stare that tended to make people nervous. He moved off, leaving her to concentrate again on *Kissing Cousins.*

Tilda, who was born during the show's original run, was one of that second generation of fans, but had made up for tardiness with enthusiasm. It wasn't the show's plots she'd loved — it had been the radical nonconformist Mercy, Tilda's first and most ardent star crush. She'd idolized the woman, or at least the character, and had done her best to emulate Mercy's bizarre combination of serenity and rebelliousness, standing in front of the bathroom mirror for hours trying to reproduce the actress's crooked Mona Lisa smile.

Though Tilda dreamed of dressing like Mercy, in the black lacy skirts and blouses that were so different from the Day-Glo colors of most teens on TV, her mother wouldn't allow it. It wasn't until Tilda went to college that she got the chance to indulge herself, wearing relentless black day and night for most of those four years.

Looking at her reflection in the subway car's window, she was reminded that she still wore a lot of black, but even her mother

31

had to admit that it suited the Black Irish coloring she'd inherited from her father. His hair had gone gray, while Tilda's was still jet black, but they had the same fair skin and startlingly blue eyes.

The train pulled into Malden Center, the penultimate stop on the T's Orange Line, and Tilda swiftly squeezed out and got to the escalator and out of the station ahead of most of the crowd. Dunkin' Donuts' coffee was still calling to her, so she took a side trip to the store across the street from the station and picked up a large black and a corn muffin for the next morning's breakfast. Or, more likely, that night's midnight snack. She could have picked up two, to cover both occasions, but not with her latest roommate. Heather ate Tilda's supplies continually, despite their carefully negotiated agreement, but at least she was polite enough never to take the last of anything. If Tilda brought home two muffins, one would be gone by dinner time. If she brought home only one, it would still be there when she wanted it.

The apartment Tilda shared with Heather was just half a block from the subway station — in fact, the location was the only thing the place had going for it. As she trudged up the two flights of stairs, Tilda

32

reminded herself that it was cheap. Someday she hoped to be able to afford her own place in Boston or Cambridge, but in the meantime, sharing a cramped two-bedroom apartment out in the burbs was the best she could do.

"Anybody home?" Tilda called out as she unlocked the door, but there was no answer. Heather wasn't due home from work for another hour, which meant that Tilda could play her music without restrictions. Once Heather got back, the headphones went on, both because Heather despised Tilda's taste in music and to drown out Heather's endless phone calls to her bevy of boyfriends. Heather was her fourth roommate in four years, and Tilda had strong doubts about the relationship making it as far as another lease. She honestly wasn't sure if she was that hard to live with, or if she just had bad luck with roommates.

She headed for her bedroom, forced open the window to get some fresh air, set up her laptop on her desk, and cranked up the Dead Kennedys on the stereo. After taking a minute to gulp down some coffee, she started going through her files on the *Kissing Cousins* cast members.

Other than the actress who played Mercy, the cast had been easy enough to track down, especially since she'd had only the Cousins to deal with. The actor who'd played Pops the crotchety grandfather had passed away a year or two after the show ended.

Jim Bonnier, who'd played Brad the jock, had become a major party animal: drugs, drinking, whatever came his way. Despite his habits, he'd managed to eke out a living doing guest shots on TV, playing the usual circuit of *The Love Boat*; *Fantasy Island*; *Murder, She Wrote*; *Diagnosis Murder*; and *Touched by an Angel.* The work had kept him in recreational chemicals right up until the night in his Pasadena apartment when he shot up too much while drinking. Tilda had managed to get a peek at the crime scene photos — it had been a nasty way to die.

It was never explicitly stated in *Kissing Cousins* that biker boy Damon was doing drugs — it was a sitcom, not an after school special — but there'd been broad hints and lame jokes ripped off from Cheech and Chong. Actor Alex Johnson really was a motorcycle enthusiast, though he'd never copped to the druggie part, and after the show ended, went on to open a bike shop that expanded to a Southern California chain. He gloried in flouting helmet laws,

34

which made him either a rebel or a complete idiot. After he was struck and killed by a hit-and-run driver while riding his Harley sans protective headgear, Tilda had come down on the side of "complete idiot." The police officer Tilda had spoken to about the incident said Johnson might have made it if he'd been wearing a helmet, but without one . . . She hadn't asked to see those crime scene photos.

Tilda hadn't speculated much about either death at the time. For one, she'd been on deadline, and for another, the facts as they were known were perfect for making her point about the difficulty actors had making the transition from teen star to anonymous adult. But with Vincent's ominous theories fresh in her mind, she started considering other possibilities.

When Tilda had spoken to the police detective investigating Bonnier's overdose, he'd stressed that there'd been no sign of foul play and no note to suggest suicide, so the official conclusion was accidental overdose. But he'd also mentioned that somebody might have been with Bonnier that evening, because he wasn't known for partying alone. Could that somebody have waited until the actor was passed out from the booze and then administered a fatal overdose?

Then there was the unknown driver of the car that hit Johnson. With hit-and-runs unpleasantly common, there was no reason to think this one was anything but another statistic, but the police had never found the driver, and there were no witnesses. Somebody could have waited for an opportunity to run the biker off the road and leave him to die.

Tilda made a face and took another drink of coffee, wondering if it was Vincent's craziness or her own urge to make splashy headlines that was making her imagination spin out of control. Then again, the story of Sherri's death — or rather, Holly Kendricks's — was lurid enough without any embellishment from her.

After spending a couple of years failing to build an acting career post–*Kissing Cousins*, Holly had moved back to her hometown of Weldon, Connecticut, and started a real estate business. She'd used her history to help move property — there was a certain cachet in buying your house from a former TV star, even a little-known one like Holly — so she'd been happy to talk to Tilda for whatever publicity she could get. With a pang, Tilda remembered the husband and kids Holly had spoken about so proudly.

According to Vincent, the former actress had been found shot in a vacant house, and Tilda guessed it was one she'd been trying to sell. Hadn't she heard of other real estate agents being lured to vacant houses to be raped and killed? It could be a dangerous job, especially for a pretty woman like Holly, who'd kept her figure trim and dye job fresh.

Three deaths of three costars in three months was a wicked big coincidence, even without Vincent's paranoia. Tilda tried to decide if the renewed curse business would make it easier or harder to find Mercy. Then she pulled the brake on that line of thought, disgusted with herself.

Some reporter she was. She'd barely started the assignment and already she'd committed the fangirl's most egregious sin — she'd confused the actor with the role. Of course, the actress had actually been named Mercy. According to *Kissing Cousins* lore, the character had originally been named Letitia, but after casting Mercy Ashford, the producer decided he preferred that name and made the change. But Tilda couldn't pretend she'd been referring to the actress — she'd been thinking about the character.

Tilda had met or spoken to the other cast

members after they'd moved on to other roles, either in other TV shows or in some semblance of real life. That had never happened with Mercy, so it was the TV character who was stuck in Tilda's mind. The only cure for that was to find out what had happened to the woman.

First, there were two surviving cast members she *did* know how to find. Noel Clark, who'd played the mad-scientist-in-training Elbert, was still in show business, with a long-running, albeit small, role on a soap opera. Katie Langevoort, who'd played the cloyingly sweet youngest Cousin, Felicia, was now a gospel singer. Though neither of them had been able to help Tilda before, it wouldn't hurt to talk to them again. The same went for the show's creator, Irv Munch.

She pulled out her Palm to start a "to-do" file for the story. Then she checked e-mail again, and found more messages waiting. The first was from Nicole, and she took a moment to read, laugh at, and delete the demand for more info about Sherri/Holly and *Kissing Cousins.* Then she turned her attention to Vincent's new messages, each subsequent one giving more details about Holly's death, and each sounding more and more desperate in his pleas for Tilda to do something. Unfortunately, he was vague about what exactly she was supposed to do.

Tilda sighed. She liked Vincent. Sure he was the biggest fanboy she'd ever met, but he was so incredibly sincere and enthusiastic about the many books, TV shows, and movies he was attached to. Moreover he lacked the all-too-common snobbery of fans who wouldn't deign to explain the significance of Spock's heritage or the intricacies of Middle-earth culture to an outsider — he wanted to share his passions, which made him an invaluable source of information and kind of sweet.

As well as being a fan ambassador to the unwashed, Vincent considered himself an activist. Unfortunately, his usual brand of activism involved sending fervent e-mails around the country that would result in online petitions destined to be ignored by Washington, New York, or Hollywood, depending on the topic. Tilda didn't think that approach would be any more successful this time, but she did send him a note asking him to marshal his resources toward finding Mercy. That would keep him occupied while she started her own search.

After reading the data Vincent had sent about Holly Kendricks's death, Tilda was sure he had to have a contact in the Weldon police department because he'd sent her the text of the preliminary police investigation. The report said that Holly had left at noon to show a house to a male caller. Normally she met with clients before she showed them a property, but in this case the caller said he was in town for a business meeting and had seen the property while driving by. He had only a short window of time before he had to head back to New York, and wondered if she could show it to him. Since the property had been vacant for several months, Holly had agreed.

According to the secretary at Holly's realty office, Holly thought she had met the man somewhere, because he clearly knew who she was. Since Holly had a habit of handing out business cards at social gatherings, this wasn't all that unusual.

At any rate, Holly went to meet the man at noon. She had an appointment at the office at two-thirty, and when she didn't show, the secretary called her cell phone. There was no response.

The secretary was alarmed, because Holly was conscientious both about keeping her schedule and answering her phone, so she got somebody else at the office to go to the house in question. That agent had been the one to find Holly dead from a gunshot wound, with no sign of the client. He called the police, and after they arrived and confirmed that she was dead, they started their investigation.

Vincent's last message, which had been sent only minutes before Tilda opened it, said that while it appeared Holly had been beaten before her death, there was no sign of sexual assault. They weren't sure about robbery. Holly's briefcase and purse were left beside the body, and both appeared to have been rifled. There was no cash in her wallet, but the credit cards were all accounted for, which would have been unusual for a pro.

The police had no specific motive in mind, but were planning to speak to Holly's husband, who was described as a local businessman. Tilda thought she remembered him being in banking. The file also listed assignments for officers to check to see if any other attractive women real estate agents had died in similar circumstances anywhere around Weldon.

Vincent pooh-poohed those lines of investigation, infuriated that the police couldn't recognize what he thought was obvious — that the deaths of the three former costars had to be connected. That meant it couldn't have been Holly's husband — why would

41

he have killed Jim Bonnier and Alex Johnson? The same went for the proposed serial killer. That meant there had to be a deranged celebrity stalker lurking, a *Kissing Cousins* fan gone bad.

Tilda appreciated the wealth of information Vincent was providing, and had to admit that there were some odd coincidences — the actors dying in the order of their characters' ages and the apparent pattern in the dates of death. But while this was more than enough to throw Vincent into a frenzy of fear, she wasn't ready to accept his conclusions, despite the striking PowerPoint presentation he'd sent, complete with a death's head border.

Three more messages had come in while Tilda read Vincent's ramblings, but two were spam and the third was an even more irate note from Nicole. Tilda deleted them all. Then she reached for her coffee, took a swallow, and grimaced because it had cooled to lukewarm. It was time to stretch and use the microwave for reheating. She was in the kitchen trying to decide if the corn muffin would be enough food for dinner when her roommate, Heather, came into the apartment.

Even before she got the door closed, the curly-haired blonde said, "Can you turn that down?"

"Sure," Tilda said, resisting an aggrieved sigh because Heather's aggrieved sighs were so much better than hers. She stepped into her bedroom to shut off the stereo, then went back to the kitchen, where Heather was already peering into the Dunkin' Donuts bag.

"Is that the last one?" Heather asked.

"Afraid so," Tilda said with a certain amount of satisfaction, even if it did give Heather an excuse to use her aggrieved sigh. "I thought you were going to go to the grocery store."

Heather kicked her shoes off. "I just couldn't handle shopping today. The boss kept me running all day, and I'm exhausted. Are you going to call for pizza?"

If she'd said, "Do you want to split a pizza?" Tilda would have gone for it, but what Heather wanted was to swipe half of whatever pizza Tilda ordered and paid for. So she said, "Actually, it's such a nice day, I think I'll go out." Before Heather could try to talk her into bringing back a doggy bag, Tilda grabbed her satchel, making sure her cell phone and Palm were inside.

Just before she opened the apartment door, she said, "Heather, who was your favorite of the Kissing Cousins?"

"Brad, of course," Heather said. "But Sherri was cool too. Why?"

"Just curious," Tilda said, already making plans to start the hunt for a new roommate.

CHAPTER 4

"Everyone's a geek about something."
— Mike Luce, artist and comic book shop
manager

The next morning, Tilda woke to the sound of Heather's usual morning frenzy, which climaxed with the slam of the front door as she made a mad dash for the subway in a probably vain attempt to make it to work on time. Tilda took a moment to gloat about being a freelancer before getting up, even though she knew the glow would last only until the day's mail arrived, with its allotment of bills that wouldn't wait until this or that magazine got around to dealing with accounts payable.

Until then, she would continue to revel in the joy of working at home by going to the computer without stopping to shower or change out of the T-shirt and the penguin-patterned pajama pants she'd slept in, pausing only long enough to fix a cup of coffee and eat her corn muffin.

With her stereo playing Green Day's album *Dookie* loudly, she fired up her laptop and zipped through the morning's crop of e-mail: an info recap from Vincent, one last appeal from Nicole, Cooper's hilarious description of Nicole's temper tantrum as she tried to find information about Holly Kendricks's death with so little to go on, notes from a couple of friends, a request for an article from a low-paying but entertaining magazine dedicated to sixties pop bands, and the inevitable batch of spam advertising Viagra, ersatz Rolex watches, and various miraculous methods for penis enlargement.

Once that detritus was cleared away, Tilda was ready to get to work. The first step was to go over her notes from when she'd hunted for Mercy before so she could figure out what it was she hadn't tried yet.

Despite the sob stories she told editors when fishing for an assignment, it usually wasn't that hard to track down former television stars. For one, actors almost always had agents. Not that an agent would give just anybody the contact info for their clients, but Tilda had enough clippings and references to loosen even the tightest grips on PDAs and Rolodexes.

Going through an agent worked just as well for nonworking actors because most of them either wanted to become working actors or to at least receive whatever residuals were owed them for previous work.

Of course Tilda had to find out who an actor's agent was, but that wasn't hard either. It wasn't as though they didn't want to be found, at least by people who could give their clients publicity. Twenty minutes on the Web or half an hour on the phone would do for sixty to seventy percent of the people she was looking for.

For the rest, she had an arsenal of other tricks. If an actor was working regularly on a series, in films, or in the theater, she could track down publicists who would nearly orgasm at the chance to get publicity without having to work for it. Then there were casting people, who had enormous databases — one of her favorite sources was a former casting agent turned mystery bookseller. Next were actors' organizations and unions, all of which would forward messages.

Sometimes it was even easier to find people who'd severed all formal ties with the entertainment industry but were hanging onto their bit of fame with both fists. Many maintained their own Web sites or frequented fan sites. They sold their own T-shirts and screen-printed pillow cases. Some hit the convention circuit, traveling all over the country to sign memorabilia and sell photos of themselves. They were happy to be found.

If those methods didn't work, Tilda had nurtured a web of contacts, fans and pros alike, who would help her track down all kinds of performers. She haunted user groups, Listservs, and online bulletin boards to find those people and cultivate them. That's how she'd met Vincent, and eventually she'd started to consider him a friend as well as a source.

The problem, Tilda realized as she went through her notes, was that she'd tried all those tricks before, some of them twice.

The woman who'd been Mercy's agent was dead, and while the agency was still collecting the actress's residual checks and taking their cut, they'd made only the most perfunctory efforts to track her down to pay her. After all, it wasn't their job to make people accept money. Ditto for the organizations and unions — Mercy had let her memberships lapse shortly after *Kissing Cousins* was canceled, and hadn't left a forwarding address or phone number. Ditto again for casting people — apparently

Mercy didn't want acting work.

As for the fans, there were a number of Web sites and Listservs devoted to *Kissing Cousins* and to Mercy in particular, but there was no evidence that she'd so much as lurked on any of them. A couple of times people had claimed online to be Mercy, but had had their claims debunked. Not only had they been thoroughly flamed in retaliation, but Tilda wouldn't have been surprised to find out that they'd been infected with every virus known to the computer world too — she herself knew better than to ever tick off a really good hacker.

Tilda had at least managed to track down Mercy's old address, where she'd lived during the filming of the show, but the neighborhood had gone through several renaissances since then. Mercy's house was gone, and none of the neighbors even knew who she was, let alone where she was.

Tilda had even gone to a private eye. Not that she'd been able to pay him, but she knew one who was an ardent admirer of seventies TV detectives like Mannix, Barnaby Jones, and Banacek, so she'd traded signed cast photos for a few hours of his time. The detective had tried the usual routes — getting Mercy's Social Security number and checking for records, digging up her automobile registration and using that, checking police files for arrests. Nada. He'd even checked death records, but there was nothing there either.

Tilda leaned back in her chair, drumming her fingers on her desk. If there was anything she'd missed, she was still missing it. So until something smart occurred to her, she was going to try something dumb, which was to do all the usual things again. She pulled up the old e-mails she'd sent to everybody she'd thought of before, updated them, and sent them again. Maybe something would come from it.

That done, she took a break for showering and dressing, hoping something else would occur to her. It didn't. Then she checked e-mail again, hoping some new lead had arrived. It hadn't. So she spent the rest of the morning polishing her witch article for *Entertain Me!*, tracking down the art she needed, and zapping it off to the magazine.

After lunch and another quick e-mail check, she rewrote the witch article, this time exploring how the television witches she'd interviewed compared to actual Wiccan practitioners, and sent it to a small Wiccan magazine. Another rewrite, and the article compared glamorous TV witches to far less attractive historical witches. That one went to a retirees' magazine that liked popular history articles. She then simplified that version for a teen magazine. Next she cut the article into individual profiles of each of the interviewees and added information that hadn't fit in the previous articles. Those went to fan magazines focusing on the shows the actresses starred in. She did draw the line at writing about how television witches subverted children's morals, though she knew of a fundamentalist newsletter that would have grabbed it in a heartbeat.

Not all of those secondary markets would buy the articles, of course, but they were worth a shot. Tilda had long ago learned that the key to survival as a freelancer was not to research and write lots of different articles, but to rewrite the same article for as many different markets as she could finagle. While the various versions started with the same basic information, each one was slanted in a way to allow the readers to see what they wanted to see.

By the time she'd done all that, what Tilda really wanted to see was Mercy's contact information, but none of the lines she'd set out had caught anything useful. She might have come up with something useful to do, like laundry or grocery shopping, but the phone rang, rescuing her from practicality.

"Hey, girl."

"Hey, Cooper. How was work today?"

"Don't ask! Nicole was in fine form, trying to get information about that dead TV star, and naturally she took it out on me and Shannon."

"Did she make Shannon cry again?"

"No, but not for lack of trying. I swear, that woman is using Anna Wintour as a career model."

"You think Nicole is hoping to work with Wintour at *Vogue* someday?"

"As if! She doesn't have the fashion sense of a gnat — instead of *The Devil Wears Prada,* it would be *The Devil Wears Nada.* No, I think she wants Jillian's job. If that ever happens, I am so out of here!"

"You and me both. Speaking of witches, did Jillian get my article?"

"She did, and I watched her read it. She nodded twice, and I'm almost certain I saw a tiny smile."

"Two nods and a smile? Bitching! My last piece only got two nods." Jillian was not known for enthusing, but then again, she wasn't a tin tyrant like Nicole either. "What are you and Jean-Paul up to tonight?"

"He's working an anniversary party up in Revere."

"Why don't you go with him? You could

be his roadie. Or better yet, a groupie."

"He asked me, but it's an Italian couple. I don't mind the doo-wop, but I can't stand all the Rat Pack music. Not to mention the fact that they specifically requested the Electric Slide and the Chicken Dance."

"I shudder in sympathy."

"Anyway, since I know you don't have plans — "

"Are you implying I can't get a date?"

"No, but if you were dating anybody, I'd know about it, wouldn't I?"

"Almost certainly," she admitted.

"Then, as I was saying, since you don't have plans, why don't you come over here? I'll order calzone and we'll watch a video."

"That's the best offer I've had all day. I'll be there in an hour."

"Ciao, bella!"

After they hung up, it only took Tilda a few minutes to change to a nicer top, pull on her battered Doc Martens, and run a brush through her hair. She was heading for the door when she thought of something, so she went back into her room to pick through her disorganized collection of videotapes until she found what she was looking for.

Tilda wasn't sure if the Red Sox were in town or not, but even without pregame traffic, she didn't care to try parking near

53

Cooper and Jean-Paul's apartment on Commonwealth Avenue. Instead she hopped the T, and thanks to some luck making the switch from Orange Line to Green Line, pushed the doorbell a full ten minutes earlier than scheduled.

Cooper buzzed her in and was standing at his open door when she got off the elevator at his floor.

"Come on in. The delivery guy buzzed right after you did."

"The cute one?"

"It sounded like him."

She tossed her satchel into the apartment and waited with Cooper for the elevator door to open. When it did, out stepped as buff an example of college student as Tilda ever expected to see, wearing tight jeans and a knowing smile. Like most people who worked in Boston's Italian pizza joints, he was Greek.

"Hey," he said. "How you guys doing?" He handed over the bag of food, and Cooper handed over the money.

"You want change?" he asked.

"Keep it," Cooper answered.

He smiled even wider and slowly tucked the bill into his pocket, his body language implying that much greater treasures than a twenty-dollar bill filled his jeans. Then he was gone.

"He is so gay," Cooper said as he closed the door.

"Straight," Tilda insisted. "He was checking me out big time."

"Please. He wants me so bad he can barely stand it."

"Yeah, he wants you to make yourself scarce so he can come after me. Besides, what do you care? You've got Jean-Paul. I'm the one who needs to get laid."

"You sure as hell do!"

"Hey! It hasn't been that long."

Cooper just looked at her.

"Okay, it has been that long. Maybe I should order more calzone."

"Forget that — I'll order Chinese. I know Ming is straight."

"He's also married, with four kids."

"Then he must be straight, right?"

They went into the kitchen for Cooper to unpack the sausage calzone and side of mozzarella sticks he'd ordered and for Tilda to get glasses out of the cabinet to fill with Dr Pepper. Then they went back to the living room and spread their food on the coffee table in front of the TV.

It never ceased to amuse Tilda that Cooper and Jean-Paul's was the stereotypical gay couple's apartment. Invariably neat, it was stylishly decorated with furniture that went together, in direct contrast to her own digs, which could be charitably described as bohemian and more accurately described as furnished with Tilda's mother's castoffs. Less stereotypical was the sizable comic book collection Cooper stored in a spare bedroom, but very few people ever saw that.

"Did you pick out a movie?" she asked him.

"I couldn't make up my mind between *X-Men* and *Pride & Prejudice*."

"Hugh Jackman or Matthew Macfadyen. You in the mood for beefcake tonight?"

"It's not for me. I thought you needed all you could get."

"Meow. I've got another idea." She retrieved the video from her satchel. "How about *Kissing Cousins*?"

"Are you kidding me?"

"It's research," she said, reaching past him to slip the cassette into the VCR.

He made a face, but didn't object, and as the show started, she heard a low sound. "Are you humming along with the theme song?"

"What? You think I don't watch seventies TV? How do you think I come up with my pop psych quizzes?"

"I bet you'd sing along if I weren't here."

"Please! The lyrics are so lame they make the *Gilligan's Island* theme sound like Gilbert and Sullivan."

"God, yes."

By the second stanza, they were both singing along. Tilda figured Cooper couldn't very well rat on her if he was singing too.

Though the episode she'd picked wasn't the first she'd seen, it was the one that had hooked her on the show. The plot, variations of which had appeared in countless sitcoms before and since, was about Mercy getting a crush on a new student and enlisting Sherri's help to get his attention. Sherri decided she wanted him herself, and gave her Cousin advice designed to make her look like a fool.

Since the boy was from Kentucky, Sherri got Mercy to adopt a Southern accent, dress in red gingham, and spout horse-racing statistics. Naturally, the guy decided Mercy was brain-damaged and asked Sherri to the dance instead. Mercy then realized what Sherri had been up to and immediately changed back to her usual ensemble of lacy black blouse, long skirt, and dark lipstick to attend the dance solo. Because the show was a sitcom, Mercy got the last laugh when she ran into Sherri and the guy at the refreshment table; he was entranced by her and blew off Sherri.

The moral, which the Cousins' grandfather pointed out in case either the Cousins or the audience were too dense to figure it out, was, "To thine own self be true."

"Shakespeare," Cooper said. "How terribly profound."

"I know it's hokey, but sometimes hokey strikes a chord."

He looked at her. "There's a story here, isn't there?"

"Yes," she admitted, "but it's even more hokey than the show, which at least has the excuse of being fictional."

"Spill, or I won't share the ice cream."

"Did it come from Toscanini's?"

"Chocolate Number 3, Dark."

"I'll spill. Do you remember high school?"

"Sadly, yes."

"Then picture this. The summer before I started high school, my mother divorced my father and moved us from Waltham to Medford. That meant I knew absolutely nobody."

"That's harsh."

"Harsh, hell — it would have been major trauma even if the divorce hadn't already thrown me for a loop. As it was, I was terrified that I'd be consigned to the geeks and nerds zone, so I decided to make myself into the perfect, perky freshman. And I used my big sister June as a model."

"Your half sister, who is as different from you as Sherri was from Mercy?"

"That's the one. Not that she was pushing it on me. In fact, I think she was freaked when I suddenly started wearing clothes like hers, buying shoes like hers, fixing my hair like hers, and even using the same colors of makeup."

"With your skin tone? June is blonde!"

"I would have been too, had Mom let me dye mine."

"Thank the Lord for small favors. Did the makeover achieve the desired results?"

"Let's just say that on a Friday night in September, I was sitting at home watching *Kissing Cousins* rather than going out on a date or hanging with friends."

"Wait a minute. That was a seventies show. Were you even alive in the seventies?"

"Just barely, but there is a magical gift known as reruns."

"More of a curse, if you ask me."

"Sometimes," she allowed. "Anyway, I was channel surfing and ended up on a low-budget indie channel and came across that episode of *Kissing Cousins* we just watched. Afterward I went into the bathroom and took a good, hard look at myself in the mirror."

"Did you cry?"

"Are you kidding? I laughed my ass off. I looked ridiculous. I washed all the gunk off of my face and took the headband off and threw it out the window. The clothes went to Goodwill the next day. By Monday morning I was back to my usual self."

"And you became wildly popular?"

"Of course not. My usual self was a geek. But I did make new friends — other geeks of course — but my kind of geeks."

"It's hard to imagine you as a geek."

She laughed. "Are you kidding? It's Friday night and I'm dateless and watching *Kissing Cousins*. Nothing has changed."

"Ah, but now you're watching it with me. That raises your coolness rating significantly."

"True enough," she said. "So where's my ice cream?"

They adjourned to the kitchen to divide the pint into thirds: one for each of them and a share for Jean-Paul when he got back from his gig.

Once they were back on the butter-soft leather couch, bowls and spoons in hand, Cooper said, "So that's why you're obsessed with that show."

"Not obsessed. Just very, very interested. Back then, my buds and I would watch the show each week just to see the popular Cousins get their comeuppance — it was cathartic. We only wished we could do something similar for the popular crew in our school."

"I know the feeling. Somehow a gay, black comic book fan wasn't exactly mainstream in my school."

Tilda took another spoonful of ice cream. "Have you ever noticed that almost everybody says they resented the popular kids in high school, that they were the geeks and nerds? Every movie and television star says he was the outsider, or at best, the class clown. What happens to the popular kids?"

"I'm guessing that a covert cadre of unpopular kids takes them out quietly after graduation." He smiled at the thought. "Wait! Your sister June admits to having been popular, right?"

"True, and she's okay. We didn't get along so well back then, but we're tight now. So there might be other ex-popular kids living among us, in hiding."

"Like mutants?" Cooper said. "That sounds like a cue for *X-Men* to me."

After that they concentrated on their ice cream and the movie, stopping the DVD occasionally to more thoroughly admire Hugh Jackman's form and argue over whether Patrick Stewart or Ian McKellan had the greater stage presence. It was midnight by the time Tilda left for home, and she went to bed as soon as she got there.

Since the next day was Saturday, Tilda slept in, then got up to tend to some wholly uninteresting errands and make her weekly duty phone calls to her mother and step-father, who had retired to Florida, and her father and stepmother, who'd retired to North Carolina.

Late that afternoon, Tilda's phone rang.

"Tilda? Vincent. Have you been reading my e-mails?"

"Every one. But I try not to work on the weekends." She couldn't avoid it all the time, but since working at home meant she was always at the office, she had to draw the line somewhere. Vincent had no such compunctions. All day long he'd been sending her details about the continuing investigation into Holly's shooting.

Either the town of Weldon was having a slow murder week, or Holly's family had some political connections, because it being the weekend wasn't slowing the cops down. Unfortunately, the legwork and forensics and whatever else it was they were doing didn't seem to be leading anywhere. There were no substantive leads in the case.

"I just found out that Sherri's body — "

"Holly's body."

"Right, Holly's body has been released to the family. They're having a wake tomorrow night, and the funeral will be Monday. Are you going to go?"

Tilda considered it. "Definitely not to the wake." For one, it was still the weekend, and for another, she already had plans. The funeral was a different story. Some of the people she wanted to talk to for her article were bound to be there. Besides, she almost felt as if she owed it to the actress, after all the years of celebrating when her character got the short end of the stick. "I think I can make it to the funeral. Do you want to ride along?"

"I can't. I've got a project meeting at work that I can't miss. I thought I'd have a private memorial service at my house Monday night, just for us fans. I'd really like you to be there."

"I don't know, Vincent." Vincent was okay, but spending the evening with a group of his fanboy homeboys didn't appeal to her. "It's a long drive to Connecticut. I'm going to be wiped by the time I get back."

"Please? I think it would mean a lot, and you could tell people about the funeral. There's going to be about a hundred of us.

Wouldn't that be good for your story?"

Tilda reconsidered. A photo or two of a hundred mourners would certainly add poignancy. One or two of them were bound to be photogenic. "Okay, if it means that much to you."

"Great. Can you make it by seven?"

"I'll do my best. See you then."

Other than checking e-mail in the vain hope of something useful turning up, Tilda spent the rest of the weekend completing her list of uninteresting errands and jobs around the house, which made the prospect of Monday's funeral almost appealing.

CHAPTER 5

"Episode 5: The Death of Mr. Floppy
The night after Sherri's beloved bunny Mr. Floppy hops into the great beyond, Elbert sees a rerun of *Frankenstein,* and decides to exhume the rabbit and revive it. He starts his experiment, but when he has to leave the lab, Brad sees the corpse. Horrified, Brad takes the body outside to bury it, but is interrupted and stashes it behind a bush. When Elbert returns, he thinks Mr. Floppy has risen, and tells Sherri the glad tidings. Then Mercy's cat Emily finds the body and drags it inside. Mayhem ensues, followed by Pop's carefully nondenominational lesson on the finality of death."
— Fanboy's Online *Kissing Cousins*
Episode Guide, by Vincent Peters

Once she was up and showered Monday morning, Tilda approached the problem of what to wear to Holly Kendricks's funeral.

As she rummaged through her closet and bureau, she realized that one advantage to having been a Goth was having so many choices. Admittedly she had to eliminate the miniskirts and artfully torn tights, but she quickly assembled an ensemble of a black thigh-length skirt, a purple blouse that was only moderately lacy, and a black wool jacket. The shoes were the toughest part — neither pair of her Doc Martens nor her Day-Glo sneakers set the proper tone. Eventually she settled for a pair of black patent leather Mary Janes she used to wear as part of a school-girl-from-hell outfit one ex-boyfriend had found alluring.

Then she added the black Coach handbag June had given her for college graduation, no doubt picturing it as the perfect accessory for the wardrobe of business suits and pumps that Tilda would soon accumulate, and she was good to go to for the three-and-a-half-hour drive to Weldon.

The listing on the *Weldon Sentinel* Web site hadn't specified that the funeral was private, so Tilda hadn't expected to have any problem slipping into the back of the service. But as she turned onto the road the church was on, traffic went from a flow to a trickle, even though her directions said she had three blocks to go. Deciding that a little walk would be easier than trying to get closer, she parked at the first available space on the side of the road. She had her digital camera, but didn't think it would look right to start snapping shots of the mourners, so she left it in her trunk. She could always discreetly take a few shots with her cell phone if something particularly juicy happened.

As Tilda approached the church, she found herself dividing the crowd into categories.

First were the actual mourners: Holly's family and friends. Of course the closest family members would arrive in limos later — Tilda didn't see a hearse, which meant that the funeral procession hadn't arrived yet — but there were some people there whose faces showed signs of actual grief. They were dressed much like Tilda, in suits and dresses in muted colors, if not all in black.

Then there were those there to pay their respects: business associates, neighbors, and church members. Tilda suspected some of them were industry types Holly had worked with back in the day. These tended to be dressed a notch better than the first group, which made sense. They were there to be seen.

Sprinkled here and there were the curious types who invariably turned up for funerals of well-known people and murder victims — with the murder of a minor celebrity they were getting a double helping of schadenfreude. Tilda's mother would have sniffed loudly at their velour jogging suits and polo shirts with chinos.

Around the edges were other members of the press, and at least the TV people were dressed decently. Tilda spotted local affiliate trucks from two of the big three networks, E!, and CNN. The cameramen were busily filming the crowd and establishing shots of the First United Methodist Church of Weldon, which was a scenic steepled one that could have been used as an encyclopedia illustration for "traditional New England Protestant house of worship." The print media representatives — newspaper and magazine reporters — were a mixed bag, with outfits ranging from the respectful to the ludicrous. Tilda noted with more than a little satisfaction that her attire was better than that of most of her colleagues.

Last there were the fans, and even though they were dressed the least appropriately — mostly in jeans and *Kissing Cousins* T-shirts — tears were running down their faces and they were hugging each other openly.

Then Tilda corrected herself to add one more group of people — cops, in uniform and out. Presumably some were there to control the crowd, but no doubt others were there scanning the crowd for suspects.

Just as she got as close to the church as the press of people would easily allow, the hearse drove up, followed by a line of black limos. Police officers started clearing the path as the pall bearers gathered, and the pink-and-white-rose-covered casket was unloaded and readied to be escorted to the church. A tall, handsome man whom Tilda recognized as Holly's husband followed directly behind the casket. He looked worn and sad and was clutching the hands of Holly's and his two children, who seemed more baffled than anything else.

If she'd been a news reporter, she would probably have felt compelled to try to wrangle an interview with him, even angling for a photo or three of his grief-stricken face. But since he wasn't a celebrity, *Entertain Me!* wouldn't be interested. Usually she deplored that attitude as being shallow, but this time she was just as glad her personal and professional needs meshed. She could leave the man and his children in peace.

Two women who looked like smudged copies of Holly came after, along with an older man and woman — likely the sisters and parents Holly had mentioned in her interview. A dozen or so others followed them, most of them probably other family members, but near the back Tilda spotted another man she recognized. Irv Munch, the producer and creator of *Kissing Cousins*, was walking with Holly's family.

Munch was skinnier than when she'd seen him last, but he didn't look so much fit as shriveled. His gray hair was still thick, and though he was dressed a bit West Coast for the Connecticut crowd, he wasn't flashy. As Tilda tried to decide if she was impressed by his coming so far to say good-bye to Holly, or suspicious that he was there to take advantage of publicity, two women near her called out to him. Munch's wince was minute, but Tilda could tell he'd heard them, even though he didn't turn their way as he walked past on his way into the church.

The crowd started to ooze toward the church doors, slowed by police officers trying to make sure rubberneckers weren't allowed in, and Tilda saw them turn away a couple of reporters. She was starting to think that she'd wasted her time driving down, when she found herself immediately behind the petite women who'd tried to get Munch's attention.

"Poor Mr. Munch," one of them said. "He's so sunken in his grief that he didn't even hear us."

"I wish we could sit with him," the other said. "I'm sure it would make him feel better."

"Gabrielle? Gwendolyn?" Tilda said hesitantly.

They turned as one, smiling in that vague way that told her they couldn't quite place her.

Most people, even stone *Kissing Cousins* fans, would have been hard pressed to place them too. Gabrielle and Gwendolyn Roman had been part of the cast, but just barely. They'd played Gabby and Gwen, the unimaginatively named twin Cousins added to the show when ratings began to slip. Just as unimaginatively, Gabby was normal and Gwen was weird, so the family feud was kept on an even footing. To give the girls credit, they'd done exactly what they'd been hired to do. They were cute. They had no discernible acting talent, even allowing for the fact that they'd only been seven, but they were darned cute.

Despite their dimples, the strategy hadn't

helped — if anything, it sped the show's demise. Most fans considered their first appearance the moment the show jumped the shark. About the only people who acknowledged them as part of the cast were some particularly imaginative slash fiction writers.

Surprisingly the two young actresses had never realized how disliked they were. They'd had very few acting jobs since the show was canceled, most of those prepuberty, and made their living taking advantage of the nostalgia market to appear at collectibles shows and fan conventions. Tilda could see that they weren't sure if she was a fan from one of their road trips or somebody worth their time.

"Tilda Harper," she said. "I interviewed you two for *Entertain Me!*"

"Tilda!" Gabrielle and Gwendolyn gushed in unison, and the three of them kissed in the airspace of each other's cheeks.

Focused as she'd been on funeral fashions, Tilda was surprised she'd missed the duo. Though they were indeed dressed in black, their dresses were well above the knees, their shoes were strappy sandals with spike heels, and they'd tied black ribbons around their perky ponytails. The overall effect was Widow's Weed Barbie.

"It's so good to see you," Gabrielle said, and Gwendolyn added, "It's been too long."

"I'm just sorry it's on such a sad occasion," Tilda said.

They nodded. "We cannot tell you how destroyed we are," Gabrielle said, and Gwendolyn lifted an actual cloth handkerchief to her eyes, searching for a tear. "Holly was one of our closest, dearest friends."

"Despite the great age difference," Gwendolyn put in. "She was like a mother to us." That made it Gabrielle's turn to wipe at her eyes.

The two actresses were just as convincing as they'd been on *Kissing Cousins.* Which was to say, not at all. Tilda wondered how many hairs had been torn from how many directors' heads in trying to get a decent acting job out of the twin moppets. Even the rawest actress could usually sob on command, but even at a funeral, Gabrielle and Gwendolyn couldn't dredge up a single convincing sniff between them. If they managed to avoid makeup stains, they'd be able to put those handkerchiefs back into their lingerie drawer as soon as the funeral was over, ready for their next performance.

Fortunately for her, Tilda knew they were no better at detecting insincerity in others, so she said, "I'd hoped to pay my respects,

but they're not allowing the press inside."
She nodded at the police officers waving off
a TV crew. "I'd love to be able to talk to
you two more after the service, but I don't
think I should just hang around — "

"Don't be silly!" Gabrielle said quickly.
"You're not just press. You're a friend. You
can come sit with us!"

Gwendolyn nodded vigorously, her hair
ribbon bobbing indignantly.

"If you're sure I won't be intruding," Tilda
said with mock reluctance.

In response, one twin took hold of her
right arm while the other took her left, and
the three of them headed for the door of
the church. The police, no doubt overwhelmed by the sheer perkiness of the
twins, didn't object as they went in and
found space in a pew a third of the way
down the aisle.

Tilda had attended enough funerals in her
life to know that Holly's was fairly standard.
The eulogies reminded her of a high school
valedictorian speech, where the speaker tries
so hard to draw on her special experiences
of high school, never realizing that her references to bad school lunches, exciting football games, favorite rock bands, and as-
sorted hijinks sounded just like every other
valedictorian speech ever given. It wasn't

that the eulogies given by Holly's best friend, neighbor, and business partner were insincere. It's just that they didn't really say anything about the woman.

Still, Holly's family and friends seemed comforted, though there were plenty of tears. That made the twins' few noticeable signs of grief all the more glaring. Then again, Tilda thought, she wasn't exactly broken up herself. Though she hadn't been friends with Holly, or even particularly liked her, she had met her twice and spoken to her on the phone several times. The least she could do in honor of the woman was regret her passing, not just mentally take note of the mourners for her article. So she deliberately shut down the reporter part of her brain and drew on the Catholic training she'd abandoned as soon as she was confirmed to offer a private prayer while the preacher did it his way.

The eulogies were followed by absolutely glorious performances of "Amazing Grace" and "How Great Thou Art." After the first few bars made it plain that this was not the usual church soloist, Tilda craned her neck to peek up at the choir loft and was surprised that she recognized the soloist. It was one of Holly's former costars. Katie Langevoort had played the insufferable Felicia, the worst specimen of tattletale, Goody Two-shoes, teacher's pet ever to foul a television set. Though she'd only been a child when the show was made, rumor had it that she'd received sacks full of hate mail every week, and she was still the unlikely star of a ridiculous amount of improbably kinky fan fiction and artwork on the Web.

Like Holly, Katie hadn't had much success in acting after *Kissing Cousins,* but she hadn't left show business. Instead she'd changed her name to Kathleen Owen and become a gospel singer, so her prissier-than-thou reputation was a help instead of a hindrance. From what Tilda could tell from her previous telephone interviews, she was making a good living at it, and after hearing her moving renditions of the funeral warhorses, she understood why.

The service ended shortly afterward, and Tilda stood with the other mourners while the coffin was taken down the aisle to the waiting hearse. As the widower and his children walked after it, Tilda heard Gabrielle whisper, "My God, they're younger than we were when we made the show." As if trying to imagine how they'd have felt in such a position, the twins finally honestly cried, and Tilda awkwardly patted them both.

Gabrielle's and Gwendolyn's tears subsided as they took their turn to leave the church and pulled out matching Ray-Bans. During the service, the minister had passed on the request that the graveside service be for the family only, so once the hearse left and the widower and other relatives climbed into their limos to follow it, most of the mourners were left standing on the church steps as if waiting for permission to leave.

The twins were apparently fully recovered from their earlier distress and were watching the crowd, Tilda momentarily forgotten. "Do you see Mr. Munch?" Gabrielle asked her sister.

"No, but there's Noel."

Noel Clark was another former *Kissing Cousins* cast member. He'd played Elbert, the budding mad scientist who was rarely seen without his white lab coat.

"Should we go talk to him?" Gabrielle wanted to know.

"Why bother? He said he could get us a walk-on on *City Hospital,* and that went nowhere." Gwendolyn looked further afield. "There's Katie Langevoort, but she's left the industry."

"Is Mercy Ashford here?" Tilda asked.

"I doubt it," Gwendolyn said with a shrug. "She wasn't at Jim Bonnier's funeral."

"Or Alex Johnson's." Gabrielle echoed her sister's shrug.

"Really?" Tilda said. "I'd have thought she'd want to show her respects."

Gwendolyn sniffed. "I don't think Mercy cared enough to bother. Do you know we've never heard one word from her in all the years since the show ended? Not so much as a phone call!"

"She pretended to like us too," Gabrielle added. "She made a point of telling us her address and phone number at the wrap party, and wrote ours down. She even gave us presents."

"Matching purses."

"But that was the last we ever heard of her. When we tried to call, the number was disconnected, and when we sent a Christmas card, it came back unopened."

"Of course, we were so much younger than she was," Gwendolyn took pains to remind Tilda.

Just then, a man came up to the three of them and said, "Gwendolyn, Gabrielle, I'm so glad to see you."

"Lawrence!" the twins said in unison, beaming at the man.

Like the twins, Tilda suspected Lawrence wasn't quite as young as he wished he were, but he was still reasonably appealing, with sandy blond hair, a decent tan, and only a few lines in his face. He was well-built and nicely dressed in his somber but stylish HUGO BOSS suit. He'd have been perfect casting for a widowed or divorced father in a sitcom — old enough to theoretically be the father of a brood of implausibly attractive teenagers, young enough that script writers would be able to inundate him with romances until one culminated in a very special two-part end-of-season wedding episode.

He completed the cheek-kissing ceremony, having bussed the twins on both sides, and then took one hand from each. "What a sad, sad day. You two must be distraught."

As if in answer to a cue, the twins lifted their hankies to their eyes again.

"Destroyed," Gwendolyn said.

"Devastated," Gabrielle agreed.

The three of them shook their heads sadly until their grief was assuaged. Then Lawrence turned to Tilda and said, "I'm sorry, I don't believe we've met. I'm Lawrence White."

"Tilda Harper," she replied.

"Tilda is an industry reporter too," Gabrielle said. "She interviewed us for *Entertain Me!*"

"Is that right?" Lawrence said. "That's an

excellent publication."

"I just freelance for them," Tilda said.

"Still, you must know Nicole Webber."

"I'm afraid I must," Tilda agreed.

He blinked, as if trying to figure out how to respond, then apparently decided to move on. "I'm always impressed by how current *Entertain Me!* is, what with being published in Boston."

Tilda bristled. "Boston is the Hub of the Universe." When he blinked again, she added, "It's Boston's nickname, the Hub City. Supposedly it's the hub of the universe."

"Interesting," he lied politely.

"Don't be such a snob, Lawrence," Gabrielle said, swatting him playfully. "Gwendolyn and I are going to be in Boston ourselves in a couple of weeks. We're speaking at a conference."

"Maybe you could cover it, Tilda," Gwendolyn said.

"I'll see if one of my editors is interested," Tilda said, but she doubted anybody who paid actual money would be. She knew that the "conference" was in fact the Beantown Collectibles Extravaganza, and the twins were only two of the slate of cult actors, costumed wrestlers, and former *Playboy* pinups who would be hawking autographs and photo ops to willing fans. However, since she frequently attended that kind of event, she politely added, "Maybe we can get together for drinks while you're in town."

"That would be great," the twins said in unison, then giggled. They really were too perky for words — Tilda was already regretting her tentative invitation, and it was time to change the subject.

"Who do you write for?" Tilda asked Lawrence.

"I'm a freelancer too — I've written for *People, EW, Hollywood Reporter,* occasionally some TV work. Keeps me on the road a lot, going back and forth between New York and LA."

"Who sent you here? No offense to the late Mrs. Kendricks, but her funeral seems a little low-profile for *People.*"

"True, but I'm sure I'll talk them into printing something — I was a big fan of the show myself."

"No kidding," Tilda said, warming to him. "Tell me, which character did you — "

Before Tilda could finish her screening question, Gabrielle called out, "There's Mr. Munch. Mr. Munch!" She clattered over, with Gwendolyn in pursuit.

"I guess they've heard the rumor," Law-

81

rence said.

"What rumor is that?"

"There's talk that Munch is trying to resurrect *Kissing Cousins*."

"There's been talk about that since the week after the show was canceled," Tilda said dismissively.

"True, but with the publicity the show is getting these days, people are returning Munch's calls for the first time in years."

"That's ghoulish."

"That's show business. That whole curse thing is great press."

Tilda sighed heavily — if Munch was a ghoul, what did that make her?

Lawrence said, "Come to think of it, didn't that curse story break in *Entertain Me!*?" He snapped his fingers. "Harper! You wrote that story."

"I did," Tilda admitted. "I'm surprised you read it."

"Have to keep an eye on the competition. I've never written for *Entertain Me!* but you never know in this business." He looked over at where the twins were enthusiastically sucking up to Munch. "Anyway, it's starting to look like there's life in the idea after all, and you know no producer ever let go of a good idea."

"Or in this case, a lame one."

"Then you're not a fan of the show?"

"I love it, but I know good from bad."

"The show should never have worked as well as it did," Lawrence admitted. "Chemistry in the cast, I think. Are you still working the curse angle?"

"Something like that," Tilda said, realizing there was no good reason to try to explain her view of the cursed title, though she did briefly consider the possibility that her epitaph would be "Concocted the Curse of the *Kissing Cousins*." "Right now I'm hoping to meet with the rest of the cast members."

"Are they here?"

"Two are. The soloist at the funeral, and that man standing next to Munch. But the last one — Mercy Ashford — is still AWOL."

"Are you sure she's not here?" he said, scanning the crowd. "I'd think she would be, under the circumstances."

"Apparently nobody has seen her in years."

"Really?"

Tilda nodded. "I'm hoping to get in touch with her for my article."

"Do you have any leads?"

"I've got a couple of things that look promising," Tilda said, which was exaggerating to the point of fiction, but she hated to admit the truth to a fellow reporter. She saw Katie Langevoort heading out of the church. "Excuse me, but I'd better go talk to people while I can."

"Work comes first of course. By the way, I was planning to take the twins out for lunch after this winds down. We could make it a foursome." Lawrence had a glint in his eye that said he wasn't thinking about tennis.

Though he'd fallen, just barely, on the right side of the line between sleazy and amusing, Tilda shook her head. She still had Vincent's memorial service to cover. "Thanks, but I've got to get back to Boston."

"The Hub of the Universe," Lawrence said, proving he had been listening after all. "Let me give you my card."

She accepted it, and gave him her own before making her way through the crowd to Katie Langevoort, or rather, to Kathleen Owen. Langevoort the child actress had been blonde and cute. Owen the singer was blonde and voluptuous, and had traded the pink ruffled dresses she'd worn on camera for a dark CHANEL suit.

"Ms. Owen? I'm Tilda Harper. I interviewed you by phone for *Entertain Me!*"

"Oh, yes, Tilda." The woman offered her

hand for a brief clasp. "How nice to meet you in person. But call me Kat."

"Your singing today was lovely."

"Thank you so much. I was so upset about Holly that I was sure my voice would crack, but the Lord answered my prayers and helped me give a good performance."

Tilda blinked twice before responding, "He certainly did."

Kat dimpled and said, "I'm sorry. Y'all aren't used to bringing the Lord into every conversation up here, are you?"

"Not unless I'm talking to a priest," Tilda said.

"It's an occupational hazard for me. People in the gospel biz are full of prayers and hallelujahs and all that. But a day like this surely puts a strain on my faith. Holly was so young, and to die the way she did . . . It's hard to understand His plan, isn't it?"

Tilda nodded.

"Anyhoo," Kat said, "it was mighty nice of you to come pay your respects."

"Actually, I'm working on a story," Tilda was forced to admit.

"No sin mixing business with other obligations," the singer said cheerily. "At least you're not hovering around with cameras and microphones. What angle are you using

85

this time around?"

"I won't be sure until I talk to everybody. That's one reason I came today, hoping I'd see you and the others."

"Well, Noel Clark is right over there with Mr. Munch, and I see the twins too. At least, I think that's them — haven't seen them in a coon's age."

"That's them. What about Mercy Ashford?"

"If she's here, I haven't seen her, but I don't know that I'd even recognize her. I haven't laid eyes on her since the cast party at the end of our last season."

"Is that right? Then you don't know where she is now?"

"No idea. It's a shame too. I always liked Mercy — she was a couple of years older than I was, but always had time for me. I used to get a lot of hate mail back then, mostly from kids thinking I was just like my character. Mercy would try to get to the mail ahead of me and toss out the nastier letters. When a bad one did get through, she'd keep me from brooding over it."

"People do sometimes blur the line between an actress and the character."

"I suppose it's a compliment, in its way. When we did live appearances, it was even worse. If I'd known then what I know now,

I'd have played it up, had some fun with it, but then I was just upset that people didn't like me. Mercy would always stick close by me and explain to everybody that I was nothing like Felicia. She made a point of saying so in interviews too. I really looked up to her, and when the show ended and she promised to keep in touch, I was so young I believed her. It hurt my feelings that she didn't." She shrugged. "That's the industry, love you today, don't know you tomorrow."

"It must be a relief to be in the gospel business, where people aren't so insincere."

Kat hooted. "Honey, you haven't ever had your back stabbed until it's been stabbed by a so-called preacher woman in blue silk choir robes. Hollywood is right civilized compared to what goes on in the gospel business."

"Really?" Tilda considered the notion. "Would you be willing to let me interview you about it?"

"That might be fun. But I don't guarantee to name names — I've got a living to make."

"Understood. I'll see if I can get an editor interested, and get back to you." Again the exchange of business cards, and Kat started down the church steps.

Tilda stopped her to say, "Oh, one other

question. I went over my notes before I came down today, and I was wondering about something. I know you changed names after leaving acting."

"Langevoort is kind of a mouthful," Kat said. "Owen is my middle name."

"I get that. But what about your accent? You didn't have one when you were working on *Kissing Cousins.*"

"I had to train myself out of the drawl for Hollywood, but I let myself use it now."

"What drawl?" Tilda asked. "You were born in Revere, Massachusetts."

Kat looked around to see if anybody else was listening. Then, in the thickest North Shore accent Tilda had heard in a long time, she said, "Tilda, you think anybody wants to hear a gospel singah from Reveah? Get outta heah!" Then she winked, and said, "Bye now," just as sweetly as any Georgia peach.

Tilda saw that the twins had managed to cut Noel Clark off from Irv Munch, so she took the opportunity to approach him. "Mr. Clark? Tilda Harper, from *Entertain Me!*"

"Tilda, of course, so wonderful to see you again." He too, had perfected the air kiss, as he demonstrated.

Noel Clark, with his tight blond curls and determinedly trim figure, could be considered the greatest success story of the *Kissing Cousins* alumni — he'd played Antoine on the soap opera *City Hospital* for over twenty years, making him the only cast member to have landed another series. Admittedly, his role was that of a chauffeur to the show's wealthy Valeria family and the lines he got in an average episode were engrossing bits like, "Will Madame be visiting her cancer-ridden child in the hospital today or making a rendezvous with her latest himbo in his skanky love nest?"

Tilda made the appropriate remarks about the sadness of the occasion, and Noel made the appropriate responses. Then she said, "It must be comforting to see Katie Langevoort and the twins from the old days." She made a show of looking around. "Is Mercy Ashford here too?"

Noel smiled sardonically. "Mercy never was one to be bothered with her old friends, not even their funerals. I know I shouldn't gossip, but . . ."

"Would you prefer to keep this off the record?" Tilda offered, knowing what his answer would be.

"No, no, I trust you."

In other words, he wasn't willing to risk losing a mention in a magazine.

He said, "It's just that some people in the

industry will give you a hand up, and others won't. After *Kissing Cousins* shut down, Mercy got a feature almost immediately. Well, I got a copy of the script and there was a part that I would have been perfect for — absolutely perfect. So I called Mercy and asked if she could put in a good word for me with the director, but next thing I know, Mercy walked off the set and left me high and dry. Can you imagine?"

Actually, Tilda could, having just heard from the twins that he hadn't bothered to help them get work, but then again, the twins couldn't act and Noel, though no Laurence Olivier, was a solid character actor. So she clucked sympathetically and said, "Do you know what happened to make her leave the movie that way? It sounds so unprofessional."

"Completely unprofessional," Noel said. "And that's not the least of it. I mean, have you ever heard of an actress who didn't bother to let her agent know where she was going?"

"No, never."

"Well, that's what she did. We had the same agent back then, you see."

"Ariel Tomilyn?" Tilda said, remembering the name from her research.

"That's right. Apparently Mercy didn't

90

even talk to Ariel personally. She just left a message with Ariel's assistant. Naturally, the first thing Ariel did was try to get in touch with her to find out what was going on, but it was as if the woman had disappeared off the face of the earth."

"Really?" Tilda said.

He nodded. "Ariel called me, she called the rest of the cast, she called everybody — she was desperate to find her. But she never did."

"That's strange. Do you have any idea why Mercy would have left like that?"

"Not a clue. But wherever she went, she had plenty of money."

"Why do you say that?"

"According to Ariel, Mercy had some money coming in for something or another — I think it was some print ad work — but by the time the checks cleared, she was gone. Later on, when there were residuals from *Kissing Cousins* — not a fortune, but nothing to pass up either — Mercy never once came looking for her money. Ariel put it in escrow with the agency — she's dead now, and I imagine the agency still has the money."

"That's very strange," Tilda said. Presumably Mercy had made a lot more acting than Tilda did freelancing, but she still couldn't imagine anybody walking away from money that had already been earned.

"So, are you working on another story about the show now?" Noel asked, knowing where his bread was buttered.

"I am," Tilda confirmed.

"Then let me just say that Holly Kendricks was one of my dearest friends, and I feel her loss more than I can possibly say." He looked pointedly at Tilda's hands, as if wondering why she wasn't taking the words down.

"More than you can possibly say," Tilda repeated after him, as if she were memorizing his speech. "Thank you. I've still got your contact information if I need to get in touch for more background or quotes."

"Great, great. And, well, I know it's tacky to mention it here, but you may be interested to hear I just got a heads up from one of the writers at *City Hospital*. It seems that I'm going to be getting a lot more airtime in the story line they're kicking off later this month. Significant airtime."

"That's wonderful," Tilda said, though he'd said the same thing every time she'd ever spoken to him. As far as she could tell, he said it in every interview he'd given for the past twenty years, almost as long as Irv Munch had been pushing for a revival of

Kissing Cousins. "I know Holly would have been delighted — when I interviewed her, she said she watched *City Hospital* faithfully because of you."

"Really? I didn't know that. It's been so long since I talked to her . . ." He honestly sounded touched. As if in some karmic payback, he said, "Could you also say that I think Holly was a fine actress, and that it was the industry's loss when she left Hollywood for marriage and family."

"Marriage and family," Tilda repeated, again pretending to memorize it. "Got it."

Noel instigated another air kiss, but before he could make his exit, he stopped and asked, "Tilda, do they sell Sky Bars in Connecticut?"

"I'm not sure." At some point in her research on him, she'd found out that Noel was addicted to Sky Bars, a candy bar made by the New England Confectionery Company in Revere, Massachusetts, and she'd mentioned it in her article.

"I just thought I could pick up some, since I'm in New England. Of course, I've got plenty at home," he added with a satisfied smirk. "When the fans found out I couldn't get them in LA, they started sending them by the case. Isn't that amazing?"

Of course, Noel could probably have

found the candy somewhere in LA or he could have ordered them on the Web, but what he really enjoyed was the fact that devoted fans were willing to send the candy to him. It wasn't just the money — though it's always partially about the money — it was the ego boost of knowing some poor schlub in East Arm Pit had gone to the trouble of buying a box of the things and shipping it to Noel at his own expense.

"You could check at a Store 24," she suggested.

"Good idea. Ciao!"

As Noel made his exit toward the parking lot, Tilda idly wondered if he ever found himself automatically getting into the front seat of cabs and limos after all those years playing a chauffeur.

The crowd was considerably thinned out by then, and though she would have liked to have spoken to Irv Munch, by the time she'd disengaged from Noel, the producer was climbing into a car. The twins were gone too — Tilda saw Lawrence White escorting them toward the church parking lot. So it was time to make her own exit.

CHAPTER 6

"I never had any problems with stalkers or anything like that. *Kissing Cousins* fans are the best! The only thing is . . . Have you ever heard of 'slash' fiction?"
— Holly Kendricks, quoted in "Curse of the *Kissing Cousins*," *Entertain Me!*

Tilda tried to smooth out some of the wrinkles from her skirt when she got out of her car at Vincent's house in Cambridge, and wished her eminently suitable shoes were more comfortable. As she walked up the sidewalk to the rambling house Vincent had inherited from his parents, she wondered if she'd gotten the time wrong. Though Vincent had said over a hundred people were expected, there were only four other cars parked nearby, and one was Vincent's. She could tell from his vanity license plate: FANBOY. Some people might have carpooled, cabbed it, or caught the bus, but even so, she'd have expected more cars.

She rang the doorbell, grinning as always as she recognized the theme from *Close Encounters of the Third Kind.* Vincent opened the door, dressed somberly in black jeans and a black *Kissing Cousins* T-shirt. Of course he pretty much always wore dark jeans and black T-shirts, so it wasn't a big inconvenience for him.

Most of the really obsessed fans Tilda had met were either overweight or underweight, but Vincent was unusually average. Average build, average light-brown hair, average-size and -shape nose, average brown eyes, and average Caucasian complexion. He was a bit paler than some, but that was easily explained, either by his living in Massachusetts or by his job as a computer jockey.

"Tilda," he said, opening his arms wide. "I'm so glad you could make it."

Though they'd never been hugging buddies, Tilda was willing to stretch a point under the circumstances. At least it was a real hug, and not an air kiss.

"I hope I'm not early," she said.

"Not at all. You're right on time."

He led the way down a hall to a large living room decorated with TV and movie memorabilia. Vincent had never seen the need to limit himself to one brand of fandom. Not only was *Kissing Cousins* well represented, but there were posters from *Star Trek, Buffy the Vampire Slayer, The Addams Family, Highlander,* and others. One wall was lined with shelves of books, videos, and DVDs, and another had enough home entertainment equipment to fill the AV department of a good-size high school. A third was lined with computers, printers, scanners, modems, and other gadgets Tilda wasn't sure about. The last was mostly those posters. The windows, including a large bay window, were thoroughly curtained to make sure the real world didn't intrude upon Vincent's world.

There were two other people in the room, sitting in the circle of couch and arm chairs surrounding a coffee table in the middle of the room.

"You know Rhonda and Javier," Vincent said.

Tilda nodded at them, both of whom she'd met through Vincent.

Rhonda fit the stereotype of fan better than Vincent did — she was a prime example of the underfed fan. She was short, and tiny in all dimensions except her head, which seemed unnaturally large to be on that thin neck. Her watery blue eyes looked even bigger than they were because of the owl-like glasses she wore. Tilda knew from earlier meetings that Rhonda wasn't just a fan — she was a collector. Her archive of *Kissing Cousins* memorabilia was the most complete one Tilda had ever seen, or even heard of.

Javier was also not what Tilda would consider a pure fan. Like Vincent, he dabbled in many brands of fandom, but his real passion was spoilers. It wasn't enough for him to watch a show to find out what was going to happen — he had to dig around and read bootlegged scripts to find out what was going to happen before the rest of the world knew. He ran a Web site — thespoilerroom.com — to share his ill-gotten knowledge with like-minded fans. He always seemed smarmy to Tilda, though, seen objectively, he was quite good-looking, with olive skin, thickly lashed eyes, and full lips.

Tilda glanced around the room again, looking for the other people Vincent had said would be there. "Where is everybody?"

"They're all here in spirit," Vincent said happily. "I've got the chat room set up, and we can log in as soon as you're ready."

"We were just waiting for you," Rhonda added.

"Vincent, are you telling me that the hundred or more fans you said were coming are only online?" Tilda said, working hard not to sound as irritated as she was starting to feel.

"Well, yeah," he said. "Did you think I was going to try to get a hundred people in here?"

"You didn't make that clear when you invited me."

"Oh, I'm sorry, Tilda. You are going to stay, aren't you?"

Though Tilda was tempted to blow him off, Vincent was one of her best entrees into the fan world and pretty good for computer news too. Besides, he was looking so disappointed. "Sure I'll stay. I just wish I'd realized — I'd have brought a change of clothes."

"Go ahead and slip out of anything you want," Javier said with a leer.

Tilda ignored him. "The only thing is, I didn't bring my laptop."

"That's okay," Vincent assured her. "I've got stations set up for all of us. We've got just enough time to grab some pizza before the service gets started."

A few minutes later, munching on a piece

of pepperoni pizza with a full glass of Dr Pepper beside her, Tilda decided it wouldn't be too bad. Sure, she'd have to jettison the idea of a tear-jerking photo of mourning fans, but she could still use the memorial service for human interest, and the fact that some of the fans were logging in from the UK and Australia would add international flavor. Plus Vincent could e-mail her a transcript of the whole "service" so she wouldn't even have to take notes. How bad could it be?

An hour in, Tilda was dying to open up a game of solitaire or Minesweeper — anything to stay awake. The chat had started out promisingly enough. Vincent, as the moderator, introduced those of them there in person, and even more than the expected one hundred fans logged in with user names like "Cousin_ Kisser," "Damon_4_Ever," and "Sitcom_Fan." Then Tilda typed in a brief report of the funeral: who'd been there, what was said and sung, and so on. Some of the questions posted in response reminded her strongly of her Aunt Tess, who liked nothing better than to critique funerals. All of that killed about half an hour.

Then Vincent opened the chat to people to tell their memories of Sherri/Holly, or of either of the other two deceased Cousins:

Brad/Jim and Damon/Alex. That's when Tilda's eyes began to glaze over.

It wasn't that the fans didn't have legitimate sorrows, and memories that were clearly important to them. It was more the fact that very few of them could write or spell decently — Tilda had a decided aversion to chatspeak, that bastardized form of code words some people insisted on using online. Worst of all, while the first tale of how much the show had meant to one of the fans was touching, the second through umpteenth were pretty much the same, meaning that they were just tedious. Admittedly, the guy who swore that the show's scripts were written in code that revealed all of the actors were actually aliens and that the dead ones had actually faked their own demises so they could return to the home world was somewhat entertaining, but Vincent cut him off quickly.

It didn't help that Tilda knew that if she'd posted her feelings, they'd have been pretty much the same as everybody else's, albeit better written and properly spelled. Part of her wanted to type in ALL CAPS that the show was HERS! Another part wanted to type in all caps that these people really needed to GET A LIFE. And a third part just wanted to go home and go to bed. She drank more soda, hoping the caffeine would keep her going.

Finally even Vincent had had enough, and after promising the people still waiting in the queue that they'd be able to post their stories on the Listserv, he said it was time to introduce a new topic.

Tilda sat up from where she'd been slumped over in her chair. He hadn't warned her about this, but whatever it was, it had to be more interesting than all the essays on "What *Kissing Cousins* Meant to Me."

Vincent typed:

<Vincent_the_Moderator> As you all know, Brad/Jim, Damon/Alex, and Sherri/Holly all died under suspicious circumstances. It's my belief — and there are those who agree with me — that a killer is targeting the cast of *Kissing Cousins* and that Mercy is next. (See my Web site for details.) Given the accelerating timeline, she may be marked for death in as little as two weeks. Tilda Harper, our professional investigative reporter, has been unable to locate her, so I'm asking all of you to help. Surely one of us here must have some idea of how to find Mercy so we can warn her and protect her. Any idea, no matter how outlandish, could help.

Tilda winced. Though she liked the sound of "professional investigative reporter," it was hardly accurate, and she wasn't at all sure she wanted a bunch of fans throwing their most outlandish ideas her way. The fans seemed taken aback too. It was a full two minutes before the first reply came.

<Damon_Luvr> This may sound obvious, but have you checked the nationwide phone books? YellowPages.com?
<TildaHarper> Obvious, maybe, but not to be ignored. I tried it.
<Back2theLab> Did you ask the other cast members?
<TildaHarper> Yes. Including Gabrielle and Gwendolyn Roman, who played the twins.
<Cousin_Fan> Mercy's agent? The producer of the show? Screen Actors' Guild?
<TildaHarper> Yes, yes, and Mercy wasn't a member.

The suggestions kept going from there. Some of them were obvious, some were clever, but all were ideas Tilda had tried before. Then came a post that took Tilda by surprise.

<Have_Mercy> Have you asked her lover?

Excuse me, LOVERS. Everybody knows she was fucking her way through LA.

In all of Tilda's research about the actress, she'd never heard anything of the kind about Mercy. In fact, none of her sources had even mentioned the woman having a serious boyfriend.

Vincent snapped, "Bullshit! I'm cutting this bastard off."

"No, wait," Tilda said. "I want to see what he's got to say."

<TildaHarper> I never heard about Mercy sleeping around. Where do you get your info?

<Have_Mercy> It was common knowledge back when the show was on the air.

<TildaHarper> Do you work in the industry? Or did you, back then?

<Have_Mercy> Not exactly. I know people who did.

<TildaHarper> Can you give me any names? Perhaps share your sources? People who slept with her, or who knew who did?

There was a longish pause, and Vincent muttered, "He's lying. He made it all up and doesn't want to admit it."

"Give him another minute," Tilda said. It

wasn't that she believed him, necessarily, but it was the first new idea that had popped up all night.

Finally he responded.

<Have_Mercy> I bet she slept with the other stars on the show.
<TildaHarper> Hard to prove now. Brad/Jim and Damon/Alex are dead, and Elbert/Noel is gay. Anybody else?
<Have_Mercy> What about the producer? He must have had some reason to hire her.

Vincent could restrain himself no longer.

<Vincent_the_Moderator> He hired her because she was incredibly talented, you dork-wad! She MADE that show!
<Have_Mercy> If she was so hot, why hasn't she worked since?
<TildaHarper> That's what I'm trying to find out. Have you got anything solid, or are you just pulling ideas out of the blue?
<Have_Mercy> She was a slut!

Tilda said, "Cut him off. He's just a troll." She'd never understood trolls herself, weirdos who posted the most inflammatory messages they could think of just to stir people up. It was the Internet equivalent of a child poking at an anthill with a stick.

105

Unfortunately, even though Vincent wouldn't let any more messages from Have _Mercy go through, the guy had infuriated the fans so much that the rest of the chat was nothing but people flaming him. If anybody had any decent suggestions for Tilda, they forgot them in their outrage.

After half an hour of indignation, Tilda said, "Vincent, I think this has run its course, don't you?"

He nodded, and posted a closing message.

<Vincent_the_Moderator> Despite SOME people, I think this has been healing for MOST of us. I'd like us all to share a moment of silence in honor of our Fallen Cousins.

He actually bowed his head over his keyboard before going on. Rhonda, Javier, and Tilda just took the opportunity to drink more of their soda.

<Vincent_the_Moderator> If anybody has any other ideas for Tilda — credible ideas, not crazy ramblings — post them on the list. Goodnight all.

After posting a few of the good-bye messages that came and responding privately to several requests for Have_Mercy's head on a platter, Vincent closed down the chat room and leaned back from the screen to stretch. The others followed suit.

Tilda said, "Funny, I don't remember asking you to solicit suggestions from the list."

"I thought somebody might have a decent idea."

"They might, but I don't have time to weed through all the spam in hopes of finding something worthwhile."

"I'll screen it for you," he promised, "and just send you the stuff that might help."

"All right," she said ungraciously. She didn't like the implication that she needed help from random fans, especially when she probably did.

"Let me know if Have_Mercy comes through with anything else," Javier said with an unpleasant gleam in his eye. "I wonder if there's any photographic evidence of Mercy doing the dirty with Brad and Damon."

Rhonda tossed an empty Coke can at him. "You don't believe that guy, do you? He's probably the one who keeps trying to post slash fiction to the list. Mercy screws Brad, Sherri screws Damon, both girls screw Damon, Sherri screws Mercy — how many possibilities are there, anyway?"

"It would depend on how many characters are involved in a scenario, and who you included in your pool of candidates," Javier said thoughtfully. "The six Cousins, their grandfather — those are a given. Then there are the twins."

"And the shark they jumped to get onto the show," Tilda couldn't resist adding.

Javier actually seemed to be considering the possibility, which was sort of freaky. "If we assume no more than three characters at a time, the possible combinations would be —"

"A math geek and a pervert," Rhonda said, going to check for leftover pizza. "What a man!"

Javier shrugged. "You asked."

"It was rhetorical!" Rhonda yelled from the kitchen.

Tilda followed Rhonda for a fresh infusion of caffeine.

"How's the writing business?" Rhonda asked.

"Not bad," Tilda said, wracking her brain to remember what Rhonda did. "You?"

"Still looking for a job. Jeez, the market is tight! I've even gone to interviews out of state — all over New England, the Research Triangle in North Carolina, Silicon Valley — but nothing."

Okay, that probably meant computers. "That's rough. Sorry I don't know anybody

I can call on your behalf."

"Thanks, I appreciate it." The woman sighed. "I'm going to have to find something soon, or move back in with my folks."

She and Tilda both shuddered at the possibility, and went back to the living room, where Javier was working a calculator.

"Should I include the Cousins' parents in the equation?" he asked.

For a moment, Tilda actually wondered if there was a place in her article for a discussion of *Kissing Cousins* slash fiction, which made her realize just how tired she was. "Vincent," she said, "it's been real, but I'm going to head out."

"Thanks so much for coming," Vincent said. "It means a lot to have friends around at a time like this."

Again he spread his arms for a hug, and again she went with it. He was just so damned sincere. But when Javier opened his arms too, she deliberately turned away to put her shoes back on. She didn't give a shit if he was sincere or not, he was still Javier, and he'd tried to cop a feel every time she'd ever seen him.

When he said he was leaving too and would walk her to her car, Tilda's first thought was that he was going to have another try at her, but he had a different passion on his mind.

"So there's really talk about a *Kissing Cousins* reunion?" he said as they walked toward their cars.

"There's been talk about that for years, you know that."

"Yeah, but it sounds as if it might have gone beyond talk this time. Was there any mention of a script or a treatment? It would be a real kick to get something like that up on my site."

"Nobody mentioned there being anything in writing."

"Do you think you could check into it? Maybe get me a copy? Even a preliminary draft would be a hell of a spoiler."

"Javier, what is the point of spoilers anyway? Why not just wait for the finished product?"

"Any loser can see it when it's released — I want to know sooner."

"Why?"

"To be the first to know."

It wasn't much of an answer, but she was willing to bet that he didn't have a better one. "I bet you peek at your presents before Christmas morning."

"Peek, hell," Javier said. "By Christmas Eve, I have them opened, taken back to the store, and exchanged for something I really want."

"If I were Santa Claus, I'd put coal in your stocking."

"If you were Santa Claus and I posted your picture on my site, I would totally own Christmas!"

Tilda didn't bother to say anything more. There was no point.

"So, what do you say?" he said. "Can you get me something? I'd make it worth your while."

"You can not possibly pay me enough to risk my reputation by giving you something like that."

"Come on, Tilda, nobody would know it was you."

"That's what they told Max Levine."

"Who's that?"

"He was a promising entertainment reporter until he got caught leaking the winner of one of the lesser reality shows. Now he works in a car wash. Does a great detail job, if you need one."

Javier smiled ingratiatingly. "I bet he was nowhere near as smart as you are."

"That's true," Tilda agreed, "because I'm not stupid enough to give out any spoilers."

Leaving him no time to argue further, Tilda got in her car and left. She wondered idly how much time he'd waste trying to track down Max Levine, and hoped it would be hours. Max was actually a friend of hers, but as far as she knew, he'd never worked as a reporter or in a car wash. Max wasn't even his real name.

CHAPTER 7

"Episode 23: Summer Camp (Part 1)
Pops sends Sherri and Mercy to summer camp, where a clueless counselor assigns them to the same cabin. Desperate to get away from one another, they play a series of pranks, each hoping the other will ask for a transfer. When Sherri's pail of water over the door douses a counselor just as Mercy's pet tarantula appears, both girls get transferred to new cabins. But when they meet their new bunkmates, they realize they've gone from the frying pan into the fire."

— Fanboy's Online *Kissing Cousins*
Episode Guide, by Vincent Peters

The drive from Cambridge to Malden seemed endless, not just because of the traffic, but because Tilda was wiped out by the day. Only cranking up The Dan Band Live on her CD player kept her awake. There was nothing like listening to girl songs of the seventies and eighties being sung by guys, only with faster tempos and more profanity. At least she found a convenient parking place, and the apartment was dark when she got in, meaning that Heather was out for the night. She didn't have to make small talk before falling into bed and into a deep blissful sleep. For all of three hours.

It was just after one when Tilda heard her roommate and a male guest arrive, obviously drunk and amorous. Despite wrapping her pillow around her head, she was soon to learn just how amorous they were, not to mention the facts that the guy's name was Doug, that he preferred to be on top, and that he probably had forgotten Heather's name, because he kept calling her "Babe." Also, he was a grunter. An hour after that, she found out that he snored.

Despite the late night, Heather somehow managed to get out of bed nearly on time and noisily started fixing breakfast. Since this woke Tilda once again, she was able to throw on a pair of jeans and a T-shirt and pull a document from her files before going to the kitchen to confront her roommate.

"Hi!" Heather said brightly, obviously going for the approach of pretending nothing was wrong. "You're up bright and early this morning."

"I hold here a copy of our Roommate Agreement," Tilda said formally. "If you will read Item 11, you will see that —"

"I know, I know. No bringing home dates without warning. I'd have called, Tilda, but it was already so late by the time I met Doug that I was afraid you'd be asleep."

"Item 11 clearly states these decisions have to be made before eleven on a weeknight, and by eleven-thirty on a weekend." Admittedly she'd been in bed by ten-thirty, but she saw no reason to mention that. "Why didn't you go to his place?"

"He's living with a girl —"

Tilda just looked at her.

"No, it's not like that. They've broken up, but he can't move out until the end of the month. It would have been really unfair to his ex to bring home another girl, don't you think?"

"Isn't keeping me up all night unfair, not to mention breaking our agreement? Again?"

"You're right, I'm sorry. Look, I'll make it up to you."

"How?"

"By letting you know right now that Doug is going to be staying over for the next couple of nights. That's more than twelve hours warning."

Tilda didn't quite see how two more nights of grunting and snoring would make up for anything, but she had to admit that Heather was adhering to the agreement. "Fine. But let me also remind you of Item 12. Your guest is not to go into my room, and is not to use any of my bathroom supplies or food. If he mistakenly uses anything belonging to me, it is your responsibility to replace it. Clear?"

"Clear," Heather said. "And I'll let you know if he decides to stay longer."

"Item 13. No guest is to stay longer than three nights without at least a month's warning."

"Does last night count? I mean, since it was unexpected."

"Yes!"

"Okay, two more nights maximum." She looked at the clock on the microwave. "Shit! I've got to get a shower."

She ran off, and Tilda started back for her bedroom. Then the door to Heather's room opened, and a bleary-eyed specimen who had probably looked good in the dim lights of whatever club Heather had found him in stepped out wearing nothing but a pair of boxer shorts.

"Hey!" he said in mild surprise.

"Good morning, Doug," Tilda said. "Sleep well?"

"Yeah, great. Where's, um, your roommate?"

"In the shower. I'm going back to bed."

"Wouldn't mind getting forty more winks myself, but you know, duty calls. I guess she, your roommate, has to get to work too?"

"I'm sure she'll tell you all about it," Tilda said. Then, taking pity on the lunk, she added, "By the way, her name is Heather."

"Heather, right. Thanks."

She just shook her head and went back into her room. Not that she could actually sleep for the next hour, as Heather got ready for work and communed with Doug, and then while Doug used up all the hot water Heather hadn't. Eventually Tilda got a couple of hours rest, but woke up with the firm conviction that it was time to spend a couple of days with her sister June.

Chapter 8

"Sometimes it's hard to pin down where inspiration comes from, but I remember exactly how I created *Kissing Cousins*. I read an article in *Teen Fave* comparing Wednesday from *The Addams Family* to Marilyn from *The Munsters,* and I started wondering how those two would get along in the same house. Just having two kids would have been too much like *The Patty Duke Show,* so I added more, but I started with those two completely different girls."
— Irv Munch, quoted in "Curse of the *Kissing Cousins,*" *Entertain Me!*

Tilda did try to call June to warn her that she was coming, but the line was busy. So instead she checked e-mail in case something interesting had shown up, and then attended to the decidedly uninteresting messages that had arrived since the day before, including negative replies to some of the calls for information she'd sent out. Next she made sure her laptop was in synch with her desk computer and packed it and enough clothes for a couple of days away. Just before leaving, she tried to call her sister again, but the line was still busy.

She got busy signals twice more during her leisurely drive up to Beverly, where June lived with her husband Glen, her two disgustingly well-adjusted kids, and an overweight cocker spaniel. Tilda had once commented that they had the looks of a sitcom family, but none of the problems or friction required for joke fodder.

June's house was in a neighborhood that straddled the line between upper-middle and lower-upper class. There were children around, but no more than two per family, and SUVs and minivans filled the driveways. The houses were comfortably old, with character and fresh paint jobs. It was clearly a "nice" place to live.

Tilda parked on the street in front of June's Dutch Colonial, glad to see that June's minivan was there. She grabbed her bags and headed for the front door, but it opened before she could reach it, and June nearly barreled into her.

June was older than Tilda, and took after her father, just as Tilda did hers. Their mother had always been nonplussed that neither of her daughters looked as if they belonged to her. June's father was plump and fair-haired, with a generous helping of freckles, all of which looked better on June than they did on him.

"Tilda!" she said happily. "What are you doing here?" Without waiting for an answer, June enfolded her into a hug.

"I was hoping I could borrow your guest room for a night or two," Tilda explained. "My roomie has company."

"Of course you can — I'm dying for some girl talk. I've been meaning to call all week, but between the bake sale for Lonnie's class and the school book fair, I've been crazed!"

"I tried to call but — "

"I know, my line was busy. You'd be surprised how many phone calls it takes to put together a lousy bake sale and book fair! Not to mention the egos I've had to stroke — I tell you, if I ever decide to leave this so-called life of leisure and go back into psychology, I'll have enough material for a dozen papers. Maybe even a book!" She shooed Tilda toward the door. "Go on in, get yourself something to eat. I made brownies for the bake sale, and you can have some from the plate on the table."

"Where are you heading?"

"Hair appointment with Tom. The so-and-so moved to a new shop! Now I've got to go all the way to Burlington to get my hair done."

Though Tilda was used to crossing town barriers for work and recreation, her sister preferred to stay closer to home. "Isn't there somebody else at his old place who can cut your hair?"

"When I find somebody who can cut my hair as well as Tom, then I'll switch. So what if I have to drive an extra half an hour each way — it's worth it. Not to mention the fact that nobody has ever been able to get the gray out of my hair like he does. When you start coloring your hair — "

"What's the matter with my hair?"

"Absolutely nothing — it's gorgeous — but you know black will show the gray a lot quicker than something lighter." June looked at her watch. "I've got to run."

"Don't let me keep you. I've got the brownies to keep me company."

June promised to be back in time for lunch and headed for the minivan. Since it was the same forest green as half the minivans in town, Tilda had found a happy-face ball to put on the antenna, knowing that June wouldn't mind the fangs Tilda added to the smile.

A thought occurred to Tilda just as her sister opened the car door, and she yelled, "June, is my stuff still in the attic?"

"Of course."

"Do you mind if I go up there to take a look?"

"Help yourself. I'm afraid it's pretty dusty up there —"

"You haven't dusted your attic?" Tilda said in mock horror. "I'm going to cancel your subscription to *Martha Stewart Living.*"

June laughed, and was gone.

Closing the front door behind her, Tilda passed through the living room — which, as always, looked like an explosion in a Fisher-Price factory — and into the kitchen, where warm brownies waited. Tilda knew the milk she took out would be fresh, unlike the contents of her own refrigerator, so she poured some into a glass without even sniffing it first. The first brownie was good, and the second was even better. She was tempted by a third, but went upstairs instead, leaving her stuff in the guest room, which also had a door leading to the attic stairway.

Unlike many attics, June's was tall enough for Tilda to stand in. June had hinted that she'd be willing to fit it out as a bedroom and even add a private bath, should Tilda be interested in moving in, but Tilda refused to consider it. Sitcom suburbia was her stock-in-trade — the real thing made her nervous. Besides, knowing how quickly she went through roommates, she wasn't willing to jeopardize her relationship with her sister. June was already going above and beyond the call of duty by letting Tilda store those boxes that she would have inflicted on her mother's attic, had Mom and her third husband not retired to Florida.

The attic was the domain of Tilda's brother-in-law Glen, and as such was as precisely organized as the living room was not. And despite June's warning, there was less dust than in Tilda's bedroom. All of her boxes were stacked in one corner, with the labels facing outward, so it took no time at all for her to find what she was looking for: the three boxes marked *Kissing Cousins.*

Tilda liked to pretend that she kept her boxes in her sister's attic because she didn't have enough closet space in the apartments she'd been able to afford, and that was certainly true, but she had other motives.

One, she didn't want any of her roommates finding out just how much of a geek she'd been about certain shows, including *Kissing Cousins,* which they'd certainly have realized if they'd seen the care with which her collection was arranged — the photos and clippings neatly filed in folders with typewritten labels and each paperback book and magazine in its own clear Mylar bag with backing board. Even the board game from the show was wrapped in plastic, and some of the jigsaw puzzles had never been opened.

Two, she didn't want anybody pawing through her treasures.

The heaviest box was filled with her collection of vintage teen magazines — *Tiger Beat, 16 Magazine,* and *Teen Fave* — and she pulled it out first to flip through pages of articles with titles like "Donny Osmond's Secret Sickness," "Rick Springfield Tells You Everything You Want to Know," and "John Stamos's Dream of a Full House of His Own." She'd carefully bookmarked the articles about *Kissing Cousins* stars, so it was easy to find them again, and she found herself wondering if green really had been Jim Bonnier's favorite color and if Noel Clark had ever found his lost first love. None of this, fascinating as it had been to the teenaged Tilda or as amusing it was to her now, was really what she was looking for. She was hoping that there would be something in the articles to give her an idea about where to search for Mercy.

Unfortunately there wasn't much to work with. Teen magazines of that era weren't really known for giving hard data — sure, she found out what Mercy's ideal date would be, but not her ideal place to live nearly three decades after the show ended. In fact, articles about the *Kissing Cousins* cast had dwindled as the show reached the middle of its third season, which had undoubtedly been a clue to the network that the show's modest popularity was waning.

The last mention Tilda found was in an issue of *Teen Fave,* a magazine she preferred over the others because of the editor's predictions about where the current crop of teen idols would be in five years, ten years, or even longer. Sophia Vaughn had had a gift for knowing who was likely to hang onto their current level of fame, or even exceed it — she'd successfully predicted long careers for John Travolta and Michael Jackson, while remaining mute on Sajid Khan and twins Andy and David Williams, and tactfully vague on many others.

Sophia had written about Mercy just after *Kissing Cousins* was canceled, and had announced that Mercy had already signed to be in *The Raven's Prey,* a feature that would no doubt be the first of many big screen appearances for the young actress. Tilda remembered renting that movie, only to find that Mercy wasn't in it after all. She'd never heard why until Noel told her about Mercy quitting.

It was a thin lead, but it was something, so Tilda pulled out her Palm and jotted down the movie's title. Maybe she could get in touch with some of the people who'd worked on it — one of them might know why Mercy had left the production.

Sophia Vaughn might remember more too, though Tilda wasn't sure if it would be worth the effort it would take to find out. The retired editor was enormous fun, and a source of information Tilda could find nowhere else, but she was eccentric and could be difficult to deal with.

Tilda was about to put the magazine back into the box when she saw a bookmark at the inside back cover. There was a picture of Mercy along with Sophia, sitting on a couch in what looked like a hotel lobby. A handsome, dark-haired man was standing behind the couch, and a young boy was sitting between the women, staring at Mercy worshipfully. Neither the man nor the boy were identified. This was an even thinner lead, but Tilda thought she might be able to find out who they were. She slipped the issue back into its protective bag, and put it aside to take downstairs.

Next was the box with photos, mostly publicity stills, each authentically autographed by an authentic studio staff member, some of whom had even managed to spell the names of the star correctly. She found the one she was looking for, a head shot of Mercy dressed as her character, all in black lace. Even if Tilda made allowances for her early adulation of the actress and whatever touching up had been done on the photo, it was clear that Mercy had been a striking young woman. Her straight black hair shone like a model's in a shampoo ad, and her dark eyes were bright. She wasn't traditionally pretty, but attractive in that strong way that promises even greater beauty in the future. Though it didn't show in this picture, she'd been tall too — several cast members had mentioned the convolutions they'd gone through to ensure that the older boys looked taller than Mercy, even though she'd been their height. By now, she'd be forty-five years old, but Tilda felt sure that unless the actress had suffered some disfiguring accident, she'd be able to recognize her. That was, if she ever managed to find her. She kept the photo out too.

Checking her watch, Tilda realized she'd

been up in the attic for nearly two hours, meaning that June would be home for lunch soon. Short of checking to see if the *Kissing Cousins* board game had a coded message that revealed a hidden map to Mercy's secret lair, she thought she'd found all she was going to find. So she restacked the boxes, trying to meet Glen's exacting standards, and went back down to leave her gleanings in the spare bedroom and wash the dust of her memories from her hands and face.

Her timing was good. June was coming in the door as she went downstairs, and Tilda dutifully complimented June's haircut, which looked pretty much the same as every other haircut she'd had over the past several years. Then she convinced her sister to abandon her plans to fix something at home and instead let Tilda treat her to lunch at the local Bertucci's.

Knowing her sister the way she did, Tilda wasn't surprised by the topic June introduced at the restaurant, only that she waited until their Cokes and hot rolls were served before introducing it.

"So?" June prompted. "Are you seeing anyone?"

"Yes," Tilda said solemnly. "I see dead people."

"Very funny. I saw that movie too."

Tilda grinned. "Actually I did see a dead person, or at least her coffin. I went to a funeral yesterday in Connecticut."

"Oh?" June said, looking concerned. "Anybody I know?"

"No, it was work. Someone I interviewed."

"Anybody I've heard of?"

"Do you remember *Kissing Cousins*?"

"The show you watched incessantly? The one you wanted to record so badly that you nagged Mom for a month until she bought a VCR? The one that inspired the board game that I spent two weeks on eBay trying to find for your birthday, because it had to be in mint condition? No, I've never heard of it."

"It was the actress who played Sherri, the cheerleader."

"That's a shame. She was still fairly young, wasn't she? Cancer?"

"Murder."

"Really? Husband or boyfriend?"

"Don't women ever get killed for money or revenge?"

"Women get killed for all kinds of reasons, but husbands and boyfriends — whether they're current, former, or estranged — are the mostly likely. Horrible, I know, but true. I may live in the suburbs, but I do read the papers."

"Cruel but fair," Tilda acknowledged, "but this time it might be something else." She briefly explained Vincent's theory, but when she saw her sister was looking worried, she quickly changed the subject to the story assignment.

"Something else for my scrapbook!" June said.

"Are you still keeping that up?"

"Of course. Times three: one for me, and one for each of the kids. You're keeping copies of everything for your kids, aren't you?"

"I don't even have a regular boyfriend." Then she swore inwardly, realizing June had managed to get the conversation right back where she wanted it. Someday she'd have to figure out how her sister did that.

"So you're not seeing anybody right now?" June confirmed.

Tilda thought briefly of Lawrence White, who'd certainly hinted that he was willing, but she didn't want to get June's hopes up. "Nobody bed-worthy, if you know what I mean."

"No, I have no idea what you mean — Glen and I sleep in twin beds and the kids appeared on our doorstep in baskets."

They both snickered, and when their food arrived, Tilda took advantage of the distraction to ask about her niece and nephew. Answering in the required amount of detail kept June talking through their chicken parmesan, the second round of Cokes, and the drive back to June's house. The kids themselves were dropped off by their carpool soon after, and getting them snacks and making sure they did their homework took up most of the rest of the afternoon.

Though she'd expected June to get back around to the topic of husband hunting over dinner preparation, instead she sent her off to the guest room "to get some work done," so Tilda went online to see what she could find out about *The Raven's Prey.* She didn't remember it that well, other than her disappointment at not seeing Mercy in it, but found that it had been about a young female spy with the code name Raven outfighting male spies three times her size and eventually falling for an enemy spy. Luckily for the plucky lass, he turned out to be a double agent, so it was okay for her to ride off into the sunset with him, which they had done in a helicopter.

According to the Internet Movie Database, Tilda's favorite movie Web site, the acting had been wooden, the writing completely unoriginal, and the action scenes unbelievable, so, not surprisingly, the movie had tanked. IMDb also listed all the cast and crew, but unfortunately, Tilda had met none of the people involved. Of course, the film industry being what it was, a little time would likely find her a connection she could use. She started searching for a link.

She came up empty on the first round and was ready to take a break when she heard Glen come home, so she went downstairs to say hello. He was in the middle of telling June how wonderful her hair looked, proving both that he was an exemplary husband and that maybe the haircut had been worth the drive after all.

Inspiration struck. "June," Tilda said, "how long has Tom been doing your hair?"

June added up the answer on her fingers. "Twelve years now. Why?"

"How many different places has he worked?"

"Three, counting the new one."

"And you keep following him?"

"Of course. He knows my hair, and he knows all about my life, so I can talk to him about anything. It's better than going to a therapist, and I should know. Do you want an appointment with him?"

"No, thanks. I just had a thought. You'd go to a lot of trouble to get to him, right?"

"Of course."

"Elizabeth Montgomery was the same way," Tilda mused, remembering the phone interview she'd had with the actress's former hairdresser. "There was this one guy she liked and she made sure he got hired to work on her movies after *Bewitched* was canceled. In fact, she still talks to him."

"I thought she was dead," Glen said.

"She is, but the guy says they still keep in touch. Anyway, it sounds as if stars are just as devoted to their makeup artists as regular people are."

"Sounds reasonable," Glen said, politely trying to follow along.

Tilda didn't take time to explain. "June, is there time for me to do some more work before dinner?"

"About fifteen minutes."

"Great!" She scooted back up to the spare room and sent a quick e-mail to Vincent, asking if he knew who'd done the makeup on *Kissing Cousins.* It was too obscure a question for IMDb or the usual fan sites, but Vincent had the answer for her in minutes.

Though there'd been a couple of different makeup people, Jasmine Fisher had done the girl Cousins, including Mercy. A little bit of Googling, and Tilda had found her Web site, which included contact information and a résumé. She even had Mercy listed as a client, which might mean that they'd been more than casual acquaintances. Fisher's address was in New York, and Tilda e-mailed a request to interview her by phone for *Entertain Me!* She knew the woman would assume that she was the intended focus of the piece, but Tilda could explain the real situation after she agreed to the interview. Besides, now that she thought of it, an article about makeup artists might be interesting — actors spent a lot of time in those makeup chairs, and there were bound to be interesting stories. She quickly composed a query letter and e-mailed it to Jillian.

Her niece Lonnie came up then to call her for dinner, and Tilda was feeling happy enough to race her down the stairs. The makeup artist might not lead to anything, but it was a new lead, one she'd missed when looking for Mercy before, and that was enough to cheer her up.

Dinner was meat loaf, one of June's specialties, and Tilda was enjoying the treat of one of the so-called normal dinners that very few people actually seemed to experience: meat and two vegetables, conversation about the day's events, and reasonably polite kids. But halfway through, she noticed that June was laughing a bit too loudly, smiling a bit too brightly, and nodding longer than necessary. There could be only one explanation. Her sister was up to something.

As June brought out the dessert of strawberries and whipped cream, she casually asked, "So, how long will you be staying with us, Tilda?"

"Well, my roommate said her —" She stopped, starting to get an idea of what June was planning. "Why do you ask? Do you need me out of the spare room?"

"Of course not," June said quickly. "We're just having some people over tomorrow night that you might enjoy meeting. Friends."

One would have thought that, somewhere along the line, a psychologist would have learned to lie convincingly, but June must have slept through that course. Tilda was sure that at least one of the friends would be an unattached male, with a good job, and attractive, at least to June. She'd introduced a number of such friends to Tilda over the past few years, and none of them had been worth a second evening. Now Tilda knew why her sister hadn't asked her to keep her company in the kitchen while she fixed dinner — she must have hit the phone faster than Tilda could get her computer booted.

"That sounds great," Tilda said as sincerely as she could, "but I'm going to New York tomorrow. I got a lead on my story, and it's not something I can do long distance. Maybe another time."

"Sure," June said, acknowledging defeat. "We'll plan something when you get back."

Of course that meant a flurry of e-mails and phone calls over the course of the night and the next morning to make sure that *Entertain Me!* would reimburse her for train fare and a hotel room. Plus she had to fend off an end run from Nicole, who wanted to force her to take the bus from Chinatown instead of the train and to stay in a cheaper hotel. When Tilda flatly refused to take the bus and pointed out that she needed a decent room in case she conducted interviews at the hotel, Jillian agreed to pay.

With that settled, Tilda could set up an actual meeting with the makeup artist instead of the phone call she'd originally planned. And, since she was going to be in New York anyway, she decided she might as well schedule dinner with Sophia Vaughn. Surely one of the meetings would bear fruit of some kind — Jillian had expressed moderate interest in a piece about celebrity makeup artists and Sophia was almost always good for an article. If not, the trip would be worth it so that Tilda could avoid Heather's noisy lovemaking and June's unsubtle matchmaking.

CHAPTER 9

"Teen Fave gave a lot of space to *Kissing Cousins.* They were never huge — they only got one cover and never a banner — but one or more of them made it into just about every issue while the show was on the air. They were good-looking kids, with that built-in feud to play with. In other words, tailor-made for us."

— Sophia Vaughn former editor of *Teen Fave,* quoted in "Curse of the *Kissing Cousins,*" *Entertain Me!*

After travel arrangements were completed, Tilda made a stop at her apartment to pick up more clothes and make sure Heather's boyfriend was staying out of her room. Then she took the T to South Station to catch the 1:15 train to New York.

As far as Tilda was concerned, the train was the only civilized way to travel from Boston to New York. Since it was an off time, she had no problem getting a window seat, and she pulled out her iPod and a paperback to keep herself entertained during the three and a half hours the train took to get to Penn Station. Between her toys and occasionally looking out the window to watch New England scenery flow by, she was completely relaxed. From past experience, she knew she needed the respite before she dove into the whirlpool of sights and sounds that was Manhattan.

As soon as she got to the station in New York, she rolled her suitcase into a semi-quiet corner and used her cell to call the doorman at Sophia's building to find out what restaurant the older woman currently favored. The Palm was still in vogue, so next she called there to see if they were familiar with Sophia's tastes. They were, and Tilda ordered heart of palm salad, prime rib, and hash browns for two. Then she headed outside to the taxi stand, and cabbed it to Second Avenue.

The price for an information-gathering session with Sophia was always the same: dinner from her favorite restaurant, whatever that happened to be. Since retirement, Sophia seemingly never left her apartment, so that meant takeout. By virtue of knowing countless famous people, Sophia was able to prevail upon even the most prestigious and popular restaurants to provide her with to-go food of the quality she considered her due. Price was no object, particularly if somebody else was paying.

Tilda didn't know why Sophia never left her apartment. She and the mutual friend who'd introduced her to the former editor had speculated about it more than once, considering agoraphobia, embarrassment over some deformity hidden by the flowing caftans Sophia always wore, fear of crime, fear of being recognized, and fear of not being recognized. Tilda had eventually concluded that Sophia never left because she liked having the world come to her.

Tilda kept the cab waiting while she went into The Palm, glaring at the man who was trying to snag it as she brought her order back out. New Yorkers might lay claim to the most aggressive attitudes on the East Coast, but Tilda was unwilling to concede the point.

A few minutes later, the cab pulled up in front of Sophia's building on East 49th Street, and the doorman came out to help Tilda with her suitcase and dinner. The marble foyer and elevator with its shiny brass fixtures were a far cry from the dingy doorway and stairs at Tilda's walkup, but

140

then again, nobody there expected a tip, as the doorman would once they reached the eighteenth floor. A slender, dusky young man met them at Sophia's door, took the shopping bag of food from Tilda, and disappeared toward the kitchen without saying a word.

"Joe, is that you?" a voice called out from somewhere out of sight.

The doorman's name tag said "Bill," but he replied, "Yes, ma'am. I brought up your guest."

"Thanks, Joe. You know where the cookie jar is."

"Yes, ma'am. Thank you." There was a tall pedestal just next to the door, the kind one would expect to hold an objet d'art or exotic plant. This one had a glass cookie jar filled to the brim with money: one dollar bills, fives, tens, even some twenties. Joe, or maybe Bill, lifted the lid and pulled out a buck. Then he tipped his hat to Tilda before closing the door behind him.

Sophia called out again. "Tilda? What are you waiting for? You don't get to dip into the cookie jar, you know."

Tilda followed Sophia's voice to an enormous corner room, framed with French doors and full-length windows that showed a gorgeous and ridiculously expensive view of Manhattan. The furniture was also gorgeous and ridiculously expensive: two couches covered with sleek black leather, glass and chrome tables, and Sophia's preferred seat: an honest-to-God chaise longue. The woman was gracefully arranged on it, wearing the expected flowing caftan. This one was green silk, which made a striking contrast to her henna-red hair and fair skin.

"Tilda," Sophia said, her arms thrown wide, and Tilda leaned over to dutifully exchange air kisses in the vicinity of both cheeks, complete with "mwaaa" sounds.

"You're getting better at that," Sophia said, "but you still lack sincerity."

"And once I can fake that, I've got it made."

"Exactly! Have a seat."

Just as Tilda sank into one of the couches, the man who'd met her at the door carried in a silver tray with two wine glasses. Sophia's actually held wine, but Tilda's was filled with Dr Pepper, which she preferred. Then he silently disappeared.

"Is he new?" Tilda said.

"Who, Juan? Cute, isn't he?"

"He looks just like the last one, and the one before that."

"Well, both of them were cute. Therefore

this Juan is cute too, right?"

"Do you clone them or put them through plastic surgery?"

Sophia laughed. "I breed them. Not me personally, but they're all brothers or cousins or something. I bring them over, give them a job, help them get their green cards, and then they leave me for better jobs." She rolled her eyes. "What could possibly be better than working for me?"

"You mean better than waiting on you hand and foot, twenty-four / seven? Maybe cleaning the bathrooms at Grand Central Station with a toothbrush."

"Tilda, Tilda," Sophia said, trying to sound disapproving, but she couldn't hide her grin. "Could an old woman hope to dream that you've come just to visit?"

"At The Palm's prices? Please!"

"Then whose dead career are we exhuming today?"

"The stars of *Kissing Cousins*."

Sophia wrinkled her nose. "Silly show. Didn't you just do them? That awful curse thing?"

"Less than a month ago," Tilda admitted, "but there's a new hook. Holly Kendricks — the one who played the cheerleader — was just murdered."

"Murder is so sordid. We never talked

143

about murder in *Teen Fave.*"

"Nobody died at all in *Teen Fave.*"

"Not so. People died all the time. There was no better way to draw in fan mail than a tragic teen idol whose mother had died in a car accident, whose father had fallen in war, whose childhood sweetheart had died in his arms after a lingering illness."

"Like AIDS?"

"Don't be vulgar. Even if AIDS had been around, childhood sweethearts would have been immune from it. At any rate, nobody we wrote about was ever murdered."

"Holly was — I saw the body myself."

"You got into the funeral? I heard security was tighter than a virgin's knees."

As usual, despite Sophia's protestations of being isolated, she knew far more than she let on. One day Tilda hoped to catch her watching TV, reading the paper, taking a phone call, or, in her wildest dreams, trolling the Internet. "Gabrielle and Gwendolyn Roman snuck me in," she said.

"And? Start talking. What was the service like? Who was there?"

Sophia was, Tilda decided, one of the few people she knew who would openly admit that a funeral was a prime source of gossip, even if you were honestly sad about the person's death. So they happily discussed

144

the mourners who'd shown up, judging which ones were sincere in their grief and which ones had less mournful agendas, and what was appropriate dress for a funeral in these decadent times, continuing the conversation over dinner when Juan came in to tell them it was laid out. Even when eating takeout, Sophia wouldn't stoop to eat on anything other than her Limoges china.

Afterward, comfortably ensconced back in Sophia's living room, Tilda felt simultaneously stuffed with good food and drained by all the details Sophia had dragged from her. Sophia, who was sipping a fresh glass of wine supplied by Juan, looked as sated as a cat who'd scored an entire gallon of cream. She leaned back in her chaise longue and solemnly said, "It's really quite sad. Holly was never a big draw at *Teen Fave,* but we ran a few photo spreads on her. She had no acting talent to speak of, but she was attractive and personable. I only spoke to her two or three times so I don't know if I can give you anything for your article."

"The article isn't just about Holly. I'm doing another piece about what's happened to all of the *Kissing Cousins,* and I've got most of what I need. What I don't have is Mercy."

"No reporter should have mercy — I

never did."

"Ha ha, very funny. I'm talking about Mercy Ashford, the actress who played Mercy on the show. I never did track her down when I was working on that other article."

"Didn't you?" Sophia shrugged. "I gave you everything I could when you were here last time."

"I know you don't know where she is, but I found something that might shake something loose in your memory banks." Tilda looked around for her satchel, and when Juan silently appeared to hand it to her, she reached inside to pull out the issue of *Teen Fave* she'd found in June's attic, and opened it to the article about Mercy. "You said in here that Mercy was going to be in a movie called *The Raven's Prey,* but she wasn't. Do you remember what happened?"

"You don't ask much, do you? That was what, thirty years ago?"

Tilda just waited. Part of the fun for Sophia was pretending that remembering these things was harder than it was.

The older woman frowned pensively for a few seconds so that Tilda would appreciate how hard she was working, and then said, "She quit."

"I heard she did that, but not why."

"Nobody knew why. There was talk about it too, because up until then her reputation had been spotless. Since the picture was low budget, people finally decided that she must have gotten a better job. Only she never showed up in anything."

"You didn't mention this when I talked to you before."

"You didn't ask about the movie. You asked if I knew where Mercy Ashford was now."

Tilda nodded ruefully. Sophia wasn't one to volunteer information when each tidbit could lead to another dinner being brought to her door. While she had a chance, she said, "Do you know anything else about Mercy that you didn't print in the magazine?"

"Like?"

"Was she as cool as she seemed to be? Is there any truth to the rumors about her wearing black all the time because she was mourning her parents or a lost love or a beloved poodle?" Remembering Javier's lurid speculations, she added, "Did she date any of the men on the show? Or the other women, for that matter?"

Sophia rolled her eyes, and sighed an aggrieved sigh that Tilda's roommate would have envied. "You realize I only interviewed her two or three times personally. The rest of the time we just mined the questionnaires we sent out to all the stars."

"Humor me."

"Fine. Yes, she was as 'cool' as she seemed to be — a very focused and creative young woman. She wore black on screen because the role called for it, and during public appearances because the fans expected it. It also suited her. When she was off duty, she wore whatever she wanted. I saw her in blue and red, and one time in yellow, which was a mistake. Her parents did die in a car accident when she was young, but she never mentioned a poodle or lost love, living or otherwise. She never dated anybody else on the show. She was seen dating a few other men in the industry, but none of those relationships were serious — two were publicity stunts I set up myself. What else?"

"Can you tell me anything I can use to find her?"

"I could try to find the questionnaire she filled out for us, but I think all that stuff went into the magazine at one point or another."

"Don't bother. I already know her favorite movie was *Casablanca* and that she liked hot fudge sundaes for dessert."

"Then you've got all I can give you."

"What about this picture?" Tilda turned to the back cover of the issue of *Teen Fave* she was still holding to show the photo of Sophia, Mercy, and the unidentified man and boy. "Do you remember who that man was?"

Sophia studied the picture. "That was taken here in Manhattan. At the Plaza, I think. Mercy was in town to ride in the Macy's Parade, and that man was her escort."

"Escort? Like a date?"

"Like a bodyguard. He got her to the parade and back to the hotel, then I came and met her for dinner. Got a nice piece for the Christmas issue out of it too, all about her holiday memories from when she was a kid. That's when Mercy told me she'd auditioned for that movie, come to think of it. She was so excited about it. It's a shame it didn't work out."

"Was this guy her regular bodyguard?" Tilda asked. Somebody who'd been with her every day could be an even better source of information than the makeup artist. But Sophia shook her head.

"No, the studio hired him just for the day to get her to and from the parade and deal with any fans who got carried away. Mercy didn't have a regular bodyguard. Not many people did, then, unlike today." Sophia handed back the magazine. "I could dig up his name, if you're that desperate. I must have gotten a release for the photo, even though he wasn't identified. We only took that shot to make the little boy happy — that's the bodyguard's son, there. I wasn't planning to use it, but the idiot photographer screwed up every other shot to get back at me for having to work on Thanksgiving."

Tilda was going to tell Sophia not to bother. A one-day encounter that many years ago probably wouldn't mean anything. Then she decided it wouldn't hurt. "I'm that desperate."

Sophia was kind enough not to mock her. She just called Juan in and gave him a complicated set of instructions about where to find a particular file. A few minutes later he returned and handed a thick folder to Sophia, who flipped through it until she found what she was looking for. "Here we go. Dominic Tolomeo, Tolomeo Personal Protection." She looked up at Tilda. "I'd forgotten this — he wasn't from New York. He's in Boston."

"Really?" Tilda said, entering the name into her Palm.

"I know — who'd have thought they'd need celebrity security in a town like Boston?" Sophia said with the unconscious but ingrained snobbery of the longtime New Yorker.

"Amazing," Tilda said dryly. Her friend's attitude reminded Tilda of another snob she'd recently encountered: Lawrence White, who'd been so surprised that a national magazine could operate out of Boston. "On a completely different subject, do you know an industry stringer named Lawrence White?"

"Only by reputation, which isn't that good. Dresses well, but writes poorly. Not only is his prose pedestrian, and his stories sycophantic —"

"This from a woman who published 'Ten Reasons to Love David Cassidy.' "

"I never pretended to be writing *Teen Fave* for anybody but teenyboppers. White claims to be a journalist." She snorted as delicately as one can snort. "Rumor has it that his real claim to fame is the ability to parlay his interviews into bedroom encounters, which he probably commemorates with notches on his bed post or something equally tacky."

"He's a star fucker?"

"We called them star collectors in my day," Sophia said primly. "Like in the Monkees song." She sighed. "Ah, Davy, Davy, Davy . . ."

"Davy Jones? Was he one of your protégés?"

Sophia just smiled. "What an adorable accent he had. So very appealing."

"Kind of short, wasn't he?"

"Height doesn't matter when you're lying down."

Tilda snickered.

Sophia said, "As for your Mr. White, I understand his greatest appeal is for those on their way up or on their way down. When you're desperate, you're more willing to trade favors for magazine inches —"

"Inches for inches, as it were."

Sophia allowed herself a small grin.

"That explains why he was trying to get close to Gabrielle and Gwendolyn at the funeral," Tilda said.

"I'm surprised he'd waste his time. They were never far enough up to be on their way down."

"No, but they're cute and desperate for attention. Plus they're twins."

"One of the perennial male fantasies."

Tilda considered it. "Actually it sounds pretty interesting to me too."

"Twins are more trouble than they're worth," Sophia said firmly. "Believe me."

Tilda did. If half the rumors she'd heard — or a quarter of Sophia's hints — were true, had Sophia descended to putting notches on her bed post, she'd have needed more bed posts. Though it hadn't been necessary for a teen idol of the sixties and seventies to sleep with Sophia to get a *Teen Fave* cover, it hadn't hurt his chances either. The former magazine editor's predilection for pretty young men like Juan was nothing new.

"Can I assume your foray into fantasy means you're without regular male company at present?" Sophia asked.

"You sound like my sister," Tilda said, "at least in theme. No, no male company. Though Lawrence White did ask me to join him and the twins for lunch, with the unspoken possibility of more activities to follow."

"And?"

"I turned him down. I was afraid his tan-in-a-can would rub off on me."

That reminded Sophia of a story about the natural coloring of an exotic-looking teen idol who was not actually a native of the Near Eastern country he claimed as his origin. During a photo shoot at the beach, his true complexion had come to light, light being the operative word. Sophia, who admitted to having enough of a personal interest in the fellow not to want to ruin his image, had effected a quick cover-up with a beach towel.

More stories followed, some of which could have been true, and all of which were hilarious. But eventually Sophia started to yawn, so Tilda said, "This has been illuminating, as always, but I should go check into my hotel before they give away my room."

"You're just saying that because you're tired — you've got no stamina for late nights," Sophia scolded. "At your age, I'd have two dates waiting for me at this time of the evening."

"Then call them up and have them come see me — your dates were always closer to my age than yours."

"Jealousy is so unattractive," Sophia said with a smile, and indicated that Tilda should practice her air kisses once again.

It was only when Juan appeared, silent as always, to escort her to the door that Tilda said, "I think I'll poke around that movie Mercy walked out on. Do you know anybody who was involved?"

"Of course I do — no movie got made at that time that I didn't know people on," Sophia said, "but offhand, I don't know who I know. I'll see what I can look up in the morning, and messenger the information to you. Where are you staying?"

"The Kimberly. You could just call me — they've got phones in every room. I've even got a cell phone."

"Don't be silly. Juan needs the exercise. Now, when you get downstairs, don't give Joe any money to call you a cab — that's his job."

Sophia had this Joe — who was named Aaron — well trained. He wouldn't take the tip Tilda offered in spite of Sophia's instructions.

Tilda always tried to stay at the Kimberly when she was in Manhattan. The location was convenient and it was small enough that the staff remembered her from visit to visit, or at least convincingly pretended to. Most of the rooms were suites, meaning that she could interview people in her room without a bed in plain view, which forestalled complications.

Once she checked in she decided to boot up her computer and check e-mail, but once she had, she almost wished she hadn't. The first item was a program Vincent had put together to count down the time remaining until the *Kissing Cousins* killer was due to execute Mercy, if Tilda couldn't find her in time. Not that Vincent was putting pressure on her or anything. She deleted it.

Next were three batches of Mercy sightings from members of the *Kissing Cousins* Listserv, thoughtfully divided into "Possible," "Unlikely," and "No Way."

As she read through the "Possible" posts, she wondered what Vincent had been smoking when he compiled it. If the posts were to be believed, Mercy was working at a Barnes and Noble in San Francisco, raising ostriches in a small town in North Carolina, running a law firm in Manitoba, and walking the streets as a prostitute in New Orleans. In her spare time, she worked for the CIA, the FBI, and other sets of initials with which Tilda was unfamiliar.

Most of the accounts were so short on details as to make them impossible to confirm, and the others could well require hours of work to disprove. She put the less unlikely ones on her mental list of things to do if she got terribly, terribly desperate.

She should have known better, but she couldn't resist looking at the "Unlikely" list. Twenty minutes of reading about aliens and government conspiracies was enough to convince her that she wouldn't have to bother with that category in the future, although she had to admit that the explanation of how Mercy was actually the last heir to the Romanov throne was particularly imaginative.

Tilda knew she was being a glutton for punishment, but she just had to look at the "No Way" list, the posts even Vincent wouldn't believe. The first one made her very glad it had been so long since dinner — the writer claimed that he knew Mercy's whereabouts because he himself had killed her and buried her in his backyard. Eventually. Tilda decided that the sicko who came up with that bit of necrophiliac porn needed some serious help.

The rest fell into that same category, though they were less graphic, and she could almost picture Vincent's look of disgust as he read the posts. She was about to delete that whole shebang summarily when she saw a familiar name. Have_Mercy had resurfaced from whatever slime pit he inhabited.

\<Have_Mercy\> Is there any progress in finding Mercy? I told that reporter what to do — talk to some of the people she slept with. One of them must know something, guaranteed.

She wanted to dismiss that one too, but damned if the guy didn't sound sincere, in a psycho kind of way. So she sent a message of her own to the Listserv:

<TildaHarper> Have_Mercy, I'm willing to entertain reasonable suggestions, but so far you haven't given me any reason to believe that your information has any merit. Lay your cards on the table, if you've got any.

Of course Vincent would be shocked when he saw the post. He was the kind who wanted his idols sealed from the world, perhaps in giant versions of the Mylar bags he used to protect his comic books.

Tilda rather liked the idea of Mercy as a femme fatale. Why couldn't the quirky girl get the guy for a change, or even several guys? Admittedly, she'd prefer to find that Mercy had worn out her mattresses for love or recreation and not for career advancement, but either version would spice up her article nicely.

With the post sent, she shut down the laptop and reached for the TV control to play her favorite hotel game: how many clicks would it take to find an episode of *Law & Order* in one of its incarnations? She caught a classic Jerry Orbach / Chris Noth episode in three clicks, a respectable showing, though not a record, and happily watched it until the last chung-chung. By then she was more than ready to get some sleep.

Chapter 10

"Episode 60: Homecoming Dance of the Seven Veils
Sherri gets into a fight with her boyfriend, Hank, and though she assumes they'll make up in time for homecoming, instead he asks Mercy to the dance. Furious, Sherri sabotages Mercy's shampoo with green food coloring so her cousin will cancel, leaving Hank up for grabs. But Mercy makes a veiled hat to match her gown, and starts a fashion sensation."
— Fanboy's Online *Kissing Cousins*
Episode Guide, by Vincent Peters

It was overcast as Tilda set off for the corner of Central Park where Jasmine Fisher was working a television commercial shoot. Not that it made much difference, really. The constant press of buildings and sidewalk businesses in Manhattan made Tilda feel as if she were always inside. Even Central Park, as enormous as it was, felt more like a backyard than the great outdoors. It wasn't that Tilda considered herself an outdoorsy person, having never earned a single merit badge during her disastrous three months as a Brownie, but New York still seemed to be missing something.

That something was definitely not traffic. There was plenty of that, complete with honking horns and festive hand gestures. Tilda was glad she'd decided to walk.

The shoot was easy enough to find, set up just past the Alice in Wonderland statue. There were a few people making token attempts to keep passersby out of the way, but Tilda walked past them with the gait of somebody who knew where she was going. It usually worked, and that day was no exception.

There were three makeup stations set up, each with a chair, mirror, and table overflowing with compacts, jars, tubes, sponges, brushes for hair and makeup, hairspray, and all the other gear it took to make actors look natural. Apparently the trio of makeup artists was temporarily off duty, because their chairs were empty and they were sucking down some of the river of coffee that flowed through every shoot Tilda had ever seen.

One of the artists was male, another

female, and Tilda wasn't completely sure about the third. Just in case, she walked up and said, "Jasmine?" in the direction of all three.

The more obviously female one, who was also the oldest, looked up. "Yes?"

"I'm Tilda Harper. We spoke earlier today."

"Right, my reporter." She turned to her androgynous coworker. "You owe me lunch, Terry — I told you I was getting interviewed."

Terry scowled, and started rearranging his or her supplies. Unfortunately, the name hadn't settled the question.

"Have a seat," Jasmine said, gesturing to a chair aimed at the bank of mirrors. When Tilda hesitated, she added, "If I leave the area, they'll dock my pay, so we have to stay here, and you may as well be comfortable."

"Won't I be in the way if you have to make somebody up?"

The three makeup artists snickered. "None of us have anything to do," Terry explained. "It's background shots today — scenery — not even extras. Somebody screwed up and scheduled us, so now they have to pay us, but the flip side is that we have to stay on call."

Tilda had heard too many similar stories

of cost management in the industry not to believe her, so she sat. It was odd watching the subject of an interview in a mirror, but she was willing to give it a try. She knew Jasmine had to be at least fifty to have worked on *Kissing Cousins,* but she didn't look it. Her bobbed hair was convincingly dark, and her complexion looked firm without the uncomfortable tightness that plastic surgery can cause. Knowing the tricks to keep one's appearance young must be one of the perks of her line of work.

Tilda pulled out her Palm and said, "As I explained on the phone, I'm looking for background on Mercy Ashford. I understand you used to do makeup for her when she was in *Kissing Cousins.*"

"All three seasons," Jasmine confirmed, "plus some outside work, but I haven't heard from her in years. Where did she end up?"

Tilda stifled a sigh. "I was hoping you could tell me. Nobody seems to know."

"Really? I hope she's okay. We were pretty tight. We used to gab the whole time I was working on her."

"What did you two talk about?"

"The usual. Guys, the show, family, the other people on the show, guys, clothes, how crazy the business is. Guys."

"You mentioned family. Did Mercy say much about hers?" Tilda's research hadn't pulled up any family connections, but she could have missed something.

"Actually, it was more about my family than hers," Jasmine said. "She was an orphan — no brothers or sisters either. Really sad. I'd be complaining about something my mother had done, and she'd listen, but then I'd remember she had nobody to complain about."

"What about the show? Was she happy working on it?"

"She adored it. Irv Munch never had an original thought in his life, but wasn't bad to work for. He hired good people, and if he'd just left them alone, they could have kept the show going longer. But he kept writing these shows with sappy endings, and they just didn't work."

Tilda nodded, remembering that her least favorite episodes were the ones Munch had written. "How about the rest of the cast? Did Mercy get along with them?"

"Absolutely. Not buddy-buddy friends-for-life, but they worked well together, and could have a few laughs afterward. Mercy made an effort to be nice to the younger ones too, kind of kept an eye on them."

"What about men? Was Mercy seeing

anybody seriously?" Tilda asked, thinking of Have_Mercy and his claims. The stories in *Teen Fave* had insisted that Mercy was still looking for the right guy, somebody down-to-earth and regular. Of course, all of the stars interviewed in *Teen Fave* were looking for somebody down-to-earth and regular — in other words, the *Teen Fave* reader, whose fantasy life would have been trampled by the knowledge that his or her fave was making the two-backed beast with everybody in LA.

"You mean on the show? Jim Bonnier tried to put the moves on her, but that didn't fly."

"What about outside of work?"

"Well . . ." Jasmine started to say, then switched to, "Are those your real eyes, or are you wearing contacts?"

Tilda was tempted to point out that even if she'd been wearing contacts, they would still be her real eyes, but she settled for, "Natural eye color."

"Nice. What color mascara do you use?"

"Black."

"Good, stick with it. But you need to get yourself a gel eyeliner in plum —"

"A dark plum," Terry put in, coming over to cast a professional eye at Tilda's face.

"Right, a dark plum. Then use a plum eye

165

shadow for the crease in the eyelid. Man, your eyes would just pop."

"Oh yeah," Terry breathed. "They'd just pop."

"Thanks, I'll remember that," Tilda said, taking notes. She saw no reason to turn down free expert advice. "Anyway, we were talking about Mercy's love life."

"Right, I got off track. You know, she really didn't date much."

"She did like men, didn't she?"

"As far as I know. She did date a few guys, but never seemed serious about any of them. When you're starring in a show, it's hard to find somebody who cares about who you are and not what you do."

"I can understand that," Tilda said.

"Besides, Mercy was very ambitious. She really wanted to move on and up in the business."

"Was she ruthless?"

"No, nothing like that. She was the kind who'd go out of her way to make it a better place to work. That gal who played the cheerleader, Holly something, she was a little bit of a diva at first. She was insecure about her looks — and you'd be surprised how many gorgeous people are — and she took it out on me. 'I don't like that eye shadow. It makes me look cheap.' 'That's too much blush. It makes me look old on camera.' 'Hurry up! I've got a big scene coming up!' These days, when I'm so much older than the people I'm working on, that kind of thing just rolls off my back."

"Either that, or you play games with their makeup," Terry put in.

Jasmine grinned. "Maybe I make a nose look a little crooked once in a while, but mostly I ignore it. But back then, it really got to me. I didn't want to say anything, not when she was a star and I was replaceable, but I was thinking about quitting. Then one day, Holly showed up with a bunch of flowers and apologized. She said she hadn't realized what a bitch she'd been — that's the word she used too. She never gave me a bit of trouble after that."

"That's impressive," Tilda said. "Most stars never admit being wrong."

"Don't I know it. Truth is, I don't think it was Holly's idea. I think Mercy took her aside and explained it to her."

"Really?"

"I never knew for sure, but I wouldn't have been surprised."

"That's even more impressive." Tilda was enjoying hearing Mercy praised, but she wasn't getting much for her *Kissing Cousins* article, so she decided to start slanting her questions toward the makeup artist article she was hoping to sell. "Were there any particular challenges with the makeup on the show?"

"Mostly it was beauty makeup, but simple, because they were kids. We did do a couple of Halloween shows, which were fun, and in one show Felicia dreamt they'd all turned old overnight. That was interesting." Jasmine went on to describe some of the techniques she'd used to transform young, attractive girls into crones. "The hardest makeup I ever had to do on that show didn't even show on camera — that's how I knew I'd done a good job." Jasmine paused for effect.

Tilda was willing to play along. "Oh? That sounds intriguing."

"It was during the third season," Jasmine said. "We were starting a new episode that day, and Mercy showed up on set with a black eye, a real shiner. They had to rewrite the episode on the fly to work around it, not to mention the costume guy having to come up with something she could wear to hide it."

"Are you talking about 'Homecoming Dance of the Seven Veils'?" Tilda asked. "Sherri spikes Mercy's shampoo with green food coloring, which gets all over her hair and her face?"

"That's the one. I had to disguise the black eye, and put the streaks of color on top of that, which helped fool the eye."

"I've watched that show a dozen times and never noticed," Tilda said. "You did a terrific job."

"Thanks," Jasmine said. "I was damned proud of that makeup job."

"How did she get the black eye?"

"She said she tripped and hit herself on the corner of the kitchen cabinet."

"Ow! That must have hurt."

"It took a while to heal too. I had to layer on the makeup to hide it for the next few weeks, and I know it must have hurt her to have me slopping on foundation, but she never said a word. A real trouper. I considered her a friend too, but I guess I was wrong."

"Why do you say that?"

"Well, she was signed for a feature right before *Kissing Cousins* was canceled, and at the series wrap party, she told me she was going to try to get me a job on the movie. But that's the last I ever heard from her." She shrugged her shoulders. "Promises are cheap in this business."

"Mercy never made it to features," Tilda said, feeling protective. "She started on that one picture, but didn't finish."

"I thought I heard something about that," Jasmine admitted. "Still, even if she couldn't get me work, I'd have thought she'd call once in a while."

Then Terry cleared her or his throat, and Jasmine hissed, "Shit!" She grabbed up a tube of makeup, squeezed a dollop onto her hand, and dabbed it on Tilda's face.

"What are you doing?" Tilda asked.

"It's the PA," she whispered. "The pissant has it in for us. He's the one who scheduled us by mistake, and he's dying for an excuse to send us home early to get back in the director's good graces. Just go with it."

The production assistant in question, a grumpy-looking guy with wrinkled khakis and a Starbucks cup, came over. "Who's she?" he demanded, looking at his clipboard. "We're not using any talent today."

"The director told me to get my face done — he's thinking of using me later on in the shoot," Tilda said. "If there's a problem, I'll be glad to go with you and confirm."

The magic word *director* was all that was needed. Tilda had never heard of a commercial or movie shoot where the rumor of a director saying frog wouldn't get the PAs practicing their long jumps.

"No problem," the PA said, and walked away quickly, staring at his clipboard as if it would tell him how to get a better job than PA.

The three makeup artists waited until the guy was out of earshot before hilarity ensued, with high fives all around.

"That was brilliant," Jasmine said. "He'll leave us alone for the rest of the day now. We might even make it into overtime."

"Glad to help," Tilda said. The guy had reminded her of Nicole, which was reason enough to put the fear of God, or at least of the director, into him.

After that, Tilda and the trio were pals. Not only did the other two makeup artists join in to dish about every shoot they'd worked — giving Tilda enough for a nice feature on what it was like to work with the rich and famous, and, even more salable, the rich and spoiled — but they combined efforts to give her the best makeover she'd ever had, complete with samples of foundation and dark-plum gel eyeliner so she could take a stab at recreating the effect.

As she stopped to admire herself in the window of a store on the way back to her hotel, Tilda was calculating how much money she'd have to make to be able to afford a regular makeup artist of her very own.

CHAPTER 11

"Back in the early eighties, *16* came out with this promotional T-shirt that said, 'Keeps Me On Top Of The Stars.' Gloria Stavers told me about it over lunch one day — she'd left the magazine by then, of course — and we laughed so hard we wet our pants!"
— Sophia Vaughn, quoted in "Curse of the *Kissing Cousins*," *Entertain Me!*

Still looking marvelous, Tilda spent the rest of the day at the American Museum of Natural History, which never ceased to entertain her, even though there was a near zero chance that she'd scrape a story out of the visit. Even freelancers had to relax sometime, she told herself.

It was evening by the time she headed back for the Kimberly. She was walking into the lobby, trying to decide if room service was more appealing than trying to find a restaurant where she wouldn't be bored eating alone, when she heard a voice say, "Tilda? Tilda Harper?"

She turned around to find Lawrence the star fucker getting up from one of the armchairs scattered around the lobby. "Lawrence?"

"It is you. What are you doing in the Big Apple? I thought Beantown was your beat."

"I bribed the border guard to let me across."

He laughed, flashing an expensive set of teeth.

"How about you? Are you in town for a story?" Tilda asked.

"Background on a series on the hot Broadway shows," he said. "You?"

"A feature on makeup artists," she said. He'd shown too much interest in her *Kissing Cousins* story at the funeral for her to want to admit to more. "Are you staying at the Kimberly too?"

"No, I'm at the Four Seasons. I was supposed to be meeting a friend here for dinner." He checked his watch. "Unfortunately he's nearly an hour late, and I can't get him on his cell, so I think I've been stood up."

"It sounds like that," Tilda agreed.

He hesitated a second. "I suppose you've got plans for dinner."

"Does trying to decide between room service and takeout pizza count?"

He laughed again. "I think I could improve on that, if you're interested."

Tilda considered the idea. He was old for her, but not bad on the eyes, and they were in the same line of work. Dinner with him would almost certainly be more entertaining than watching *Law & Order* reruns. "I'm definitely interested," she said.

"Excellent."

"Just let me run up to my room and drop off some things." She started toward the elevator and noticed he was walking along with her. "Don't you want to wait down here, in case your friend shows up?"

"Honestly, no. If he does make an appearance, I'll feel obligated to go out with him, and now that I've got a better option . . ."

"Flatterer," she said, but added firmly, "You wait here. I'll be back in a minute." If his reputation as a star fucker was accurate, her virtue was probably safe with him because she wouldn't be worth a notch on his bedpost, but why take chances? Room service might be what he had in mind after all. She glanced at him as he walked away, noting that either he worked out or he'd been gifted with naturally firm thighs. Maybe he wasn't as old as she'd thought.

Ten minutes to pull notes and makeup samples out of her pocketbook, brush her hair, and use the facilities, and she was good to go. The face Jasmine and her cohorts had layered on showed no signs of cracking, so she left it alone, other than to add fresh lipstick.

When she got downstairs, Lawrence was chatting up the concierge. "That was fast," he said when he saw her. "Most women I know would take twice as long, without nearly so delightful a result."

It was one of those half-gallant, half-condescending comments that Tilda was never sure how to answer. Should she thank him for the compliment, chide him for insulting untold numbers of women, or point out that some of those women might have been stalling so they wouldn't have to spend as much time with him? Since she hadn't decided how much she liked Lawrence, she settled for, "I've always strived to be a fast woman. Did you have a restaurant in mind for dinner?"

"I was just asking Inez here for a recommendation," Lawrence said, gesturing to the desk clerk. "There's a Mexican place around the corner she says is quite good, and I was waiting to see if that suits you before calling for a reservation."

"Mexican sounds muy bueno," Tilda said.

It turned out the restaurant had no wait list, so they strolled the half block there. The night was warmer than in Boston, but not hot — perfect for a stroll. On the way they played the question game: how were they both enjoying New York, where were they from originally, weren't New York prices outrageous, and so on. Once at the restaurant, they ordered margaritas to go with the chips and salsa the waiter brought to the table, and moved on to the writer-specific part of the game: how long had they been writing; wasn't it a crime that writers made so little, though neither one volunteered an actual dollar figure; and weren't most celebrities spoiled or boring or both. By the time their enchiladas arrived, they were well into sharing horror stories about interview subjects who showed up late or not at all, who'd lied or refused to answer questions, who'd made passes at them, and, worst of all, who'd not given them anything interesting to write about.

Tilda was surprised by how much she was enjoying herself. One of the problems of being a freelancer was that she had no water cooler or break room to hang around to compare notes with her peers. Mostly she worked via phone, fax, and computer. When she did get face time, like at the *Entertain Me!* offices, it was with editorial, not other writers. The only time she did meet other writers was when they were covering the same event, and that wasn't a situation that lent itself to sharing war stories.

Over flan for dessert, Lawrence said, "The nostalgia bit is an interesting niche. How did you pick it?"

It wasn't the first time Tilda had been asked, but it wasn't a question she could answer easily, so she fell back on her standard reply. "I was on the features staff of the college newspaper. We got a fair number of guest lecturers and speakers, but never the A-list — it was always the up-and-comers and the formerly famous. Nobody else on the staff was interested in the old timers — researching their backgrounds was too much work — so I ended up with them. So when I went looking for work, all my clippings were about baby boomer stars. It just went on from there."

"Interesting," Lawrence said.

"How about you? How did you get into this line?"

"I was rich," he said simply. "Dad was busy making us richer, Mom was into charities, so I went to parties. We were living near LA, and since you can't have a good

LA party without a star or three, I started making connections. I didn't have anything in mind other than having fun, but when I got out of college, I realized Dad was serious about my coming to work for him. I headed for Europe to hide, but I knew that wouldn't last. Then one day I met a gossip columnist at a party, and she paid me to slip her a few tidbits. When I read the woman's columns, I realized she wasn't doing anything I couldn't do. So I moved back to LA and told Dad I had my own career plan."

"Interesting," she said, echoing him.

"It's a living," he said. "And, no offense, but I think there's more money in the big stars than in the old-timers angle." He picked up his glass, and swirled what was left of his margarita. "If you ever want to switch tracks, maybe I could make a few calls, introduce you to some people."

"Are you sure you could handle the competition?"

He smiled expansively. "Not a problem. I'm turning down work now."

Tilda wasn't sure if she believed him, but it wouldn't have been polite to say so after he'd offered her work. "That's generous of you, Lawrence, but wouldn't that kind of work be hard to keep up from Boston?"

"You mean you want to stay there?" he said.

"The weather is awful, the traffic worse, and if I hear one more morose discussion of what's happened to the Red Sox, I'll probably scream. But it's home."

He shrugged his shoulders, clearly lumping Boston with the countless towns he flew over on his way between LA and New York. "Well, if you change your mind, I'll be glad to help."

The check arrived, and after a bit of polite wrangling, he picked it up. After all, he said he had more work than he could handle, whereas Tilda doubted she could talk Jillian into paying for her margaritas.

During the walk back to the hotel, they talked about what it was that made some shows classics, some cult favorites, and others forgotten except by the composers of trivia quizzes. As they walked into the lobby, the front desk clerk said, "Ms. Harper? Room 417?"

Tilda nodded.

"A messenger dropped something off for you." The clerk reached under the counter, produced a thick manila envelope, and handed to her.

"Thank you," Tilda said, recognizing the handwriting on the envelope as Sophia's. It

179

must be the information about *The Raven's Prey* she'd promised to dig up.

Lawrence was now moving his weight from one foot to the other. "So," he said meaninglessly.

"This was great," Tilda said. "I almost never get to talk shop."

"Me too. Shall I walk you to your room? Maybe we can order nightcaps from room service?"

"Just a drink?" Tilda said.

"Absolutely."

She didn't believe him for a minute, and since she'd fully expected him to make the attempt, she'd spent the odd moment during dinner deciding what her response would be. On the plus side were his definite charm and good looks, despite the age difference. On the minus side was his reputation — experience was appealing, but not that much experience. Then there were his offers of work and help in making contacts, both of which could have been construed as ways to get a lot more than a drink. Adding all of that together led her to say, "I don't think so."

"Just a drink, a chance to talk more." Then he added, "I've got no plans to get you horizontal, if that's what you're worried about," and grinned a roguish grin.

Tilda hated roguish grins, and that made her decision final. "No, thank you." Wanting to avoid further debate, she gave him a quick peck on the cheek and said, "Thanks for dinner," before stepping into the open elevator. But as the door started to shut, she added, "By the way, I like getting it when I'm vertical too."

CHAPTER 12

"Keeping people waiting is the most popular sport in the industry. The principle is simple. The hotter you are, the shorter the wait. People used to accuse me of typing up a chart of each week's wait times to keep it straight. Baloney! I kept it all in my head."

— Sophia Vaughn, quoted in "Teen Idol Worshippers" by Tilda Harper, *Entertain Me!*

Once Tilda read the message from Sophia, she abandoned her plans to check e-mail that night and instead packed and hit the sack so she'd be ready to check out obscenely early the next morning, at least by her standards. Matthew Boardman, the director of *The Raven's Prey,* had retired to Sonoma Valley in California, and Sophia had helpfully arranged for Tilda to interview him by phone the next morning at nine-thirty. With the time difference, that would be half past noon, Boston time. So Tilda figured she could get back to Boston and book it to the *Entertain Me!* office to make the call from there.

The first part of the plan worked just fine. She got up and moving in time to catch the eight o'clock express from Penn Station, which would put her into Boston at eleven-thirty. But at eight-thirty, just as she was about to eat the muffin she'd grabbed from the snack car, her cell phone rang.

"Ms. Harper? This is Inez from the front desk at the Kimberly Hotel. A messenger just dropped off an envelope for you, and I wondered if I should mail it to your home address or your business address."

The messenger was almost certainly Juan with something else from Sophia — maybe a clue to Mercy's whereabouts that she'd dredged up from who knows where. So Tilda wasn't inclined to wait for the post office. "Inez, can I ask a favor? Could you open it and read it to me? I would really appreciate it."

"Of course." There was the sound of an envelope being slit open. "It says, 'Tilda love, it turns out Matthew can't take your call until eleven-thirty, California time. Hope that doesn't cause any problems.' It's signed 'Sophia.' "

"Shit!" Tilda said. Then, realizing that Inez might not be accustomed to her style of manners, she said, "Sorry. It's just that I would have made other plans if I'd known that my call was going to be delayed."

"No problem. Should I mail you the letter for your files?"

"Don't bother. Just trash it. And thanks again."

"Shit!" Tilda said again as she put away her phone, this time to nobody in particular. She could have slept later instead of rushing out the door, and had a real breakfast. The muffin she'd been looking forward to no longer appealed to her, but after glaring at it for a few minutes, she decided she might as well eat it anyway. It wasn't bad.

Tilda drummed her fingers loudly on the arm rest, stopping only when the older man sitting across the aisle looked her way plaintively. She wanted a way to fill the time between getting to Boston and making the call to Boardman — the inefficiency of going home to Malden and then back to Boston rankled. So she got her case from the overhead rack, unpacked her laptop, and fired it up to look back over her notes, trying to find an alternative.

Okay, she hadn't had a chance to talk to Irv Munch at the funeral, and she probably should. But when she called his number, his assistant said he'd be out of the office for a few days. The woman grudgingly promised to give him Tilda's message, but would not bend far enough to give Tilda his cell phone number.

Tilda went back to her notes to look for the next loose end, but all she found was the name of the Boston-based bodyguard whose picture had been in *Teen Fave,* which was too skimpy to even call a lead. She drummed her fingers on her armrest again, forgetting the other passenger until he cleared his throat loudly.

Okay, it was a lousy excuse for a lead, but what the hell. She'd never interviewed a bodyguard before. So she pulled out her cell phone once more to get the number for Tolomeo Personal Protection, then called and arranged to come by the office after her train arrived in Boston.

Maybe it would be a waste of time — in fact it probably was going to be a waste of time — but it was better than sitting around doing nothing. She came up with a few questions to ask Tolomeo and Boardman, and with that done, put everything away again, hoping to nap for the rest of the ride.

She'd just closed her eyes when her phone rang again. She didn't recognize the number, but at least it wasn't the Kimberly with a message postponing the phone call with Boardman until next month. "Hello?"

"Tilda? Lawrence. How are you this morning?"

"Not bad," she lied.

"Great. I just called the Kimberly, and they said you'd checked out already. I hope that doesn't mean that you're not available for lunch."

"Even worse," Tilda said, looking out the window. "I'm somewhere in Connecticut, I think, on the train back to Boston."

"Damn!" Lawrence said. "I should have asked you about lunch last night. I might have been able to talk you into staying in town a little longer."

Tilda was impressed. He'd taken her refusal better than she'd expected, and persistence was always encouraging. "It's just as well," she said. "I've got appointments lined up as soon as I get back — I'm going to have to go straight to a meeting from South Station." Then she added, "Things are really heating up on my story," which was lying to herself as well as to Lawrence.

"That's great," he said, sounding sincere, "but it doesn't make me any less sorry to have missed you. Maybe another time? I want us to keep in touch."

"Absolutely," she said.

As she put her phone down one more time, she wondered if she'd misjudged Lawrence. Maybe he really was interested in her. Or maybe he was interested in stealing her story. Either possibility was flattering.

With that pleasant thought to beguile her, two leads to follow up on when she got to Boston, and her phone shut off, Tilda finally managed to get to sleep. No doubt the man sitting across the aisle was as grateful for the restful interlude as she was.

CHAPTER 13

"Q: What's the most exciting thing being on TV has given you a chance to do?
A: That's easy — riding in the Macy's Thanksgiving Day Parade. I've always loved watching the parade on TV, and to actually be there was the coolest thing ever. And I couldn't believe how many cute girls there were in New York!"
— *"Kissing Cousins'* Brad Answers Twenty-five Personal Questions,"
Teen Fave

Since Tilda never considered how a security firm went about decorating their offices, she wouldn't have thought she had any preconceived notions, but as she opened the glass front door of Tolomeo Personal Protection, she realized she had expected something more butch. Bars on the windows, an armed guard in uniform, an office that looked particularly secure. Or since they specialized in celebrity protection, perhaps it would be like a well-appointed lawyer's office with a miniskirted receptionist who would supply cappuccino and suggestive banter to waiting clients. Instead the place looked like nothing so much as the office space at the shop where Tilda got her car serviced.

It had the same metal desk with a rubberized work surface, stacks of papers and invoices covering most of that work surface, battered PC, and half-filled coffee mug on top of the PC. Just like at the repair shop, copies of the *Boston Globe* from when the Red Sox won the World Series and from all three times the Patriots won the Super Bowl were pinned onto a cork board, and there were framed eight-by-ten photos haphazardly arranged on the wood paneling. The only difference was that when Tilda looked more closely she saw that the pictures weren't of company-sponsored soccer or softball teams. They were signed photos of Bette Midler, Aerosmith, U2, Ben Affleck, Matt Damon, Clint Eastwood, and other famous folk. Each photo included a lean man in a dark suit who aged his way through the pictures from a handsome, dark-haired stud right up to the handsome, gray-haired man sitting at the desk, talking on a headset as he typed into the computer.

He nodded at Tilda and continued his phone call. "Sure, we can handle that. How many people are traveling with Mr. Bloom? . . . Uh huh. . . . Does he want to arrange his own cars, or are we providing limos? . . . Good enough. Which hotel will your party be staying at? . . . Yeah, we've worked with them before. They know the drill. Are there any other activities you want me to cover? . . . No, I don't need specifics yet. Just give me a heads-up before you leave LA, and we'll take it from there. You've got all our contact numbers, right? . . . Great. Send me your flight numbers, and we'll meet you at Logan." He hung up the phone, pulled off the headset, then stood to offer Tilda his hand. "Ms. Harper? I'm Dom Tolomeo."

"How'd you know it was me?" Tilda asked, wondering if maybe there were video cameras or retina scanners hidden behind the wood paneling.

"Just a hunch," Tolomeo said. "Most of our clients don't carry their own suitcases."

"Sorry," Tilda said. Since she'd come straight from the station, she was still towing her rolling bag. "I just got in from New York."

"No problem. Even without the luggage,

I'd have guessed it was you. We don't get much walk-in traffic. The big shots are too busy to actually come here — that's what phones, fax machines, and e-mail are for. Which is fine with me. I don't have to waste money fixing the place up."

"I guess Steve Tyler wouldn't just drop in."

"Actually, Steve might. He's pretty down-to-earth. But others I could name, you'd think they were God's gift to the world." He waved one hand. "You didn't come to hear me complain. Or maybe you did, but if you did, you've wasted a trip. We practice discretion at Tolomeo Personal Protection, so don't expect me to help you dig up dirt for your magazine stories."

"I don't want dirt," Tilda said firmly. "I am working on an article, but I'm not interested in your current clients. What I'm trying to do is track down an actress you escorted to an event in 1979."

"That's a long time for me to remember anything."

"I realize that, but frankly, I'm running out of leads. I'm trying to find Mercy Ashford, who used to be on —"

"*Kissing Cousins?*"

"Color me impressed. I wouldn't have thought you'd remember her that quickly."

191

"I can't take any special credit this time. I was just talking about that show with my son this morning. I guess you already know that another actress from *Kissing Cousins* died recently."

Naturally Tolomeo would follow entertainment news. "That's the hook for my story," she admitted. "I've talked to the other surviving cast members, but not Mercy. Nobody seems to know where she is. As far as I can tell, she disappeared off the face of the earth back in 1980."

"Is that when the show was canceled?"

"A few months afterward, actually. She got a movie deal, but never finished the picture, and then she fell off the radar."

"Maybe that's the way she likes it."

"Maybe so, but it's my job to find her."

"Uh huh," he said, clearly not swayed.

"Besides, there's more to it than that. First, I'm a big fan of hers, and I've always wanted to meet her." Before he could point out the fact that most fans want to meet their idols, she added, "Second, she may be in danger. Three of the show's cast members have already died."

"Jeez, the curse business. I read that article. Was that you?"

"Yeah, kind of. My editor dreamed up the curse stuff. Which I don't believe in, but still . . ." She sighed. "I know it sounds crazy, and I guess you get a lot of people coming up with lame stories to try to get to the stars through you."

"A few, but this is a new one."

"Mr. Tolomeo, you don't know me, but I swear that if I were going to make up a story, I'd make up a better one than this."

Tolomeo tilted his head and looked at her for a stretch of seconds. Then he nodded. "People think being in security means you've got to be some kind of super fighter, or carry an attaché case full of James Bond gadgets. But that's not it — I've known black belts who weren't worth a dime as a bodyguard, and gadgets don't mean squat if you don't know when to use them. The important part of this job — the part you can't teach — is judging people. I think you're good people."

Tilda felt the oddest sense of satisfaction from having passed Tolomeo's test.

"You really think she's in danger?" he asked.

"I don't know, but I do know how I'll feel if she gets hurt because nobody warned her."

"Probably about how I'd feel if somebody I was supposed to be protecting got hurt. So you go ahead and ask your questions, but honestly, I just don't know how much I can help. Miss Ashford didn't make arrangements with me personally. It was handled by the studio. I never had her address or phone number, and even if I did, they'd be no good now. And I never had any contact with her other than that one day at the parade."

Though Tilda hadn't really expected that the security man and Mercy had been exchanging Christmas cards all these years, she had hoped he'd have something she could use. "Could you tell me about that day? What she was like, who was with her, anything at all."

"Tell you what. I had an associate with me that day, and I bet he's got every detail memorized." He picked up the phone, pushed a speed-dial number, and said, "Nicky? You got a minute to come up front? There's a pretty lady standing here who'd like to talk to you."

He hung up, and said to Tilda, "That'll get him moving. Nicky's got an eye for the ladies. No offense."

"None taken. Sounded like a compliment to me."

A moment later, Tilda was startled to see the young man from the pictures on the wall walk in the room. At least, it could have been him: same dark hair and eyes, same aristocratic nose, same lean build, and just as much a stud as the man in the pictures. He was a little shorter than the men Tilda usually favored, and she couldn't help but remember what Sophia had said about Davy Jones.

Tolomeo grinned when he saw Tilda comparing the pictures to the real man. "Tilda Harper, this is my boy Nicky."

The younger man offered his hand. "Nick Tolomeo."

They shook hands and exchanged "pleased to meet you," and at least in Tilda's case it was perfectly sincere. If the man had halfway decent taste in music and movies, she'd gladly take him home.

"Nicky, Tilda wants to know about that lady you met at the Macy's Parade back when you were a kid."

"Mercy Ashford from *Kissing Cousins*?" Nick asked. "What a great show. At least she was great in it. I thought she was the best part."

Tilda suddenly felt less enthusiastic. No straight guy could be that gorgeous and like Mercy too — Nick had to be gay. Still, he might be a good source. "I'm a big fan myself," she admitted.

"Nicky, you remember that day, don't

you?" Tolomeo said.

"Are you kidding? Meeting Mercy was the biggest thing that had ever happened to me. When the kids at school found out, I was the big man on campus for weeks afterward — not an easy thing for somebody my size."

"Good," his father said. "Then you can tell it all to Tilda." He looked at his watch. "Look, it's lunchtime. What do you say we go grab a bite — we can talk and eat at the same time. It's on me."

Though that muffin had been hours earlier, unlike some of the staff members at *Entertain Me!*, Tilda wasn't accustomed to freebies. "That's very nice of you, but — "

"But what? It's a business lunch. You meet people in the entertainment industry, right? So I hand you a stack of our business cards, and when you get a chance, you give them out. If you send the right client my way, I can make enough to buy you a dozen lunches. You can even leave your suitcase here."

"In that case, thank you," Tilda said. "That sounds great."

"Great! You good to go, Nicky?"

"Sure," Nick said.

Tolomeo started ushering them toward the door, but then slapped himself on the forehead and said, "What am I thinking?

My receptionist has the day off for her daughter's orthodontia — I can't leave the office alone."

"Turn on the machine — you can get the messages when we get back," Nick said.

"Machines! That's no way to do business. You two go on, and bring me back something to eat. Nicky, use the company card." He practically shoved them out the door, and Tilda found herself alone in the hallway with a handsome man. The day was looking up.

Nick rolled his eyes, but said, "So, what kind of food do you like?"

"Surprise me."

With his last name she'd expected him to head for an Italian place, but a few minutes later they were at Jacob Wirth's, with pints of dark German beer in front of them while they debated the relative virtues of the bratwurst or the fish cakes special. Tilda eventually decided on a pastrami sandwich with a side of German potato salad.

Once they'd ordered, Nick said, "I should apologize for Pop. He's not exactly subtle, is he?"

"Not terribly. Which one of us was he trying to get rid of?"

He laughed. "Neither. He was setting the two of us up."

Maybe Nick wasn't gay after all. Then again, why would a hunk like that need to be set up by his father, unless his looks were just an appealing facade for a pathetic loser?

"I just broke up with my girlfriend," Nick explained, as if guessing her thoughts, "and Pop is trying to get me involved with somebody else right away so we don't reconcile."

"Is reconciliation likely?"

"Not in a million years," he said, which Tilda didn't necessarily believe, having heard too many similar protestations, including a few she'd made herself. "But Pop isn't taking any chances," Nick went on. "He hates my ex."

"Why is that?" Tilda asked. It was nosy, but he'd brought it up.

"Hard to say. He disliked her the minute he met her. He's got this radar about people. He usually makes his mind up about them the first time he meets them, and he never changes it."

"Is he usually right?"

"Always. I should have known better."

Tilda waited for Nick to explain what terrible things his ex had done to make him agree with his father, and her estimation of him rose considerably when he skipped over the past and said, "Not to be pushy, but what about you? Are you seeing anybody?"

According to a conversation she'd once had with Heather, this was her chance to coyly hint that she had a posse of eligible men impatiently waiting for their turn to escort her to the best clubs in Boston. Tilda sent a mental raspberry toward her roommate and said, "Not a soul. Does your father like me?"

"He wouldn't be paying for lunch if he didn't."

"Do you like me?"

He blinked, but recovered enough to grin. "It takes me a little longer to make up my mind, but I'm thinking he's right again." The waitress brought their order, and Nick turned his attention to his meal. Tilda did the same. The witty badinage could wait.

When her sandwich was well on its way to becoming a fond memory, Tilda said, "Tell me about meeting Mercy."

Nick smiled like a Red Sox fan remembering the final game of the 2004 World Series. "I couldn't believe my luck when Pop said he was going to be Mercy's escort that year for the Macy's Thanksgiving Day Parade in New York. I promised I'd clean my room, wash the car, finish my homework on time, and make straight As for the rest of my life if he'd take me with him. Of course he'd planned all along to let me go, but he enjoyed torturing me for a while."

"Did you keep your promises?"

"I got the grades, did so-so on the home-work, and washed the car twice, but my room still looked like the parade had gone through there instead of down 34th Street. Pop should have got it in writing." He ate a french fry before going on. "Come Thanks-giving morning, we were at Mercy's hotel bright and early. It was the Plaza, right off Central Park."

"Eloise's stomping ground," Tilda put in.

He fixed her with a stern look. "In my day, young Italian guys did not read Eloise books."

"Then how did you know who she is?"

"Because these days, Italian men do read bedtime stories to their nieces. So do you want to talk about children's literature or the greatest moment of my life?"

"Sorry."

"We were at the Plaza early enough to grab breakfast, though I was too nervous to eat much. Which at that point meant I only ate three eggs, bacon, and toast. At eight on the dot we were outside her room, and I was so nervous that I was sure I was going to throw up every bit of that breakfast on her feet. But then she opened her door and smiled at me. That was it. I was in love." He looked at Tilda, and warned, "Don't say it was sweet."

"Wasn't even thinking it," she said, more or less truthfully. "I was just wishing she'd have made it onto the big screen — with that kind of charisma, she'd have been big."

"Real big," Nick said. "So Pop told her who we were, and he made it sound like I was working too, not just tagging along. Mercy shook our hands and treated me the same as Pop had, like I was a bodyguard too. I think that was when I decided I was going to go into the business with Pop — up until then I'd been thinking fireman or rock star, but the idea that I was responsible for keeping somebody safe really got to me. And not just anybody, but somebody famous who I'd just fallen in love with. Man, what a rush!"

As the waitress returned to take their empty plates and get their coffee orders, Tilda filed away a story idea for later consideration. She'd always wondered why somebody would risk life and limb to prevent inconvenience to some spoiled star, and now Nick had given her part of the answer. She knew a market or two that might go for a feature about Dom and Nick, or celebrity security in general.

"So?" she prompted once they were alone

201

again. "What happened next? I want details."

"You want details? Details I got. She was wearing black of course. A black lacy dress — just like she wore in the show — and a long black wool coat, but she'd added a red beret and gloves for Christmas. She looked sharp too. We had a car to take us to the beginning of the parade route, and once we got there we reported in and got her settled onto a float. Pillsbury was sponsoring *Kissing Cousins* and she was riding their float. It was all cookies and gingerbread men, with people dressed from nursery rhymes. The gingerbread castle had a balcony in front, and that's where Mercy rode. I told Pop I wasn't sure it was sturdy enough, so he let me go up and jump around just to be sure. I must have looked like an idiot, but Mercy thanked me for watching out for her."

Tilda wondered if he even knew he was grinning at the memory. "Did you ride on the float with her?"

"She invited me to," he said, "but I thought I better walk alongside with Pop, to keep an eye on the crowd. I tell you, I was taking it seriously." He looked at her as if again daring her to accuse him of being sweet, so she just nodded. "Jim Bonnier — the guy who played one of her Cousins on the show — was supposed to be riding with her, but he didn't show until about two minutes before start time. The woman in charge of the float was about to have a heart attack too, worrying that something had happened. When he finally got there, it was easy to tell what had happened." He shook his head in disgust. "Even then, I knew a hangover when I saw it. The dude had been out partying the night before, and he looked it. If he hadn't been such a jerk, I'd have felt sorry for him having to ride behind the Marching Trojans from Charlotte, North Carolina."

"Was he that bad? I talked to him a few times, years later, and he seemed okay."

"That was when he was craving his fame fix, and you were how he was going to get it," Nick pointed out. "When I met him, he was at the top of his game and he knew it. He blew off the woman in charge and sent his escort to get him coffee while he went over to Miss Muffet and Gretel and tried to cop feels."

"Charming."

"Tell me about it. About halfway through the parade, Pop sent me up to stand with Mercy after all, to make sure Bonnier kept his hands off of her. Anybody could see she wasn't interested, but he wasn't picking up on it. Pop figured having a kid standing there would calm him down."

"Did it?"

"More or less. Not so much because I was a kid, but because I planted myself between them, which cramped his style. Especially when I kept stepping on his foot. Accidentally of course."

"Of course."

"So there I was next to Mercy, waving at the crowd like I was somebody. My mom saw me on TV, and so did everybody else in the family. It was awesome."

"What did you and Mercy talk about? Every time I see people in parades talking and laughing between waves, I wonder what they're saying."

"Nothing earth-shattering. 'Are you as cold as I am?' 'Aren't your arms tired from waving?' That kind of thing. Plus Mercy asked me what grade I was in, and what my favorite subject was, and how many girlfriends I had. The kinds of questions people ask kids when they're being nice. All Bonnier talked about was the people we saw, especially the girls. 'Isn't that one a porker?' and 'I hope that chick playing the trombone is rich, because it's the only way she'll ever get laid.' Mercy kept trying to get him to shut up, but he ignored her."

"Had Mercy not already inspired you to join your dad's business, I suppose encountering Bonnier would have pushed you toward becoming a gossip columnist."

He grinned. "I could have dished some dirt on him, without a doubt. After the parade, Bonnier tried to get Mercy to go out with him so he could, and I quote, 'Stuff her turkey.' "

Tilda sputtered inelegantly. "Get out of here!"

"Scout's honor," he said, holding up three fingers in the time-honored way. "She refused much more politely than she should have, and he got pissy and stomped away."

"Did you get his autograph?"

"No, but he did give me his used coffee cup. He said I could use it to get some action with the girls in school."

Tilda allowed herself a smaller sputter. "What an asshole!"

"Yeah, but you know, he was considerably younger then than I am now. If I'd had that kind of money and attention when I was that age, I'd have been an asshole too."

"Mercy was younger than he was," Tilda pointed out, "but she wasn't an asshole."

"No, she definitely wasn't." He got a dreamy look in his eye.

"You had it bad, didn't you?"

"Oh, yeah. It wasn't just that she was a looker — though she was — or sexy — though she was that too. She had presence. You don't see it often in person, even in my line of work — plenty of performers are talented and do good work but don't have that kind of effect on me."

"Star power," Tilda suggested.

"That's it. She was the first person I met who really had it. She should have hit it big."

Tilda agreed, and wished she could find out why she hadn't. "What happened after Bonnier slithered away?"

"Dad had the car waiting, and we drove Mercy back to her hotel. We'd been booked for the whole day — or at least Dad had been — but she said she was going to have dinner with a friend there at the hotel and said she didn't want to keep us from our family. After Dad made sure she meant it, we caught the next train back to Boston. We even made it in time to carve the turkey."

"That's it?"

"Well . . ."

"Are you holding out on me?"

He grinned like a little boy caught with his hand in grandma's cookie jar — knowing he'd done something he shouldn't have, but proud of himself just the same. "She kissed me good-bye."

"I'm surprised you needed a train to get home. I bet you could have floated back."

"Oh, yeah."

"What about the photo?"

"Photo? Right, I almost forgot about that. When the friend showed up, she had a photographer with her. I think she was a magazine editor for one of those teen magazines."

"*Teen Fave?*"

"That's the one. How did you know?"

In answer, Tilda reached for her satchel, pulled out the copy of the magazine with the photo of Mercy and Sophia, alongside the man and boy she now knew were Dom and Nick.

"Hey, I never saw this," he said.

"This picture is how I tracked you and your father down. I had dinner with that editor recently, and she still has her files with the release form he signed."

"No kidding? That's nice detective work."

"It's what I do," she said nonchalantly.

"I'm just sorry it didn't pay off this time."

"I wouldn't say that," Tilda said, smiling.

"Yeah? That sounds encouraging."

"I meant it to. I'm not much into subtlety."

"Me neither." They shared a moment that might have gone on longer had the waitress not shown up with a pot of coffee for refills.

Though the mood was broken, Tilda had a hunch it could be rekindled with a minimum of effort. The fact that Nick's next move was to ask about her work convinced her of it.

He said, "Do you only write this kind of piece? The 'where are they now?' thing?"

"No, I write other entertainment articles, but nostalgia is my specialty. People like knowing what happened to their old favorites. The formerly famous, I call them, as opposed to people who've stayed in the public eye."

"Which story sells better? The big star settling down to a quiet life or the big star hitting the skids?"

"It depends on the market. Some magazines — the women's and family-focused ones — want actresses who've abandoned the glamour of Cannes and Hollywood for the rewarding life of changing diapers and making Hamburger Helper for dinner. This reassures women who stay at home. They either think 'if it's important enough for a big star, it's important enough for me' or 'I could have been a big star too, but I heard the noble calling of motherhood.' The more cynical markets want the 'hitting the skids' stories — the cost of fame, see how the mighty have fallen, plus general schaden-freude. Inspirational magazines want stars who've left the Sodom of Hollywood in order to follow God, or Buddha, or whoever. Men's magazines want the ones who were babes to still be babes. And fan magazines want to know that their stars still love them."

"What about you?"

"It doesn't matter to me. I pick out a likely candidate to hunt down, or get a lead on somebody, and when I find out what their situation is, I figure out which market will want their story and slant it that way. If I'm lucky, I can slant it several ways and sell different versions of the article to different markets, as long as they don't compete."

"I mean, what do you want to find out about them? That they've had a good life, a rotten life, or a Godly life?"

"I just want to find them. That's the fun part for me."

"Have you ever hunted somebody who didn't want to be found?"

"They all want to be found," she said firmly. "Maybe they've turned their backs on the industry, but part of them still wants to be famous, at least for a little while." Tilda thought back to the image she'd had at Holly's funeral, of fame as a kind of drug. "Fame can be very addicting. It's hard to lose it — even those who complain about it seem to crave it when it's gone."

"Like crack?" Nick said.

"Exactly. I suppose that makes me a pusher."

Nick took a swallow of coffee, apparently thinking it over. "No, a pusher would keep selling the drug they're hooked on — you're bringing them down gently. More of a methadone thing."

"Mental methadone. I can live with that."

"It must be frustrating when you can't find somebody you're looking for."

"Mercy is the only one I haven't found. So far, anyway."

"Is that right? No wonder you're so determined."

"That's part of it." Maybe she'd tell him about how much Mercy meant to her personally another time, assuming there was another time, which she certainly wanted to assume.

The check came then, and Nick dutifully pulled out the company credit card to pay for it. "Next time, it'll be on me personally," he assured her.

"Next time?"

"Hey, I told you I'm not subtle."

On the walk back to his office to pick up Tilda's suitcase, Nick asked, "Did I answer all your questions about Mercy?"

"I think so," she said. Once it became plain that Nick didn't have any idea of Mercy's whereabouts, the rest of lunch had just been for fun anyway. Then she thought of those smarmy posts from Have_Mercy. "There is one thing. I know you probably weren't around her enough to have a opinion about this, but I've heard some vague rumors that Mercy slept around."

"Really?" He frowned as he considered it. "I was young, but I sure didn't pick up any vibes that she was that way. I told you how she kept Bonnier at arm's length."

"That could have been because they worked together — even promiscuous people sometimes know better than to mix business with pleasure. Or maybe he just wasn't her type."

"I guess. Let's ask Pop when we get back to the office. It's like I told you before — he's got this sense of people."

Dom was still at the front desk, and when asked, he was positive that the rumor was wrong. As he put it, "I couldn't answer to what she was before or after, but when I met her, she was a good girl. Not naive, and I'm not saying she was a virgin, but she wasn't a tramp, either."

Then both Tolomeo men promised to call

if they came up with any ideas to help find Mercy, and Nick added that he'd be calling early next week even if he didn't. Tilda liked the sound of that.

CHAPTER 14

"I used to run these columns predicting who'd still be around and what they'd be doing — 'Five Years From Now,' 'Ten Years From Now,' and so on. I never worried about being right because our readers outgrew us long before that. Anyhow, the one I did for the kids in *Kissing Cousins* came pretty close, but I blew it with Mercy Ashford. I was sure she'd be a big star."
— Sophia Vaughn, quoted in "Curse of the *Kissing Cousins*," *Entertain Me!*

At two-thirty Tilda was sitting at the spare desk at the *Entertain Me!* office, ready to call the director of *The Raven's Prey.* She'd arrived with fifteen minutes to spare, enough time to get herself and her laptop arranged comfortably and to tease Cooper by telling him she'd dined with two different men since she'd seen him last.

Plus she got to watch shit flow downhill

as the magazine staff made last-minute arrangements for a cocktail party they were hosting as part of the Boston Film Festival. First Bryce sniped at Jillian because it was threatening to go over budget. Then Jillian scolded Nicole for spending too much on the contents of the swag bags. Next Nicole tried to lay the blame on Shannon, but Shannon started crying. Tilda didn't know whether Shannon honestly got upset that easily or if it was a political ploy. Whatever it was, Nicole found herself with nobody to dump her load of shit on, and when she looked at Tilda speculatively, Tilda picked up the phone and started dialing, once again devoutly grateful to be a freelancer.

Had she not already known Matthew Boardman was retired, she'd have guessed it when he answered his own phone. Working directors have assistants for chores like that. Sometimes their assistants have assistants.

"Mr. Boardman? This is Tilda Harper from *Entertain Me!* Sophia Vaughn suggested that I call you."

"Yes, she spoke to me about you yesterday. I must thank you for that — I haven't spoken to Sophia in an age. I didn't even realize that she knew where I live, but of course Sophia always did know everything.

And I'm always happy to talk to a friend of Sophia's."

"Thank you. I'm working on an article about the former cast members of the seventies sitcom *Kissing Cousins.*"

"That rings a vague bell," Boardman allowed, "though my work was always in film, not the small screen."

Having checked him out on IMDb, Tilda could honestly say, "I realize that of course, but at one point you worked with one of those cast members. Mercy Ashford was originally slated to work on *The Raven's Prey.*"

There was a pause long enough to make Tilda wonder if the connection had been broken. Then Boardman said, "Yes, I remember Miss Ashford." His voice had lost the warmth it had held when talking about Sophia. "I'm afraid I couldn't say anything positive about her. If you're working on a retrospective of her work, you'd be better off talking to somebody else."

"Perhaps I should explain. I'm trying to locate Mercy. You see, she dropped off the radar right after she left your production, and hasn't been seen since."

"Really? Even her agent doesn't know where she is?"

"No, sir. Even though her agent passed

away, she's still officially a client of the agency, and they have no idea."

"How peculiar."

"I was hoping you might have some insight as to what was going on with her at that time, since you were one of the last people in the industry to see her."

"Was I? Then I wish I could tell you more. You already know that Mercy was signed to play the lead in *The Raven's Prey*. In the few days of film we shot with her, I was very pleased with her work. I'd worked with former television people before, and generally I hadn't been impressed. But Miss Ashford had genuine screen presence, and though her acting wasn't world-class, she was working very hard to improve. The script wasn't particularly good — I only took the job because I was short of funds — but with Miss Ashford showing such promise, I had some hopes for the completed film. She rose above the material, frankly."

"How long did she work with you?"

"Throughout preproduction, and for the first two weeks of filming. She called in sick on the Monday of the third week, but we weren't alarmed — these things happen. We simply rearranged the schedule and filmed scenes in which she did not appear. On

Tuesday, she called again. That time it was harder to work around her absence, and it was harder still on Wednesday. We actually had to shut down for the rest of the week, which I'm sure you realize is an expense any director prefers to avoid. That weekend, Miss Ashford's agent called to tell us she was leaving the production. The producer was understandably enraged. He made the usual threats about Miss Ashford never working in films again, and so forth, but the agent didn't even try to explain her client's actions. She seemed as nonplussed as we were." He sighed. "Production was shut down for two more weeks while we recast the part, and we ended up with a lead who was not quite up to the challenge. Box office receipts were poor, and I always blamed Miss Ashford for that."

"You had no warning that she was planning to leave the production?"

"Not an inkling. She was very enthusiastic, and seemed delighted to have graduated from television work. And you could see the spark of something in the rushes. I remember that when I went home at the end of the second week, I was sure that we'd be seeing a lot more of her in the future. But after such unprofessional behavior . . . Well, I'm afraid I minced no words when I discussed the incident with colleagues."

In other words he'd trashed her to anybody who would listen. "I don't think anybody could blame you for that. It must have been very trying." Tilda shook herself. She was picking up the man's tone. "The producer's threat came true, as it happened. Mercy Ashford never worked in the industry again."

"What a waste," Boardman said.

"You'll get no arguments from me. I imagine that since you weren't working together that long, you didn't learn much about Mercy's personal life."

"She was unmarried, but I presume you know that. Other than that, there's not much I can tell you. I maintained somewhat formal relationships during shooting."

Tilda wasn't surprised. "Do you remember her mentioning any friends, or if she ever brought a friend to the set?"

"No, I don't believe she did. She did do an interview on set — with Sophia Vaughn, as a matter of fact — but that's the only time I saw her with a guest."

"What about the other people on the film? Did she seem particularly close to anybody?"

"Not really. She was friendly with everybody, but the scenes she worked on were mostly solo, so she didn't have much interaction with her costars. As for myself, the only time I recall speaking to her about a non-work-related issue was when she asked how we went about hiring makeup people. Apparently she had a friend she was hoping to get onto the production. I referred her to the appropriate person, but that's all I know."

Tilda made a note to let Jasmine know that Mercy hadn't forgotten her after all.

Boardman went on. "Now I feel a bit guilty for the unkind thoughts I've had about Miss Ashford over the years. Do you suppose something happened to her?"

"I have no idea," Tilda had to admit, "but if I find out, I'll be sure to let you know."

"That would be most kind. Is there any other way I can help you?"

She looked over the list of questions she'd come up with earlier. "I don't think so. Thank you, you've been very frank, and I appreciate your taking the time to speak with me."

"It was my pleasure. When one retires, time is all one has left to share."

Tilda left her contact information with him, just in case he remembered anything, and hung up.

"Damn it!" Her last lead, and it had led

nowhere.

"Having problems with the story?" Nicole said, almost managing to sound honestly concerned.

Tilda glared at her.

"I thought you had hot leads to follow? Did they not go anywhere?"

Tilda glared at her.

"If you're not going to be able to produce, we need to know soonest so there won't be a hole in the magazine."

Tilda glared at her. She might have spent the rest of the afternoon glaring at her if Jillian hadn't called the woman away. Only when Nicole was out of earshot did Tilda allow herself another, "Damn it!"

"No luck?" Cooper asked with real concern.

"Plenty, but it was all bad." She noticed he'd shut down his computer. "You heading out?"

"Yeah, Jean-Paul is working a really classy party out in Newton, and I'm going along to keep his admirers at bay. How about you?"

"Nothing special," she said. "June wants me to meet some guy she's dug up." That was true enough — it was continuously true — though it had nothing to do with her plans for the evening. Or rather, her lack of plans, which she didn't intend to admit to in Nicole's hearing.

She gathered up her own stuff and walked with Cooper down to the lobby and out to the street, which was enough time to fill him in on Lawrence and Nick before they went their separate ways.

CHAPTER 15

"Episode 23: Summer Camp (Part 2)
Sherri finds herself bunking with a crew of
jocks while Mercy is trapped with a trio of
constantly studying drudges. Realizing
that being bunkmates wasn't so bad, they
request transfers, but two other campers
have been given their spots. When they
realize those campers are the ones who
encouraged their feud in the first place,
they team up to get those girls in trouble
so they can get their places back."
— Fanboy's Online *Kissing Cousins*
Episode Guide, by Vincent Peters

Tilda was not exactly jolly on her way
home. Not only had Boardman given her
nothing, but the lunch with Nick had been
a waste of time too. Or rather, it had been
personally satisfying, but professionally?
Nada. She didn't need Vincent's countdown
program to remind her that time was tick-

ing away.

Her mood wasn't improved by having to negotiate the subway during rush hour, still pulling that damned suitcase behind her. Moreover, it was Friday night, she had no plans, and it was too late to try to set anything up without sounding desperate.

When she made it home, the stack of mail waiting for her on the kitchen counter was hardly cheering. There were a couple of checks in the midst of the bills and shills, but both were small — her income had definitely not kept up with her outgo for the week.

After checking to see how much of her food had survived Doug, and being further annoyed to see that a nearly full box of corn flakes had disappeared, she went to her room, only to stop at the doorway. Somebody had been in there.

It wouldn't have been screamingly obvious to anybody but Tilda, but she could tell. The drawer on her dresser that stuck was partially open, as was the closet door, though she always closed both of them tightly. Some of the papers next to her desktop computer weren't where she had left them, and her bed looked rumpled. Damn it, if Heather and Doug had been porking in her bed, Heather was going to be paying for a new set of sheets! Fortunately, Tilda's careful examination showed no sign of that, for which she was exceedingly grateful.

Next she looked at the dresser — a previous roommate's boyfriend had been a foot fetishist — but it looked like all her socks and stockings were present and accounted for and had not been molested in any way. The same was true of the rest of her clothes, both in the drawers and hanging in the closet. Everything was intact, but she was sure somebody had been rummaging. Maybe it was nothing more than Heather looking for clothes to borrow. It would have been yet another violation of their agreement, but she'd rather imagine Heather in her room than Doug.

The thing was, she was sure somebody had been sitting at her desk, and Heather would have had no reason to fiddle with her computer — she had her own. Tilda booted up the computer and checked the security files. There it was — somebody had tried to log into her system. She smiled in malicious satisfaction. Her system was protected nine ways from Sunday, thanks to Javier — he'd set up security for her after hearing her complain about a roommate who was too cheap to pay for Internet service when she could sneak onto Tilda's computer instead. Maybe a dedicated hacker could have broken in, but it wouldn't have been easy, and she didn't think Doug had the brains to attempt it.

Tilda heard Heather come in the front door, and went to intercept her. "Heather, we've got to talk."

"Glad to see you too," Heather said in an irritated voice. "I'll buy you a new box of corn flakes, okay? Doug didn't like my Weetabix."

"Forget the cereal. Somebody's been in my room."

"Well, it wasn't me!"

"I didn't say it was, but somebody was in there. I'll show you."

Tilda led the way back to her bedroom and pointed out all the unmistakable signs.

"I don't see anything," Heather said flatly. "Are you turning into that guy on TV who has to have everything just so?"

"I am not like Monk," Tilda said indignantly. "I'm just particular about my things."

"More like peculiar, if you ask me," Heather muttered.

"Fine, if it makes you feel better, pretend that I'm obsessive-compulsive. But somebody did try to use my computer — I can tell from the security files. If it wasn't you, it must have been Doug. Unless you had another guest I don't know about, that is."

"What, and violate your precious agreement? No, I haven't had any other guests. And maybe Doug did come in to check his e-mail. For all I know, the son of a bitch wanted to troll the Web for porn sites."

"Trouble in paradise?" Tilda asked.

"The bastard was supposed to take me to a nice dinner tonight, to pay me back for letting him stay here these past few days, but he called and left a damned voicemail to tell me he's decided to work things out with his live-in. He swore to me that their relationship was over! Fucking bastard!"

"Shit, I'm sorry," Tilda said awkwardly. "It's his loss, anyway."

"Damned straight." Heather sighed. "Maybe he did come in here. He could have done it when I was in the shower or something. He didn't take anything, did he?"

"I don't think so," Tilda admitted, "so I guess there's no harm done."

"Well, I'm sorry he violated your personal space."

"Forget it," Tilda said. Maybe she was overly particular about her room — or overly peculiar — but even if she was right, this was hardly the time to rub salt in her roommate's wound. "Forget him too. Tell you what — since he blew you off, why don't you and I go out to dinner?"

"That's sweet, but I met this guy on the T on the way home, and he asked me out. I'm giving you notice right now that if things work out, he might spend the night." She glanced at her watch. "Shit — he'll be here in fifteen minutes." And she rushed off to transform herself by means of a cyclone of primping.

Tilda sighed and wondered if the subway suitor preferred corn flakes or Weetabix.

CHAPTER 16

"Q: What's your favorite day of the week? A: Friday! The show almost always wraps early, so I have a chance to relax and get ready before I go out. Sometimes it's dinner and dancing or a movie with a date, but most of the time it's just hanging out with friends, listening to music, and eating pizza. That's my idea of a good time."

— *"Kissing Cousins'* Sherri Answers Twenty-five Personal Questions," *Teen Fave*

Once Heather was off on her date, Tilda was free to crank up the stereo and call up Town Pizza House to get dinner delivered. Her pepperoni pizza arrived just as she finished attending to the mail, and she was feeling lazy enough that she didn't pull out a plate, just ate it from the box while watching TV, substituting a beer for her usual Dr Pepper to emphasize what a good time she was having, eating alone in front of the boob tube on a Friday night.

Once the pizza, the beer, and the beer's twin brother were gone, she decided she'd had enough of frivolity and went to her room to check e-mail. Vincent had sent a new version of the Mercy murder countdown program, this one with animations, to remind her that less than a week remained until his hypothetical killer was expected to strike, plus more Mercy sightings, again categorized for her convenience. This batch included Mercy teaching drama in Los Angeles while dressed as a man, Mercy married to an Arabian prince and kept in seclusion, and Mercy abandoning Hollywood to embrace the life of a Buddhist nun.

Tilda even took half an hour to investigate one fan's claim that Mercy was working in the porn industry. After all, plenty of actresses on their way up or down had been known to detour into that line of work. But when she tracked down photos of the actress the fan insisted "looked just like Mercy," she found that the woman didn't in fact resemble the actress in any way and was at least six inches shorter. After watching some film clips on an aficionado's Web site, Tilda also concluded that she was more agile than most women Mercy's age would be.

There were no new posts from Have _Mercy.

That done, she leaned back in her chair to recap her progress. It didn't take long — she hadn't made much.

That wasn't completely true. She actually had more than enough information and quotes to write her article. If anything, Mercy's mysterious disappearance would only add to the woo-woo factor of the *Kissing Cousins* curse. Jillian would eat it up with a spoon, Nicole would be even more bitchy than usual, and all would be right with the world.

She didn't need to find Mercy. She just really wanted to.

It was intensely aggravating to admit even to herself that she was no further along in finding that actress than she'd been over a week before, when Holly Kendricks was found dead. Even though she knew it was ridiculous, she kept thinking about that damned countdown of Vincent's marking off the time until Mercy became a target, which was currently at 136 hours, plus or minus 12 hours. It was ridiculous! There was no crazed killer stalking nearly forgotten actors and actresses. The three deaths were purely coincidence. She shouldn't even be wasting time thinking about it — she should be concentrating on finding Mercy.

So where the hell was she? What had happened to her? Why couldn't Tilda find some trace of her?

Nobody, especially not a TV star, could disappear that thoroughly unless they worked at it. Tilda had told Nick over lunch that the formerly famous always wanted to be found, but maybe she was wrong. Maybe Mercy didn't want to be found. Maybe the actress had purposely disappeared, and was purposely staying hidden. That changed the question from "Where is she?" to "Why did she go away?"

Tilda thought over Mercy's last known appearances. There was the cast party at the end of the final season of *Kissing Cousins* where she'd promised to keep in touch with the other members of the cast and Jasmine the makeup artist. Each one of those people had sounded surprised when she hadn't. Even though Hollywood was notorious for broken promises, they were still surprised. So if she assumed that Mercy really had intended to stay friends, something must have changed.

The next confirmed sighting was on the set of *The Raven's Prey,* where something made Mercy give up a starring role in a feature, which some actresses would kill for.

That reminded her of the money Mercy hadn't collected over the years. Tilda didn't know exactly how much it was, but Noel had implied it was well worth the effort of collecting. Why would anybody ignore free money?

Tilda ran her fingers through her hair. There had to be a logical answer. Or, given the mental state of all too many actors, an illogical one. Okay, Tilda had interviewed dozens of actors who'd left show business for one reason or another. What had happened to them?

Sometimes they got dumped. Their show got canceled, their movie bombed, whatever. For some reason, the people that mattered stopped calling them and they no longer got the good tables at Spago. But that hadn't happened to Mercy. She'd quit a job, a good one, apparently without anything else waiting in the wings. That was hardly the act of somebody desperate for work.

Then there were the actors who'd grown old and wanted to retire. That definitely wasn't the answer. Mercy was young, and again, wouldn't she have wanted her money if she were retiring?

Some actors decide they want to do something else with their lives. It's not an easy business, after all, and there was even a phrase for it: walking away from it all. That could explain Mercy leaving her movie role, and even abandoning her friends if she didn't want to be part of that world anymore. But there was that money again! If she was starting a new life, she'd need it more than ever.

Tilda hesitated over the next possibility, not even wanting to think it. Sometimes actors died. Maybe Mercy was dead. That would explain why she'd never called her friends or collected her money. If she'd been taken ill, that would account for her abandoning the movie too. Except that if she'd been that sick, wouldn't a doctor or a hospital have been involved? It wasn't easy for a star to get so much as a hangnail without somebody finding out. Most entertainment magazines — including *Entertain Me!* — had sources at the major LA hospitals, and that had been just as true back when Mercy disappeared. Even if Mercy had died alone at home, her body would have been found.

Okay, Tilda thought, suppose Mercy got ill, and that made her decide to leave the movie and her friends. Make it a disfiguring disease, so she wouldn't want to call them for comfort. An STD would be even better, especially if Have_Mercy was telling the truth. So Mercy went away and died, and didn't care about the money because she was dying anyway. Of course, when Tilda used that private investigator, he'd checked for death records, and Mercy wasn't listed. But if she'd run off to die alone, she could have done so under an assumed name and been buried in an anonymous grave somewhere. It fit. It was awful, but it fit.

There was just one problem. It didn't match what Tilda knew about Mercy Ashford. An orphan with no money or connections who'd managed to break into Hollywood and who had a promising career ahead of her did not crawl into a hole and die! More importantly, Tilda didn't want to believe it and she wasn't going to. Who said that actors were the only ones allowed to be illogical?

So scratch the mysterious illness. Mercy could still be dead. What about a car accident? There had been cases of cars going into canals or over cliffs, and then not being found until years later. There were plenty of places in California where that could have happened.

Even nastier, Mercy could have been murdered and her body hidden, or mutilated enough that it couldn't be identified. Then the killer quietly closed up his victim's house and life, and stole away into the night.

Either theory could be tweaked to fit the facts, but Tilda shook her head as vigorously as if somebody had been trying to talk her into it. There was one piece that wouldn't fit into the jigsaw of facts: the other deaths.

Damn Vincent for making her think the deaths were connected! Sometime over the past week, the idea had sunk into her brain and she didn't think she'd ever pry it loose again. Two unusual deaths she could accept. Three deaths — one of them definitely murder — and a bizarre disappearance? Fifteen years of therapy wouldn't make her come to terms with that!

All right then, what could make Mercy disappear and motivate the murders of her former costars nearly thirty years later?

Why were people ever killed? Crimes of passion? Definitely not — maybe Jim's or Alex's deaths could have been spur-of-the-moment, but Holly's had been well planned.

Revenge? For what? Tilda had never heard of anything nasty going on with the cast back then, and even admitting that she could have missed it, she didn't think Sophia would have.

Money? No hint of it being involved.

Sex? Despite Javier's wet dreams, she'd

never heard about canoodling on the set. But for the sake of argument, what if Holly had slept with Jim Bonnier back in the day, and her husband only recently found out. Enraged, he flew to California, talked himself into Jim's apartment, got the man drunk, and administered a fatal overdose, all while wearing gloves so there would be no fingerprints. Then he flew home to Connecticut, with nobody the wiser.

A month later, Holly made another confession, or the husband found another volume of her diary, or whatever, but somehow he found out she'd slept with Alex Johnson too. Back to California to lie in wait for Alex to zoom by on his motorcycle so the vengeful husband could run him down, again leaving no clues of any kind, and go back to Connecticut.

Two weeks after that, he finds out there were more guys on Holly's hit parade, and he decided it would be easier to kill his wife than to try to track down all of her former bedmates. And one more time, this hitherto blameless businessman managed to cover his tracks completely.

It could have happened. And monkeys could have flown out of his butt to transport him between California and Connecticut! Not only was the tale terminally lame, but it did nothing to explain Mercy's disappearance.

Tilda mentally ran down the motives from every mystery movie she could think of, trying to think of what was left. A serial killer with a hatred of seventies sitcoms? Mistaken identity? Killing a bunch of people to hide the motive for killing the last one? All theoretically possible, but all unconvincing. Guilty knowledge? Of what? Again, neither Tilda nor Sophia had gotten wind of any scandals or mysteries. Other than Mercy's disappearance of course.

Other than Mercy's disappearance.

Tilda sat up straight. Could the connection between the deaths and Mercy's disappearance be Mercy herself? Could something have happened back then, something so awful that it would make her disappear for all those years and now she was taking her revenge? Or suppose Mercy had some reason for disappearing that she didn't want anybody to know, and she was afraid her former castmates were going to reveal the truth or her hiding place. How far would she go to keep her secrets, whatever they were? Could Vincent actually be right about somebody targeting the cast members?

Could Mercy herself be killing the Kissing Cousins?

CHAPTER 17

"Most of us have a hero, be it an athlete, historical figure, TV or film star, musician, or even an author. The manner in which one engages with one's accumulated cognitive schema of that person relative to their known history is highly indicative of one's relative maturity. In other words, mature people recognize their idols' feet of clay."
— "Idol Worship as a Maturity Measure: Maturity Correlates of Personal Heroic Figures' Cognitive Schemata Complexity," by Lorinda B.R. Goodwin, PhD, and June O'Reilly, PhD.
Psychological Science

The pizza Tilda had eaten for dinner turned to cement in her stomach. How could her idol be a murderer? The idea was obscene!

It also made a certain amount of sense. Considering Mercy's history with Jim Bonnier, it would have been no trouble to convince him to invite her into his apartment so she could kill him. Alex Johnson had been riding his motorcycle without a helmet for years — it would take no particular skill or strength to run him off the road. As for Holly, she'd been a petite woman — someone as tall as Mercy could certainly have subdued her. Speaking purely from a physical perspective, Mercy could certainly have killed all three.

But would she have? Tilda grabbed her satchel, pulled out the photo of Mercy with its ersatz signature, and stared at it. All she could think was that Mercy didn't look like a killer. She threw the picture across the room in disgust. God, what an idiot she was! Mercy wasn't the girl in the picture any more. Hell, she'd never been that girl. She'd been an actress playing a part, and no matter how much Tilda knew about her, she still didn't know the woman. How could she be so sure she wasn't a killer?

Admittedly, she had talked to a lot of people who'd known Mercy, and they'd all liked her and trusted her. But they were talking about somebody they'd known nearly thirty years ago. The people who'd known Mercy then didn't know the Mercy of the present day any more than Tilda did.

Then again, Tilda hadn't known any of the dead Cousins very well. For all she knew, they could have done something terrible to Mercy. They could have deserved what happened to them.

Damn it! She was doing it again. Even when faced with the idea that Mercy killed three people in cold blood, she was trying to come up with more reasons to admire her. She'd thought Vincent was an incurable fan. It would have been funny if it hadn't been so pitiful.

All right, Tilda decided again, the only way to get at the truth — to figure out who and what Mercy Ashford really was — was to find her.

The first step was to connect her laptop to her desk computer so she could back up the notes she'd taken since she left for New York. Then, stopping only for a trip to the kitchen for a glass of Dr Pepper, she starting going through every interview, every phone call, every bit of data or random musing she'd entered, looking for some thread that she could worry at to get closer to Mercy.

Two hours later, she'd found nothing she hadn't already followed up on. Then she remembered that she hadn't transferred the notes from the interviews with Jasmine the makeup artist or Nick the bodyguard. Again she dove for her satchel, this time to get out her Palm, and moved over everything Jasmine had said about Mercy. Then she read it. Nothing.

Next, she put in what she'd learned from Nick. These notes were sketchier — she'd been eating and enjoying herself too much to be thorough — but she remembered details as she went. Then she read that all over again. All she'd learned was that Mercy was nice to a little boy who was a big fan and reasonably tactful in resisting the advances of a horny costar. So not only had she not found any new leads, but she'd put paid to the idea that Mercy slept her way through Hollywood, no matter what Have _Mercy claimed.

Or had she? Sure, nobody else had confirmed it — in fact, those Tilda had asked had denied it — but she didn't really know that Mercy wasn't an easy lay. As she'd pointed out to Nick, maybe she didn't believe in mixing business with pleasure or maybe she hadn't liked Jim Bonnier. Maybe she was particularly skilled at hiding her bedroom antics, being an actress and all. So if Have_Mercy really had the inside scoop, he must have been pretty close to her.

Tilda frowned. It wasn't much to work

with. The way Have _Mercy had avoided giving more details, even when asked repeatedly, made her suspect he was lying. He could have an ax to grind or he could be a random nutcase. But since she had nothing, she was willing to go with next to nothing. Besides which, given a choice, Tilda would gladly believe that Mercy was a tramp instead of a murderer. Come to think of it, there was no law that said she couldn't be both.

No more speculation, Tilda told herself — she needed facts, and maybe Have_Mercy would have some she could use. There hadn't been any communications from him in Vincent's latest report, so she was going to try to approach him directly. Since the Mercy sighting transcripts listed only the guy's user name from the Listserv, she needed his e-mail address, which Vincent should be able to dig up for her. She checked her clock and saw that it was after nine. By the rules of business and personal etiquette, she couldn't call him until at least ten o'clock the next day. So she e-mailed him instead:

Vincent,
Call me ASAP.
Tilda

Then she went to get a refill on her Dr Pepper. The phone rang before she got the refrigerator open. She didn't need to check caller ID to know who it was.

"Hi, Vincent."

"Have you found Mercy yet?"

"And a lovely evening to you too."

"Sorry, but your message sounded urgent."

"It is, but not like that. I need to get the e-mail address of one of the people from the *Kissing Cousins* Listserv."

"No problem. Which one?"

"Have_Mercy."

"The guy who said Mercy slept around? Are you kidding me? I couldn't believe it when I saw that you'd posted a message to him. He's lying through his teeth."

"Probably."

"They why are you wasting time on him?"

She didn't want to tell him that she had nothing better to spend her time on, so she said, "I want to find out where he got the idea in the first place."

"He made it up," Vincent scoffed.

"Maybe, or maybe he heard it somewhere and doesn't want to give up his source. Maybe, just maybe, he even knew her himself."

"You think?"

"I don't think anything yet. Can you get me the address? Are you at your computer?"

"Of course," he said, as if there were nowhere else anybody would possibly be on a Friday night. There was the sound of rapid typing. "Have_Mercy@hotmail.com."

"Got it," she said, jotting it down. "Thanks, Vincent."

There was a pause. "Tilda, you don't really think Mercy was a bad person, do you?"

For a heart-freezing moment, Tilda thought he'd had the same thought that she had, that Mercy herself was the killer. "What do you mean?"

"You know. Sleeping with people. Men."

She relaxed. It was only the sex that alarmed him. Tilda would never understand how Vincent had managed to stay so innocent, considering the amount of trivia and biographical data about any number of stars that he had stored in his brain and on his hard disk. "Vincent, whether or not Mercy had a lover or a hundred lovers has nothing to do with her being a bad person. So what if she wasn't a virgin? Neither am I. Does that make me a bad person?"

"Of course not."

With almost any other friend, she'd have followed up with, "You're not a virgin, either, and I think you're a good person," but for all she knew, Vincent was a virgin. She didn't even know if he was straight, gay, bi, or asexual. "Today I met a man who rode with Mercy on a float at the Macy's Thanksgiving Day Parade when he was a little boy, and she went out of her way to be kind to him."

"Really? He got to ride the float with her?" Vincent said. "God, I'm jealous."

Of course he was, Tilda thought. "Anyway, a woman who'd go out of her way to be nice to a little boy couldn't be all bad, right?"

"Right," he said, sounding as if he felt better. "Thanks, Tilda. Let me know if you need anything else."

"Will do. Thanks."

She realized she felt a little better herself, as if in telling Vincent about Mercy's virtues, she'd almost convinced herself.

Though the message Tilda intended to send to Have_Mercy was brief, it took her a good half an hour to word it just the way she wanted it. She was aiming for polite and interested in what he had to say, but skeptical.

I don't know if you remember me, but we exchanged posts during the online memorial services for Holly Kendricks, formerly of *Kissing Cousins.* As I mentioned then, I'm trying to locate Mercy Ashford, and you suggested that I get in touch with Ms. Ashford's former boyfriends. Unfortunately, I have been unable to track down anybody who dated Ms. Ashford or who knows who she dated. Do you have any names of any of Ms. Ashford's dates? Failing that, do you have other contacts who might have those names? I'm anxious to find Ms. Ashford, and would really appreciate your help.

She read over the message a few times and even considered adding a veiled offer of a bribe, but decided to send it as it was. Either Have_Mercy was just a whacko, or he had something — all she could do was wait to see if he responded.

It would, of course, have been completely ridiculous to check e-mail every thirty seconds for the rest of the night. So she set her e-mail program to do it automatically and played Quake for an hour. Unfortunately, she couldn't play for shit, probably because she switched over to e-mail every time a piece of spam came through, which didn't do much for her concentration. Finally she called it a night. Anything Have _Mercy had to say could wait until the morning.

The apartment was strangely quiet, Tilda realized as she got ready for bed. Either Heather had gone to her new boyfriend's or she was staying out even later than usual. Now all Tilda had to do was get to sleep with pictures of a murderous Mercy — older, but still dressed in black lace — running through her head. She woke up the next morning feeling vaguely dissatisfied, though she didn't remember her dreams.

Before making coffee, Tilda checked her e-mail, but there was nothing from Have _Mercy. Not that she intended to sit around waiting for him, of course. She showered and ate before checking again. But she had to admit that checking again after drying her hair was overkill.

After that, she took herself firmly in hand. Even though it was the weekend, she had other work in the hopper, and it would be unprofessional to wait around for a source that might not have anything to tell her. So she did some preliminary work on her story on makeup artists, including some online research on the history and techniques of theatrical makeup. Then she wrote a more detailed query for the article she had in mind and sent it to Jillian to see if *Entertain Me!* wanted it.

Sure, she kept the e-mail window open while she worked, just in case something came in, but she often did that. And maybe she did jump every time the computer twanged to let her know e-mail had arrived, but that was because the apartment was still quiet.

That done, she did some research on the gospel music business to try to decide if a profile of Kathleen Owen would be salable, or if maybe she should try for a bigger feature on the industry. Eventually she came up with three different slants and sent off query letters to markets she'd worked with before. That distracted her fairly well for the rest of the day.

Tilda made herself go out for a bite to eat at dinner time so she wouldn't be tempted to keep checking e-mail, and for once she was glad she hadn't been able to afford the BlackBerry she'd been lusting after. If she'd had one, and had been able to get e-mail no matter where she was, she'd probably have sprinkled crumbs on it during dinner.

Saturday night was a continuation of Friday night's doldrums. Tilda never saw Heather, though the disarray in the bathroom told her that her roommate had made a pit stop between dates while she was at dinner. Tilda pretended to work, but she could only fool herself so long. Finally she gave up the pretense and played Quake until it was time for one last e-mail check and bed.

When she woke up late Sunday morning, she decided she was being an idiot, despite her best efforts. For all she knew, Have _Mercy was partying all weekend or only checked his messages at work. So she did her laundry, cleaned the apartment a bit, caught up on her bills, and made the usual calls to her parents. Then she watched TV, which almost counted as work for her.

Late Sunday afternoon, as she was about to fall off the wagon and check e-mail, the phone rang and she grabbed it gratefully.

"Hey, stranger," her sister said.

"Hi, June. What's up?"

"Just thought I'd call to see how the trip to New York went."

"In other words, you talked to Mom. She told you I sounded as if something was bothering me, and asked you to check on me."

"Bingo!" June said cheerfully. "So what's the problem?"

"This damned story is making me crazy."

"Then let me put on my old psychologist hat and see if I remember how to diagnose crazy people."

"You weren't a clinician — you were a researcher."

"And you're a whole lot more interesting to run through a maze than any rat ever was. Spill it."

Tilda did, detailing what she'd learned about Mercy and her terrible suspicions, plus how she'd been waiting for some word from her one possible source as desperately as a sixteen-year-old girl hoping the cute boy she'd met at the mall would call to ask her out.

"You sent him the e-mail Friday night?"

"Right."

"So what have you done in the meantime to verify his story?"

"Haven't you been listening? He's all I've got. Otherwise I'm dead in the water."

"Okay, you're the reporter, not me, so maybe I don't understand the process. This online guy is the only one who seems to know anything about Mercy sleeping around?"

"Apparently."

"Then you've already asked the other people who knew her about her sex life."

"Well, not all of them. I asked Nick and Dom Tolomeo."

"Who spent, what, one day with her?"

"And I asked the director of that movie

she was in."

"Who knew her for a few weeks. Right?"

"Right," Tilda said faintly.

"What about the people who worked with her on the show?"

"None of them ever mentioned anything about her boyfriends."

"Did you ask them?"

"Not directly, but . . . Hell, no, I didn't ask them and I haven't gone back to ask them. I can't believe I didn't think of that. I'm an idiot!"

"No, you're not."

"It was the obvious next step, and I didn't even see it. I am one shitty reporter."

"Nope, not that either. But if I were a psychologist — which I am — I'd wonder what was keeping you from seeing the obvious."

Tilda wondered about that herself. "You know what? I don't think I even want this guy to respond to my e-mail. If he doesn't, I can tell everybody I tried and move on. Even better, I'd like him to send me something so ridiculous — like a theory that Mercy started seeing Elvis and now she and he live in Area 51 and only leave their cozy shag-carpeted bunker to race their matching Cadillacs across the desert. Either way, I'd be able to write him off."

"And why would you want to write off a source? Are you that sure he's lying?"

"Honestly, no, I have no particular reason to think he's making it up. Sure, nobody else has hinted at anything like that, but that doesn't mean anything. Did I ever tell you what I found out about that one guy who directed some episodes of *Werewolf Hunter*? He used to take his dates onto the set at night, and make out in the woods with them. Howling, no doubt."

"Are you trying to change the subject?"

"No, I actually have a point."

"Which is?"

"Which is that I interviewed a dozen or more people about that show and that director, and nobody mentioned this fact except one lowly production assistant. A couple of people managed to miss that bit of gossip, but most of the others knew. They just figured somebody else had spilled the beans. That could be the case here, or the network or Irv Munch asked people to keep it quiet that Mercy was so sexually active back then, given that she was so young and was playing somebody even younger."

"So, what do your journalistic instincts say about Have_Mercy's story? Is it possible?"

Tilda snorted. "I don't have any journalistic instincts, June. All I've got is a decent ability to tell when people are lying or covering their asses — like when you pretended you weren't trying to fix me up again, and when my roommate didn't want to talk about her three-night-stand's live-in girlfriend. Most people can do that, because most people lie, not just the stars. But I haven't got enough from this guy to guess whether or not he's lying."

"So why are you letting this one guy kill your story?" June gave her a couple of minutes, then said, "This is the place where you have an insight into yourself."

"I thought that's what the psychologist was for."

"How many psychologists does it take to change a light bulb? One, but it has to want to change."

"Are you calling me a low-watt bulb?"

"Stalling . . ."

"Okay, here's my insight. I don't want to hear from this guy, and I'm not chasing after the other sources who might confirm his story, because I don't want to find Mercy anymore."

"Why?"

"Because I don't want to find out that she's a killer. I'd rather keep my untainted memories of the woman intact. It's that simple. Not to mention pathetic!"

"There's nothing pathetic about it!" June snapped. "Is it pathetic that your niece still pretends to believe in Santa Claus, and that the rest of us go along every year? She knows the truth — she just wants to hold onto the magic. What's wrong with your holding onto the magic?"

"Then you think I should just write the article without finding out what's happened to Mercy?"

"I'm not saying — I'm asking. Why don't you do just that?"

"Because it's too late. My memories are already tainted," she said. "Besides, three people are dead. Maybe Mercy really is the killer or maybe she's the next target. Either way, I can't let my idol — hell, she's not just some teen idol and she's not Santa Claus. She's a person. I can't let another person keep killing, or let her be killed, just so I can keep my little *Kissing Cousins* fantasy going. She needs to be found." Tilda took a deep breath. "I'm not giving up until I find her."

"You go, girl!" June said. "Or is that out?"

"June, you can say any damned thing you want. And tell you what — when this is all over, I'm going to let you fix me up again."

"Really? You won't be sorry."

Tilda doubted that, but it was the least she could do to repay her sister for the much-needed kick in the ass. In the morning, she was going to get back in touch with every *Kissing Cousins* source she had, and she was going to do her level best to dig up every bit of dirt, scandal, and smut about Mercy, if that's what it took to find her.

CHAPTER 18

"Q: What's the secret to your success?
A: Never giving up! My mother taught me
that. If you keep trying, you'll always suc-
ceed."
> — *"Kissing Cousins'* Elbert Answers
> Twenty-five Personal Questions,"
> *Teen Fave*

Though Tilda didn't always wake up as
determined on a course of action as she'd
been on going to bed, this time she did. As
soon as she was done with what her father
had always called her morning ablutions,
she made a list of everybody she thought
worthwhile to contact. That included producer Irv Munch, the surviving cast members, and a few others she'd spoken to over
the years: a costume designer who'd worked
on the show, the man who'd directed more
episodes than any other, a secretary at
Mercy's talent agency, and the widow of

the man who'd played Pops. She stopped with that, at least for the time being. She'd already pumped Jasmine about Mercy's love life, and Matthew Boardman and the Tolomeos had made it plain that they'd known next to nothing personal about the actress.

Then she booted up her computer, pausing only briefly to see that Have_Mercy hadn't answered her note, and started digging up contact information. Though it would have been less embarrassing for her to send e-mails with the impertinent questions she was going to ask, it would also have been that much easier for people to lie or ignore her. She did cater to her embarrassment by deciding to call from home instead of going to the *Entertain Me!* office — she didn't think she could take any more of Nicole's veiled hints. Instead she was planning to see just how unlimited her unlimited cell phone calling plan was.

Since she had to allow for time differences, at nine o'clock she started with people on the East Coast. She hit it lucky with her first try. Pops's widow was at home when she called.

The costume director had moved to Chicago, so Tilda took a break for breakfast before calling him. Kat Owen was performing in Branson, she learned from her Web site, but Tilda managed to get her at eleven-thirty.

She gleaned a couple of names of more people to call from those three calls, and took care of them next.

After that, there was still a little time to kill before she could start calling the West Coast crowd, so she hit the Web harder than she'd ever hit it before, checking every Web site and user group for mentions of Mercy and a man, any man. She looked at every picture she could find online too, seeing if Mercy had ever been photographed with a date. After two hours of that, Tilda wondered if it was possible to make her eyes bleed.

After a quick break for lunch and a warm compress for her eyes, she got started on the California contingent. Irv Munch was still out of town, and while his assistant again expressed reluctant willingness to pass on a message, she still wouldn't cough up his cell phone number.

Tilda had better luck with the twins. She wasn't sure if it was Gabrielle or Gwendolyn who answered their phone, but since the one on the phone constantly consulted the one who wasn't, it really didn't matter.

The secretary from Mercy's old agency was out, but Tilda left a message asking her to call back.

Oddly enough, Noel Clark was the only one whom she reached who wouldn't take time to answer her questions. He was home, so obviously he wasn't working, but he insisted he couldn't talk and that she would have to call back the day after next. With Vincent's countdown haunting her, Tilda had to grit her teeth, but she made an appointment for the call.

A few minutes after she hung up from Noel, the agency secretary called back. This resulted in one brief follow-up call.

That was the last of the phone calls she could make while waiting for a return call from Irv Munch and the scheduled call with Noel Clark. So she went back to the Web, following every link she could find.

By four-thirty, she could honestly say she'd left no stone unturned. And, as she explained to Cooper, whom she'd called at work, she knew exactly where to look for Mercy.

"Where?" Cooper asked excitedly.

"It's going to take some legwork, but I'm going to start with a list of every convent in the United States."

"Convents?"

"Since it is now plain that Mercy never went on a date with a guy more than twice, and never so much as held hands in public, I think it's safe to assume that she was a fucking nun!"

Cooper made sympathetic noises.

"I did find three guys she went out with," Tilda added. "One was a star from another sitcom that wasn't doing so well, and he admitted it was a fix-up for publicity. They only went out twice. The other two were behind-the-scenes guys — a continuity guy and a cameraman — and though they both thought she was great, they just didn't hit it off. That's it!"

"I know what happened to her — she exploded from sexual frustration."

"It's as good an explanation as any."

"Then there's just one thing to do."

"What? Give up? Let it go? Get a life?"

"Nope. Drink heavily."

"Thanks, Cooper, but I'm so not in the mood."

He ignored her. "I'm going to grab a cab and pick you up — shouldn't be more than half an hour, forty-five minutes, so get dressed. We're going to the Border Cafe and see how many margaritas we can drink."

"Cooper . . ."

"You're right. It's rush hour and it will be just as quick on the T — we'll call a cab when I get to your place. I don't want you driving when you're drinking. And you are going to be drinking!"

"Cooper!"

"Hasta la vista, chica!" He hung up.

Short of locking the door, there wasn't much she could do but start getting ready. In fact, even that wouldn't have worked. She'd given Cooper a spare key for emergencies, and she had no doubt that he'd use it. So she covered the bags under her eyes with some of the makeup she'd brought back from New York and put on something tight and low-cut. She just might meet somebody promising at the Border Cafe, and she didn't want to risk exploding from sexual frustration.

CHAPTER 19

"It was a great cast to dress because every character was different: hip stuff for Brad, vintage rock T-shirts for Damon, miniskirts for Sherri, Victoriana for Mercy, and corduroy jumpers for Felicia. But I did get tired of Elbert's lab coats."
— Robert Peppler, costume designer, quoted in "Curse of the *Kissing Cousins*," *Entertain Me!*

Though Tilda found nobody promising of the male gender at the Border Cafe, she did find several excellent margaritas. In fact she found at least one more than she should have, but she had to admit that she was exceedingly relaxed by the time the taxi deposited her at her apartment. At least she remembered to drink a lot of water and take a vitamin in hopes of avoiding a hangover the next day.

When she finally woke up the next morning, long past her usual time, she was happy to realize that she'd been mostly successful, and a long shower and a couple of Advil took care of the small hangover she did have. Then she went to face her computer. As frustrating and as useless as all her efforts had been the day before, she fully intended to continue, calling even more distant connections to Mercy and Googling variant spellings of her name, but the phone rang before she could get started.

"Tilda Harper."

"At least you're answering your phone," Nicole said with a sniff. "I just checked the RSVP list and saw that you haven't bothered to respond. Are you coming or not?"

"Coming to what?"

"Hello? To the cocktail party honoring the attendees of the Boston Film Festival? The one we host every year? Is this ringing a bell?"

"Ding, ding, ding. But I didn't get an invitation."

"Are you sure? We sent one. Hold on." There was the sound of keys being pounded. "You live on Clifton Street in Malden, right?"

"No, I'm on Summer Street. Clifton Street was two apartments ago."

"Did you ever consider sending in a

263

change of address form?"

"I did —" Tilda stopped. It wasn't worth the time. Besides, she knew the magazine had her current address — it was where they sent her checks. "Okay, my address is —"

"There's no time to mail an invitation now! The party is tonight! Are you coming?"

Tilda thought about it quickly. "Sure, I'll be there. Where and when?" She jotted down the information Nicole grudgingly read out.

"Remember, you'll be representing the magazine, so dress accordingly."

"I'll wear my least patched jeans," Tilda promised.

Nicole ignored her. "And about your plus-one —"

"My what?"

Nicole sighed heavily, and Tilda could almost hear the eyes rolling in her head. "The invitation is for you plus one."

"Fine. What about him?"

"Bring somebody presentable. Remember, you're —"

"I know, I'm representing the magazine. I'll see you there."

"I can hardly wait," Nicole said, and hung up.

Tilda's first reaction was satisfaction.

First, that Jillian had decided it was worth the catering fee to invite her, and second, that Nicole's attempt to keep her away had failed. She was sure the other woman had mailed her invitation to the old address out of spite, but Jillian must have seen that she hadn't responded and made Nicole call her.

Then she looked at the clock. It was ten o'clock in the morning. The party was at five o'clock. That left her seven hours to find an appropriate outfit and a plus-one.

Clothes first. She picked up the phone and dialed Cooper's extension at *Entertain Me!*

"Cooper? Tilda. Are you still copyediting that fashion magazine on the side?"

"Why?" he said.

"I've got a fashion emergency."

"A fashion emergency? And you assume that I, as a gay man, am knowledgeable about women's fashion?"

"No, I'm assuming that you, as a gifted copy editor, retain enough information from your editing to have some pointers about current clothing trends."

"And?"

"And that since you always look fabulous, obviously you have an innate fashion sense."

"And?"

"And . . . Cooper, I don't have time for more sucking up. Can I owe you one?"

"Make it two."

"Fine. Two major bouts of sucking up. Now tell me what to wear to the *Entertain Me!* party tonight."

"I didn't know you were invited."

"I didn't either, which is why I've got to come up with a decent outfit right away."

"How much can you spend?"

"Nothing. No, wait, I've got fifty bucks from my mother that I've been saving for an emergency."

"That might get you a decent scarf at Filene's Basement," he griped.

"I think I need more than a scarf to wear."

"That would depend on the party, but in this case, you're probably right. This is going to take some thought. The one thing you don't want to wear is a little black dress."

"I thought a little black dress was good for every occasion. I thought that was the whole point of having a little black dress. We women spend all this time and money finding the perfect little black dress, and now I can't wear it?"

"You don't even have a little black dress, do you?"

"Nope."

"Then stop bitching. Even if you had one, you wouldn't be wearing it tonight because two thirds of the women there will be wearing their little black dresses because they are appropriate for every occasion."

"Of course."

"For you, I've got one word. Vintage."

"Vintage?"

"Vintage. Meet me at Harvard Square Station in forty-five minutes — we're going to Oona's."

"Thanks, Cooper."

As she got ready to go, a little voice in her head said that she was using party preparation as another excuse to stall her hunt for Mercy, but a different internal voice pointed out that this was work-related. When the first voice argued, the second started repeating, "La, la, la — I can't hear you!" Tilda went with the second voice.

Oona's Experienced Clothing in Cambridge was a Mecca to bargain hunters and broke college students alike, and while Tilda had been there many times before, she'd never gone with a master of the shopping arts like Cooper. He flipped through skirts and blouses on racks at lightning speed and dug into boxes of scarves, belts, and purses with wild abandon. In forty minutes, including time for trying clothes on, he had what he assured her was the perfect outfit for the occasion: a steel-blue dress of floaty chiffon with a layered hemline, an old-fashioned sea-foam green and aqua-blue scarf to drape from shoulder to hip, and a beaded clutch that somehow still had ninety-nine percent of the beads attached.

With all that, Tilda still had enough of her fifty dollars to pay for their lunch at Bartley's Burger Cottage afterward. Picking up the check and complimenting Cooper's new haircut and his really bitching shoes paid off her sucking-up debt too. She even sprang for his new copy of *Astonishing X-Men* at the Million Year Picnic, the comic book store where Cooper nursed his secret addiction to buff mutants in spandex.

After issuing firm instructions about shoes, Cooper headed back to work while Tilda went back to her apartment to consider the next problem: a date for the evening.

In thinking over her available male friends, she could come up with two she was reasonably sure would make a good impression that she could call at the last minute. The problem was that one of them would see the invitation as an opening gambit to reestablishing a relationship, and the other would see it as a way to get laid. She really didn't want the relationship with the guy — it had taken her a month to let him down easily the first time, and if she had to do it again, she was afraid she'd need a restraining order. As for the second, he just wasn't that good in bed.

Then there was Nick Tolomeo, the security consultant with a father who approved of her. In his line of work, he'd certainly know how to act around industry types, and he was more than presentable. She wouldn't mind it if he saw the call as the start of a relationship, and the idea of him in bed had appeal too. It being on such short notice was problematical, but it couldn't hurt to ask.

The receptionist, presumably the one who'd been missing the other day, answered and quickly connected her with Nick.

"Tilda!" he said, sounding pleased to hear from her. "How are you doing? Did you come up with some more questions about Mercy?"

"Actually, I was wondering if you're free tonight."

"Professionally or personally?"

"Definitely personally." She explained about the cocktail party, including an apology for the invitation coming so late.

"Let me check on something." He must have meant to put his hand over the receiver, but didn't quite cover it all the way, because Tilda could hear every word that was said. "Pop, can you cover for me on the airport job tonight?"

"What for? You got a hot date?"

"I hope so. You remember Tilda Harper?"

"The magazine writer? The one with the nice ass?"

"Pop!"

"What? I'm old, but I know a nice ass when I see one. When I met your mother, that was the first thing I noticed about her."

"Pop! I don't want to hear that. I just want to know if you can cover for me."

"Damned straight I will. Don't let that one get away!"

Tilda was snickering when Nick came back on the line.

"Just how much of that did you hear?" he asked in resignation.

"All of it."

"Do you still want me to come with you to the party?"

"Absolutely." They arranged a place to meet, and just before she hung up, Tilda added, "By the way, thank your father for me, and tell him he's got a great ass too."

CHAPTER 20

"Rule number one for cocktail parties: eat before you go. You're there to see and be seen, not to eat. The food is usually terrible, and you don't want to drink on an empty stomach. In vino veritas doesn't go over well in the industry."
— Sophia Vaughn, quoted in "Teen Idol Worshippers," *Entertain Me!*

Other than brief breaks to check e-mail, Tilda spent the rest of the afternoon following the advice given to her by the trio of makeup artists, not willing to take the risk of modifying their game plan. By five before five, she was standing next to the John Adams statue in front of Faneuil Hall, awaiting her plus-one.

She'd hoped that Nick would know how to dress, perhaps in the male equivalent of the little black dress, and was more than satisfied when he showed up in a suit that even she could tell was Armani. If that weren't enough, his shirt was crisply starched, his tie stylish without being flamboyant, and his shoes were freshly polished. All those years of squiring fashionable celebrities must have taught him a few tricks.

"You look amazing," he said when he saw her.

"Thank you. You look ready for the red carpet yourself."

"Is there going to be a red carpet?"

"Come see for yourself."

The annual Boston Film Festival, though not nearly so glitzy as Cannes or Sundance, did bring an intriguing batch of films to town once a year, which of course meant an eager batch of actors and filmmakers looking for publicity. Though Tilda found some of the festival's offerings needlessly artsy, she usually tried to catch some of the screenings and a celebrity or three for interviews.

In addition to the screenings, there was always a flurry of prescreening cocktail parties during the festival, usually held at chi-chi restaurants or ritzy hotels. Jillian had decided on something with more attitude. *Entertain Me!* was hosting its party at Durgin-Park, the Boston landmark restaurant with the slogan, "Established before you were born." Situated in the middle of tourist-laden Quincy Market, the place was famous for prime rib, Indian pudding, and rude waitresses.

They really had laid out a red carpet on the cobblestones outside the entrance of the restaurant, but then had to station a man to keep the tourists from trampling over it or, even worse, posing for photos. Tilda and Nick walked onto it as if they belonged there, and Tilda had to admit it was neat in a snotty kind of way.

Shannon was standing just inside the door, clipboard in hand, wearing a little black dress.

"Hi, Shannon," Tilda said.

"Tilda! I didn't know you were coming." She checked the list, not finding Tilda's name until she got to the end. "Tilda Harper plus one." She checked them off. "Aren't you going to introduce me to your friend?"

"Shannon, Nick. Nick, Shannon is one of the staff editors." They shook hands, and Shannon waved them in. Tilda took a quick peek behind them and caught Shannon checking out the view of Nick from behind. She couldn't blame her — Nick's ass was even better than his father's.

It was still early, so none of the real celebrities had arrived yet. Though Tilda had never been invited to an *Entertain Me!* party before, she'd been to enough other parties associated with the film festival to know how they worked. Despite the fact that the party would last for only two hours, thereby allowing time to get to an eight o'clock screening, the various stars and directors weren't likely to show for another half an hour. Tilda preferred getting there on time, when the hors d'oeuvres were hot and the line at the bar was short, and then placing herself strategically to watch people as they came in.

Of course, usually she was working, and this time she was there with a plus-one, so she felt obligated to socialize. The fact that she and Nick both looked fabulous had nothing to do with her making a beeline for where Jillian and Bryce were muttering at one another. She thought she heard the familiar refrain of "No, fuck you!" before they saw her.

"Tilda, terrific outfit. Glad you could make it," Bryce said.

"I wouldn't have missed it. Nick, this is Jillian Carroll and Bryce Delaney, editor in chief and managing editor respectively. Jillian, Bryce, this is Nick Tolomeo. He's a personal security consultant."

Hands were shaken, the air in the vicinity of cheeks was smooched, and small talk was exchanged. A few minutes later when Cooper and his husband, Jean-Paul, joined them, the ritual began anew.

Cooper checked out Nick thoroughly, and when he got a chance, flashed Tilda a thumbs-up and said, "Tilda, we're still on for lunch tomorrow, right?"

They had made no such plans — Cooper just wanted to debrief after the party and ask nosy questions about Nick. But since the reason she looked halfway decent was Cooper's expertise, Tilda was willing to go along. "Absolutely," she said.

After a few more moments of meaningless chat, Jillian said, "Look, we can visit at work. I'm going to talk to some of the real guests. The rest of you — go mingle!"

Tilda was worried Nick would be offended, but he just chuckled, and the group dispersed to do as they'd been told.

When she and Nick ended up close to the door, Tilda was both surprised and delighted at one of the familiar faces she saw arriving — Irv Munch had just come in with a woman wearing a very stylish little black dress. No wonder he hadn't been available to take her call — he'd been in Boston! His lady friend looked young enough to be his daughter.

Nobody else seemed to notice them, so she said, "Nick, let me introduce you to somebody else. I think you'll get a kick out of this."

She led him to where Irv was surveying the room, and said, "Mr. Munch? Tilda Harper. It's good to see you again."

It took him a second, which wasn't bad considering how many people he must have rubbed shoulders with over the years he'd been in the industry. "Tilda, sweetheart. You're looking incredible."

"Thank you. Are you doing something with the festival?"

"Not me. My baby here has a film showing later this week. Rachel, Tilda Harper. She works with *Entertain Me!*"

If Rachel minded being referred to as Irv's baby, she showed no sign of it as she took Tilda's hand and said, "Glad to meet you."

Tilda went on, "This is my friend Nick Tolomeo. Nick, this is Irv Munch, the man who created *Kissing Cousins,* among other shows."

"A pleasure to meet you, sir," Nick said with obvious sincerity. "I've been a fan of your work for many years."

"That's always good to hear," Irv said,

beaming, "but this week is Rachel's time to shine. Mark my words — in five years' time, Rachel Munch is going to be a bigger name than Irv Munch ever was!"

Tilda mentally bitch-slapped herself for assuming the worst of the older man. No wonder Rachel looked young enough to be his daughter — she was his daughter. Now that she knew, the family resemblance was obvious, though, fortunately for Rachel, it extended only to their shared eye color, brow shape, and strong chins. The bulbous nose, prominent ears, and thinning hair were Irv's alone.

They talked a few minutes about Rachel's film, a roman à clef about a young Jewish girl growing up in Hollywood that could easily have been tedious but which sounded as if it had been done with a mix of humor and charm. When Rachel mentioned that the party was the first festival event she'd attended, Tilda extracted her from Irv and introduced her to some of the other film-makers so she could get started on the all-important job of schmoozing and making contacts. Meanwhile Nick kept Irv occupied and thoroughly buttered up while she was gone.

"Nothing's in writing," Irv was saying when she got back, "but it's looking good, it's looking real good."

"Tilda, Mr. Munch —" Nick started to say.

"Irv!" Munch corrected him.

"Irv, then. Irv was just telling me that he's been in talks about a revival of *Kissing Cousins.*"

"Is that right?" Tilda said, trying to sound as pleased as she'd actually been when she first heard the rumor, years back.

"As God is my witness. It's a terrible thing, what's happened to my kids these past few months, but the publicity . . . You know what this business is like — any publicity is good publicity. Sometimes the worse the news is, the more attention it gets. When Jim Bonnier died, I got a couple of calls and sympathy cards. With Alex Johnson, I got a few lunches. Tilda's article came out, and people wanted me to take a meeting. Now, with poor Holly, my phone is ringing off the hook. I hate like hell to have it happen this way, but I can't turn down the work when it comes." He did look sincerely contrite, for a vulture anyway. "Your business is the same way, am I right?"

"If it bleeds, it leads," Tilda admitted. She could hardly throw stones at Irv — if Bonnier and Johnson hadn't died, nobody would have bought her article about *Kissing*

Cousins, and Holly's death had led to her current assignment. If Irv was a vulture, she and he were birds of a feather. "Are you aiming for a one-shot or a new series?"

Irv waved his hands around airily. "Everything is still on the table at this point. There's even talk of making a feature, with the kids all grown up. Wouldn't that be a gas!"

They played cast-the-movie for a few minutes: would Matt Damon or Heath Ledger be better as Brad, Johnny Depp or Paul Bettany as Damon, maybe Lindsey Lohan as Sherri.

"What about Mercy?" Tilda asked. "Do you suppose you could get Mercy Ashford herself to reprise the role?"

"Do you know where she is?" he asked eagerly.

"Don't you?" she countered.

"I wish I did. I've had a couple of projects over the years that she'd have been perfect for, but I never could track her down. I did a pilot the season after *Kissing Cousins* went off the air, and I wanted to cast her, but she'd disappeared. I know she signed for a feature —"

"*The Raven's Prey,*" Tilda put in.

"That's the one. Only she left the production, and nobody's seen her since. It's a cry-

279

ing shame."

"She hasn't been in touch at all? She didn't come to any of the funerals?"

"She didn't even send flowers. It surprised me too. Mercy always had real class." Irv shrugged. "Maybe she didn't hear about the deaths — nobody knew how to call her."

"That's odd," Tilda said, trying not to sound as disappointed as she felt. She hadn't really expected anything more, but she had hoped.

"You're telling me. Even her agent couldn't get in touch with her. When an actress doesn't let her agent know where she is, you know something is off-kilter."

"She didn't have any family you could get in touch with?" Nick asked.

Irv shook his head. "Poor thing didn't have any family."

Tilda hated to do it in front of Nick, but she had to try one more time to confirm Have_Mercy's claims. "What about boyfriends? I've heard stories that she, you know, partied a bit."

"Who said that?" Irv demanded.

"It was somebody on the Web," she said vaguely.

"It's a damned lie! Sure she dated, but Mercy was a good girl."

Tilda was surprised by his vehemence,

which seemed to go beyond the usual damage control instincts of a producer. Besides, what damage could it cause now? As Munch had said himself, any publicity was good publicity. Was he honestly upset by the idea, or protesting too much?

She quickly changed the subject back to *Kissing Cousins* revival possibilities, and after a few more minutes, Irv went to join his daughter.

"You're really determined to find Mercy, aren't you?" Nick said.

"I'm sorry — I didn't invite you to watch me work."

"It's okay. It's been interesting to observe your technique."

She snorted. "Not much technique going on, other than to nearly get Irv Munch mad at me. Nobody seems to have a clue where Mercy is or why she left acting or what she's been doing all these years. I've been trying everything I can think of, and I've had no luck whatsoever. Maybe you were right. Maybe some people don't want to be found. But I can't even find out why she doesn't want to be found!"

"Do you have to locate her to write the article?"

"No. In fact, since Jillian wants me to keep playing up the curse business, it's almost an advantage to have her disappearance to talk about, since Holly's death will be old news by the time the article comes out." She winced at her own words. "I am a vulture, aren't I?"

"No more than I am when I get extra security jobs every time a celebrity stalker makes it into David Letterman's house."

"You're sweet to say that."

"Damn! I was going for bitterly cynical — I hear the chicks go wild for bitter cynicism."

She had to grin. "Anyway, no, I don't need to find Mercy for the article."

"But . . . ?"

"But I really want to." She didn't know him well enough to tell him all of what she'd been thinking, so she said, "I want to know what happened to her, I want to know where she's been all this time, I want to know her." She paused. "Great, I've mutated from a vulture to a celebrity stalker. Is that an attractive picture or what?"

"Absolutely," Nick said. "The idea drives me wild."

"You are too damn perfect for words," Tilda said flatly. "Hey, if I do find her and write an article about my experiences as a celebrity stalker, maybe that will help your business too."

"You're being even more bitterly cynical than I was. I think we should drink to that."

On the way to the bar they ran into a cluster of *Entertain Me!* editors carefully evaluating the success of the party. Since Nicole was part of that cluster, Tilda took the opportunity to introduce Nick, and was in turn introduced to Nicole's plus-one. She was pleased, in a very shallow way, to see that Nick was much cuter than Nicole's date, and better dressed too. To make it even more shallow, she was inordinately pleased to see that Nicole noticed it too.

Tilda said, "Jillian, I was thinking about interviewing Rachel Munch about her new movie, maybe with something about being second generation Hollywood. Do you think you'd be interested?" She was asking casually, because she knew a couple of other magazines who'd be happy to take it, though they didn't pay as well as *Entertain Me!*

"An actual working director," Nicole said, laughing far too loudly as she turned to her date. "Tilda specializes in old shows, the older the better! *The Brady Bunch, Gilligan's Island, Kissing Cousins* — all the has-beens!" She laughed even more loudly.

It was nothing Nicole hadn't said before, and if Irv Munch hadn't been in earshot, Tilda would have ignored her the way she usually did. But even though his back was to them, she saw him stiffen. So this time she snapped, "Don't call them has-beens!"

"Excuse me?" Nicole said with feigned politeness.

"Those people are just as talented as they ever were. Maybe they can't get as much work anymore, because they're out of style or because people think they're too old, but the fact is that at one time in their lives those people were famous, and whether or not they ever do anything else to make themselves famous again, they still achieved a level that some of the people in this room would sell their souls for." She gave Nicole a pointed look. "Their work entertained people, comforted them, and gave them happy memories. Maybe *The Brady Bunch* and *Kissing Cousins* weren't high art, but people remember those ridiculous characters and those hokey plots. I bet there's not a filmmaker in this room who doesn't know the work of those so-called has-beens, and they've learned from it and been inspired by it."

Nicole, for once, was speechless, but Jillian jumped in with, "That's good. Tighten it a bit, and you've got your lead."

"My lead?"

"Give me a piece on how the TV shows of

yesterday have inspired the young filmmakers of today, using Rachel Munch and her father as the focus."

"I wasn't pitching —" Tilda started to say, but Jillian had moved away.

Nicole, still not speaking, looked daggers at her, then stalked off, her plus-one following in her wake.

"If I were here professionally tonight," Nick whispered in Tilda's ear, "I'd be keeping a close eye on that one. She really doesn't like you."

"I don't like her either," Tilda said savagely.

Rachel Munch came up to them. "Thank you for what you said. Any time you want or need anything from me or my father, just call. Anything at all." She pressed a business card into Tilda's hand. "And if you'd like to see my film next week, there will be two tickets waiting for you at the box office." She smiled and went to rejoin her father.

Tilda looked around the room and realized that she was the focus of considerably more attention than she was used to, and she was momentarily taken aback.

"Did I just make a fool of myself?" she asked Nick.

"Speaking as a professional who has seen

quite a few celebrities making fools of themselves, I can assure you that you did not. Do you want to sit down?" Nick said.

"Only if there's a drink next to the chair."

As they headed for the bar with the shortest line, Tilda heard snatches of conversation starting with, "Did you know that the seven castaways were designed to represent the seven deadly sins?" and "I read that Carol Brady was the first divorcee in a television series — it was never stated explicitly, but —"

Maybe the article she'd inadvertently pitched had a valid point to make.

The party started winding down soon after that, with most of the attendees leaving to get to that night's screening. Tilda was thinking it was time for Nick and her to go, too, when she was shocked to see Lawrence White coming their way, making for an awkward situation. What was the proper way to introduce a man whose amorous overtures she'd rejected to a man whose amorous overtures she was cultivating? She wasn't sure there was a chapter on the topic in any of Miss Manners's books, though perhaps there was something on the "Miss Gothic Ann Landers" Web site.

In the meantime, she settled for, "Lawrence, this is a surprise." Once they'd completed the air-kissing ritual he seemed to expect, she added, "Did the plane from New York to LA stop to fuel up here?"

He laughed. "I decided to come for the film festival. I've got a hunch that a couple of these new directors are going to hit it big, and I wanted a shot at them now. I was also hoping I'd get to see you while I'm in town." He looked at Nick questioningly.

"Nick Tolomeo," Nick said.

"Lawrence White," the other man answered, and they went into a round of competitive hand-squeezing. As far as Tilda could tell, Nick won.

"Lawrence is a colleague of mine," Tilda explained. "I met him at Holly Kendricks's funeral."

"Terrible thing," Lawrence said. "Have the police made any headway in the case?"

"I don't think so." With Vincent on the job, she knew she would have been told promptly about any developments.

"What about your investigation then? Have you found Mercy yet?"

"I sound kind of like Diogenes, when you put it like that," Tilda said. "He was looking for an honest man — I'm looking for Mercy."

Both men laughed, but she thought Nick was honestly amused while Lawrence was only being polite, which convinced her that she'd done the right thing in turning him down. That might have prompted her to sound more positive than she was when she answered, "Actually, I've got some very promising leads. A couple of things have turned up, and . . . Well, I don't want to say too much to the competition. Just watch for my article in *Entertain Me!*"

"I'll be looking forward to it. Be sure to let me know if there's anything I can do to help."

"Thanks, I appreciate that."

They chatted a few minutes about the night's screening, which Lawrence was attending, and then he had to leave to get there in time. As soon as he was gone, Nick said, "Promising leads? Whatever happened to 'I've had no luck whatsoever'?"

"Maybe I had a sudden epiphany."

"Liar, liar, pants on fire."

"But Nick," Tilda cooed, "I'm not wearing any pants." She smiled when he swallowed heavily, then gave him a break by changing the subject. "It looks as if things are winding down."

"So it does. Since you supplied the cocktails, can I buy dinner?"

"That would be great. Just let me stop at the restroom." She had the traditional reason for going to the bathroom, plus the nearly-as-traditional reason of checking out her hair and makeup. But perhaps the most important reason was so she could call home to warn Heather that she was hoping to have an overnight visitor.

After an extremely pleasant dinner, she made the appropriate suggestion to Nick, and he accepted with enthusiasm.

CHAPTER 21

"Rumor had it that my competitor Gloria Stavers at *16* would bed anything in pants. I was never like that. I always made them take their pants off first."
— Sophia Vaughn, quoted in "Teen Idol Worshippers," *Entertain Me!*

"And then what?" Cooper prompted Tilda as she told him about her evening with Nick the next day over lunch. They'd met at Charley's, just down the street from the *Entertain Me!* office.

"We went back to my apartment."

"And? And?"

"What do you think? I pulled out my copy of *Sense and Sensibility* and he read aloud to me. It was most diverting."

"Don't be a tease!"

"Nick likes being teased."

"Aha! Then you did do it."

"Cooper, not only is that an unclear

antecedent, but let me point out that most people outgrow that particular euphemism in high school. What Nick and I did was have initially awkward, moderately noisy, but eminently satisfying sex."

"What was the awkward part? Did he have requests you weren't interested in?"

"No, nothing like that. It's always awkward the first time — negotiating positions, foreplay, birth control."

"How romantic. Did you get it all in writing first?"

She made a face at him. "I'm just saying it wasn't the best bout of lovemaking I've ever had." Then she grinned like the Cheshire Cat would have if he'd caught the Dormouse alone in an alley. "But it was in the top ten."

"More, give me more."

"That's what he said."

"You slut!" Cooper crowed, pounding his fists on the table. "Does he have any tattoos? Scars?"

"No tattoos, one scar on his leg."

"From defending somebody from a stalker?"

"From defending himself from his grandmother's poodle Pixie."

"I thought maybe he'd have some bodyguard scars. A gunshot crease or something."

"So sorry to disappoint you."

"But he's in shape, right? He looked like he was in shape. A bodyguard has to be in shape."

"He works out, most definitely. His endurance was right on up there."

"Did he carry you into the bedroom like Kevin Costner carried Whitney Houston in *The Bodyguard*?"

"No, Cooper. I carried him like Sam carried Frodo in *The Return of the King*."

"Bitch," he said amiably. "I'm just saying that if I had a hunky Italian bodyguard, I'd take advantage of the situation." He took a bite of his cheeseburger. "Did he bring his handcuffs?"

"No, we used mine," Tilda replied, then pounded her friend on the back when he choked on the burger.

Once he was breathing again, Tilda asked, "How about the rest of your evening? You two went to the screening, right?"

"It was okay — a little slow for my tastes, but Jean-Paul loved it. Then we went home like a boring married couple. Our being so damned monogamous is why I have to live vicariously through tramps like you."

"I'm happy to help."

"By the way, what happened with Nicole

292

last night? She's been even bitchier than usual today. She made Shannon cry twice!"

Tilda told him about her impromptu defense of so-called has-beens, ending with, "I may have had too much to drink."

"Damn, I wish I'd heard it. I thought it might have been something you said, because I heard your name muttered more than once, but I was thinking it might be because her date was too friendly with you."

"I don't think I even spoke to him, other than when she introduced us."

"I thought I saw you and your Italian stallion talking to him. Older guy, nice suit, better shoes."

"Oh, Lawrence. He wasn't Nicole's date. He's that freelance reporter I had dinner with last week in New York. And before you ask, we did not do 'it' or 'that' or 'whatever.' Now that you mention it, he said he knew Nicole."

"That must be it. I saw the two of them talking in the corner right before Jean-Paul and I left. She never introduced me to her date, but she never talks to me at parties if there's somebody else around she thinks will do her more good."

"You must adore coming to work with her every day."

"Today has had its moments," he said with

293

a grin. "Bryce was ripping Jillian a new one because the party went over budget, and Jillian aimed him at Nicole because she was in charge of the guest list and must have gone over quota. Bryce ripped her a new one too!"

"And I missed it!" Tilda said. "Was it good?"

"Spectacular! Like Charlton Heston throwing the Ten Commandments at the Israelites. I think Bryce was hungover — that's when he gets really inspired."

"Next time, call me on your cell so I can listen in."

Cooper had to go back to work soon after that, and Tilda headed for Malden. She tried to work up some enthusiasm for her plan for the afternoon, which was to continue the tedious hunt for clues to Mercy's love life that she'd started two days before. The preparations for the cocktail party had given her a full day's reprieve, and since Nick and she had slept late, they'd barely gotten out of her place in time for him to make an appointment and for her to meet Cooper for lunch. That meant her computer lay in wait.

She did manage to stall for a little while when she got back to her apartment, but checking the mail, changing into sweats, and getting a glass of Dr Pepper could be stretched only so far. Eventually she had to bite the bullet and boot up her system. Deciding another couple of minutes wouldn't hurt, she checked e-mail before going onto the Web.

There was a message waiting from Have _Mercy. It was short, but not at all sweet:

Well? Had any luck tracking down Mercy the slut? You must have found SOME of her lovers by now. It shouldn't be hard.

Tilda drummed her fingers on her desk, considering how she should respond. The bastard still wasn't giving her anything to go on.

If you know something definite, just tell me. I have checked a number of sources, and there's no sign that Ms. Ashford slept around. Unless you can give me something solid to go on, I'm going to close down this line of investigation.

Tilda read it over, decided it sounded just irritated enough, and sent it. Then she assumed an air of martyrdom and went back to the Web for more Googling and bloodshot eyes. Considering how long she'd waited for the first reply, she wasn't expecting to hear from Have_Mercy any time soon, but a few minutes later, another message arrived.

How naive can you get? I was there — I saw what she was like. She was a whore. You're swallowing this "holier than thou" shit the studio pumps out, like every other fangirl in the world, and you still have the balls to call yourself a journalist? What is wrong with you? You want names? Get out there and hump for them! It worked for Mercy!

"That's it!" Tilda snarled. She'd been polite long enough. If he wanted flames, he'd get them.

If you really know anything, prove it. Give me something to go on. Tell me your name. Tell me how you know Mercy. But if you're just a n00b, go away and quit bothering the grownups.

She'd have slammed the send button if it had been physically possible, but settled for sending the message and stewing over it. Who was this asshole? She'd spent hours trying to prove there was something in his not-so-veiled hints, and the only one who seemed to know anything about Mercy's promiscuity was him. The hell with

Googling every variant spelling of Mercy Ashford. She was going after Have_Mercy!

Since he was being so damned coy, her only connection was the *Kissing Cousins* Listserv, which meant she needed to talk to Vincent again.

As soon as he answered the phone, she said, "No, I haven't found her."

"I wasn't going to ask," he said, sounding injured.

"Sorry. Have you got a minute?"

"Of course. What's up?"

"There is something very odd about this Have_Mercy guy."

"You mean beside the fact that he lies through his teeth?"

"Lying is one thing — the guy sounds seriously deranged. What information do you have on him?"

"I already gave you his e-mail address. That's all we keep on file."

"You don't have his real name?"

"Some people enter theirs, but it's optional, and he didn't list his."

"Can you track down his previous posts in the archives? Maybe he let something slip."

"I'll see." She heard the tapping of keys. "Okay, here's his user record." He paused. "That's interesting. No data."

"Lack of data is interesting? You must find *The Jerry Springer Show* fascinating."

"Seriously. Up until now, he's just been lurking. The post during the memorial service was his first time posting, and that snide comment to you was his second and last. Of course, every list has more lurkers than posters — we've got some members who've never posted anything at all. But two years is a long time to lurk."

"Is that how long he's been on the list? Trolls don't lurk. How can you post outrageous comments and flame people when you're lurking? Why would this guy hang around all this time?"

"Do you think he's the killer?" Vincent said, sounding panicked.

"Two years is a long time to wait to start killing people," she pointed out. "Mercy has been impossible to find, but the other cast members haven't been. I suppose it could be another reporter, but that's just as unlikely. Deadlines don't wait that long."

"You've been on the list that long."

"I was a fan of the show long before I became a reporter. I don't know what this guy is." She thought for a minute. "I'm probably not asking this correctly, but isn't it possible to track down people from their IP addresses or something like that?"

"Sure, it's possible, but I don't know how."

"I thought you were a computer whiz."

"Tilda," he said, exasperated, "that's like saying you know how to write screenplays or kids' books because you write magazine articles. I do Web design — I don't do computer forensics."

"Well, shit!"

"Javier could probably do it — that's more his line."

"Shit," she said again, but less emphatically. Javier was sleazy, but he did have his uses. After all, he'd set up her computer security system, which he claimed was a virtual Fort Knox to protect her golden prose. Since he'd been hoping to get into her pants when he installed it, he'd probably been telling the truth. She'd only gotten him out of her bedroom by threatening him creatively. Though she herself didn't find toenail clippers all that frightening, obviously they stirred something primal in Javier. "Okay, I guess I'll have to call him. Thanks, Vincent."

"Any time. And Tilda?"

"I know. I'll tell you right away if I find her." She disconnected long enough to look up Javier's number and dialed it. "Javier? Tilda Harper."

"Did you get the *Kissing Cousins* script?"

She'd forgotten about his latest fixation, and briefly considered stringing him along, but decided it wasn't a good idea to completely alienate him. "No, this is something else. I've received some e-mails, and I want to find out where they came from. Vincent says you can trace them."

"What's in it for me?"

"It's because of Mercy. This is the guy from the memorial service who claimed she slept around, but he won't give me any details. I need to see if he really knows anything or if he's just jerking me around."

"What's in it for me?" he repeated.

"Jesus, Javier, Vincent has spent hours tracking down leads, and he hasn't asked for anything."

"And your point is?"

She hadn't thought it would work, so she already had an appropriate bribe in mind. "Did you hear that HBO is hosting a media event in Boston next month to hype their new season? I hear they're going to be screening part of the new *True Blood* series." She knew Javier was a sucker for vampires.

"So? That show is based on Charlaine Harris's books, which I've already read, including the galley for the next one in the series," Javier said. "There won't be any spoilers."

"Yeah? I hear Alan Ball has changed a few characters. Beefed up one or two, even changed the race of one."

"Which characters?"

"I'm not telling. If you want to know, you'll have to come to the reception."

"With you?"

Her stomach churned, but she said, "I have an invitation for two."

"I don't suppose I could sneak in a camcorder."

"Not on your life."

"I don't know. . . . If all you media types are going to be there, there won't be any spoilers left."

"Maybe you're right. Did I mention that the woman who's playing the female vampire —"

"Pam? The assistant manager at the vampire bar?"

"Yeah, that's the one. She's going to be at the reception."

"It's a deal!"

"You will have to scrape up a suit."

"I have a suit," he insisted. "And you better dress hot. I want to impress Pam."

"Javier, you remember what I told you the last time you tried to cop a feel?"

She swore she heard him swallow. "The

toenail clippers?"

"That's right."

"Message received. Will you at least dress semihot?"

"Javier, I'll dress so hot you'll be sweating all night long, but I'll have those toenail clippers in my purse."

"Jesus, you are such a ballbuster!"

"It's part of my charm. Now, about this guy . . ."

"What's his e-mail address?"

"Have_Mercy@hotmail.com."

"Shit!"

"What?"

"Don't you know what hotmail is?"

"Sure, it's a free e-mail service."

"Right. Which means he didn't have to give his real name or address or credit card number when he created the account."

"Does that mean you can't find out anything about him?"

"Did I say that? It just makes it harder. You say he sent you e-mail?"

"That's right."

"Good. I want you to send the e-mail to me, but you have to do a couple of things first."

Though Javier's words were mostly gibberish to her, Tilda had to admit that he walked her through it smoothly enough, and she sent it along as instructed. Then she listened while he muttered to himself as he received the info and did whatever it was he did. He really was good at his job, despite the high sleaze factor. The security system he'd installed had protected her data from Heather's boyfriend du jour the other day — no telling what Doug could have accidentally done to her hard drive while he was trying to get his e-mail or whatever he'd been up to.

After just a few minutes, Javier said, "You're out of luck."

"Why?"

"Because he's sending from an Internet café, not his home system."

"Shit! Then I'm screwed."

Javier must have been concentrating — he didn't say anything inappropriate in response. "Pretty much. Unless you want to stake out the Internet café to see if he shows up again. Wait, didn't you say he's sent you more than one e-mail?"

"He sent the first one the other day, and two today. I only sent you the most recent one."

"Forward the other two to me, same procedure as before." He had to explain the steps to her again, but it was faster the second time around. The pause as he typed was shorter too. "Damn, he's a sneaky bastard. He sent the first message from a different Internet café."

"Great, so unless I stake out every Internet café in the country, there's nothing I can do!" For a moment she wondered how many *Kissing Cousins* fans she and Vincent could round up for the job, so it took a while for Javier's next words to sink in. "What did you say?"

"I said you'd only have to stake out the ones in the Boston area. The first message came from Boston, and the other two were from Cambridge."

"Have_Mercy is local?"

"He could have enlisted somebody around here to send you the e-mails locally, just to mess with your head, but why bother when there are so many cafés around? Not to mention wifi zones."

It had never occurred to Tilda that Have _Mercy would be local — with his claims of insider knowledge, she'd assumed he was in Los Angeles. The idea of him being closer to hand made her uncomfortable, especially considering how snarky her last e-mail to him had been.

"Tilda, are you okay?" Javier asked.

"Yeah, fine. I'm just not happy about this guy being nearby."

"He doesn't know where you live, does he?"

"Of course not," she said. "All he's got is my e-mail address. He can't get into my system with that, can he?"

"Not with the security I put on your system," Javier said confidently. "You're bulletproof. There's no way he could hack you remotely."

"Good." Then she had a chilling thought. What if it hadn't been Doug who'd tried to get into her computer? What if Have _Mercy had been in her apartment? "Javier, what if he was here? At my desk?"

He paused. "It's still nearly bulletproof, but I could break it, so somebody else could too, if they were good enough. You think you've been hacked?"

"I don't know. Could you tell?"

"Probably, but I'd have to look at your system. What's in it for me?"

"Javier, I'm already getting you into an exclusive party to meet a sexy starlet!"

"What's your point?"

"My point is that the guy who's doing the vampire series is the same one who did *Six Feet Under.* If you come check out my system, I'll forget to mention to him that you're the one who ran the spoiler about what was going to happen on the series

305

finale three nights before it aired."

"Shit! You play dirty."

"And you love it that way." But she relented enough to add, "I'll throw in dinner."

"Deal. I'll be there after work."

She hung up, then looked around her room, as if a historical marker proclaiming "Have_Mercy Was Here" was going to lower itself from the ceiling. It hadn't occurred to her that anybody other than Doug or Heather could have been in her room — nothing had been stolen, after all. Of course Heather had denied it, but that meant nothing — she'd have denied it if she and Doug had filmed a remake of *Debbie Does Dallas* on Tilda's bed.

Tilda went to the living room, opened the apartment's front door, and looked at the lock. Had those scratches always been there? Was the lock one of those that could be opened with a credit card? How could she be sure somebody hadn't broken in while she was in New York and Heather was at work?

She closed the door, making sure it was locked, and went to get her phone. She'd called Javier to check out computer security, and it just so happened she knew somebody she could consult about personal security.

But she stopped in the middle of dialing Nick's number. Nick was in the Boston area. He was a *Kissing Cousins* fan, and even admitted to having known Mercy. How did she know he wasn't Have_Mercy?

Okay, that was crazy. Irv Munch was in the Boston area, at least temporarily, and he'd definitely known Mercy. Why not suspect him? Or even Noel Clark — he was in LA, but as Javier said, he could have used somebody in Boston. What about Vincent? She snorted. Okay, not Vincent.

Still, she had no idea who Have_Mercy was, and there was no more reason to suspect Nick than there was to suspect anybody else connected with *Kissing Cousins.* So she dialed his number and asked him to come over to check out her door. He responded with both concern about her problem and enthusiasm for seeing her again, both of which were gratifying and only mildly suspicious.

Tilda was worried enough about her computer security having been compromised that she didn't want to touch it, not even to play games. She could have used her laptop, but she'd recently hooked the two systems together to transfer files, so that didn't seem safe either. A nap would have been nice, considering how little sleep she'd had the night before, but she couldn't stop wondering how secure that locked front door really was. Short of jamming a chair under the knob, which wouldn't have been a good thing if Heather showed up, she didn't know how she could make it safer. So, without admitting the reason to herself, she spent the rest of the afternoon watching the door. Sure, the TV was on, but she was a lot more interested in that door than she was in the shows she'd recorded.

Nick showed up before Javier, and once she saw him again, all her suspicions melted. It was hormones, she knew it was hormones, but she couldn't help it, any more than she could help falling into his arms. She didn't know if he interpreted it as wanting comfort, but comfort was the last thing on her mind. It was those damned hormones! They made it difficult for her to disengage, but she forced herself to do so.

"Are you okay?" he asked.

"A little freaked," she admitted. "I've never had a break-in before. Not that I know for sure that I've had one now, but just the idea has me antsy."

"Then let's take a look at this door and see what we've got. Is this the only door into the place?"

"It is, but there's also a window that opens

onto the fire escape. The fire escape is on the front of the building, though, so I don't think anybody would try to sneak in that way."

"I'll check it too, just in case."

He'd carried in a soft-sided leather briefcase, and he unzipped it to pull out a small but powerful flashlight and a large and powerful magnifying glass. Tilda stood out of his way as he took a full five minutes to examine the door lock. Then he pulled two odd-looking wire doohickeys from his briefcase and started fiddling in the lock.

"Are those lock picks?" she asked.

"That's right. You'd be surprised how many stars forget their keys or lock themselves out when they're distracted by their work."

"Not to mention when they're drunk or high."

"Oh, I'd never mention that." He fiddled some more, until Tilda heard a click. "Did you know that this lock is extremely easy to pick? It must be thirty years old."

"Don't tell the landlord — he'll call it a classic and raise our rent."

"Come here and look at this." He pushed the pick toward the door, missing on purpose, which left a tiny scratch on the metal of the lock. "Same kind of scratches. I'm afraid somebody did pick this. He wasn't very good at it, though — I'd never scratch up a lock this way."

"Somehow an incompetent burglar isn't terribly reassuring."

"I'd have to agree," he said. "You always know what a pro is after — amateurs aren't as predictable." He closed the door and locked it. "Let's look at that window."

It was of doubtful comfort, since whoever it was had come in the door, but Tilda didn't mind that Nick checked most of the windows and verified that nobody had come in through any of them. The only ones he didn't check were in Heather's bedroom.

When he started to open that door, Tilda stopped him. "Better not. I can't very well complain about her letting her boyfriends come into my room if I let mine into hers."

Nick grinned. "Does that make me your boyfriend?"

"Not yet. It takes serious work to earn that title."

"Such as?"

She was demonstrating some of the requirements when the doorbell rang. "Hold that thought for later."

After making sure it was Javier and not a burglar returning to polish the scratches on her door, Tilda buzzed him in.

He entered with a smirk on his face. "So, I was thinking that if you buy the dinner, maybe I can supply dessert." He waggled his eyebrows suggestively, but then saw Nick. The smirk disappeared and the eyebrows wilted. "Who's this?"

"Nick, this is Javier Rivera, my expert in computer security. Javier, meet Nick Tolomeo, my expert in physical security."

"You hired a bodyguard?" Javier said.

Nick put his arm around Tilda possessively. "No, this is personal."

"Ah. Then I'll just get to work." He scurried toward Tilda's bedroom.

Once he was out of earshot, Tilda said, "I suppose I should be grateful you didn't lift your leg to mark me as part of your territory."

"Sorry," Nick said sheepishly. "I just thought it would be easier on you if I drew the lines right away. Was I too heavy-handed?"

"I'll let it pass this time, as long as you keep an eye on Javier while he's in my bedroom. I found him rummaging through my underwear once."

Nick saluted sharply. "Shall I mark your underwear drawer, ma'am?"

"Don't make me get out my toenail clippers!"

Despite Nick watching his every move, or perhaps because of it, Javier worked quickly. Though he mumbled to himself the whole time, since he was mumbling in a mishmash of Spanish, English, and computerese, Tilda had no idea what was going on until he hit the return key particularly firmly and leaned back in the chair.

"Okay, I've got good news and bad news," he announced. "The good news is that your system is secure. It's free of viruses and spyware too."

Tilda let out a breath she hadn't even realized she'd been holding in. She did everything on her computer: work, personal letters, bills. Not to mention the fact that there were a few Web page bookmarks she'd rather nobody else knew about. "What's the bad news?"

"Somebody has definitely been messing with your computer."

"You're sure?"

"Does it ever take you more than five times to remember your password?"

"Never. Not even early in the morning."

"Then somebody else was making a stab at it." He gave her a stern look. "You don't use your birthday, your name, or the word 'password,' do you? Or any of those backward?"

"Of course not."

"Good — you'd be surprised how many people pick one of those. It looks like your guy wasn't savvy enough to actually get past the security program, so he tried the obvious passwords first, and then started guessing. Of course, he wouldn't have known that security won't allow more than six tries in a two-hour period until he tried the seventh time. By the way, what is your password?"

"It's —" She stopped. "I'm not telling you."

"Good girl. Tell no one." He looked over his shoulder at Nick. "No one! It's a good idea to change it frequently too." He pushed back from the desk. "What's for dinner?"

Though Tilda asked him a few more questions, Javier said there was nothing else he could tell her. The intruder hadn't been able to get into her system to read it, and he hadn't damaged anything either.

Deciding neutral territory would be more comfortable for all concerned, Tilda suggested eating at Pearl Street Station, the restaurant across the street, and they walked over and got a table. Normally she took the role of hostess seriously, but this time she was too distracted to take much of a part in the conversation. Fortunately the two men turned out to have a lot to talk about. Not sports, for which Tilda was grateful, but security. They had similar outlooks — Nick was just as paranoid in the real world as Javier was on the computer.

Only neither of them sounded as paranoid as she would have thought twenty-four hours earlier. Now she knew that somebody had been in her apartment. Not a burglar — nothing had been taken. He'd been looking for something, and his attempts on her computer made her think that it was information he was after. Theoretically it could have just been a psycho or an enterprising identity thief — Tilda would almost have preferred that — but she was sure that whoever it was had been there because of her work on the *Kissing Cousins* article.

None of her other projects would have sparked that kind of intrusion, unless it was the makeup artist mafia or the gospel singer goon squad. Moreover, she'd written articles about *Kissing Cousins* before. The big difference with this one was her focus on finding Mercy. Was it too outrageous to think that somebody was interested in that search? Even if it hadn't been Have_Mercy, somebody was damned interested in finding out what she knew.

So who cared that much? Rival reporter Lawrence or rival-in-general Nicole came to mind — either one would probably enjoy beating her to the punch. Was Mercy herself trying to stop her? Or was the *Kissing Cousins* killer hoping to get to Mercy before she did? Who'd have thought that there would come a time when Nicole breaking into her apartment would be the best-case scenario?

By continuing to nod in the appropriate places, she managed to make it through dinner. Then Javier left, and Nick escorted Tilda home, alert for anybody suspicious. He even examined the door to make sure no fresh scratches had appeared and checked the entire apartment to make sure nobody was lurking.

Since Heather was home by that point, he went into her bedroom, and Tilda could tell by the way her roommate eyed him that he could have spent all night there if he'd so much as crooked his finger at her. Under normal circumstances, Tilda's ego would have been purring in satisfaction when Nick made it plain that the only bedroom he was interested in inhabiting was hers, but this time, she just had the creeps. So when he gently hinted, she gently put him off. He was too polite to push, though clearly he thought having a bodyguard around could only make her sleep better. After extracting her promise to get a better lock installed, he left. Heather looked at her as if she was crazy for letting him go, and retreated into her room.

That left Tilda with no better way to spend the rest of the evening than to wander through the apartment, looking for more traces of Have_Mercy's invasion. She found nothing. Finally, she headed for bed, but left the lights on in the living room, kitchen, and bathroom, in flagrant disregard of her written roommate agreement with Heather.

CHAPTER 22

"Everybody knows about fan mail, but I was pure out shocked by presents kids would send: beaded bracelets, cookies, hand-drawn pictures, T-shirts. I've still got the stuffed bunny a little girl sent when my character's rabbit died."
— Katie Langevoort, quoted in "Curse of the *Kissing Cousins,*" *Entertain Me!*

Though she'd slept poorly, Tilda was up early to call the landlord and demand a new lock. They wrangled a bit, but after Tilda pointed out that she knew people at the *Boston Globe* who would like nothing better than to write an exposé of shoddy security in area apartment buildings, he got a locksmith out there to fix things up.

Other than supervising the locksmith, Tilda wasted her day on the Web. She found nothing and received no worthwhile messages. Instead she got hourly updates from

Vincent, reminding her that this was the date Mercy was fated to die, which did not improve her mood.

At four o'clock, one o'clock in LA, Tilda called Noel for their scheduled phone interview. Naturally, he wasn't ready.

"Sorry, darling," he said, "I've been learning my lines, and I completely lost track of the time. Damn it, there's the doorbell. I'm expecting a script from my agent — it's for a feature — and I've got to take a look pronto. Call me back in half an hour, okay? Ciao!"

Since he'd answered on the first ring, Tilda would have guessed he was blowing her off even if he hadn't done the same thing every time she'd ever spoken to him. He wasn't the only celebrity who got off on making people wait. So she hadn't even bothered to get her notes or list of questions ready. The waiting time was plenty enough to prepare, and she dialed Noel's number again at four-thirty.

Again, he answered on the first ring. "Tilda, you doll! How did you know?"

"You said to call back in half an hour."

"Not the time, the Sky Bars!"

"The what?"

"The box of Sky Bars. The ones I had went stale."

Now Tilda knew what he was talking about, at least partially. "Did somebody else send you some?"

"Yes, 'somebody' did. You did!"

"What?"

"And I'm eating my second right now — I'm going to be so fat tomorrow." He sighed much the way Tilda did when thinking about Nick. "They're wonderful. I was worried they'd be stale. FedEx dented the box and tore the plastic wrapper — you should complain."

"But I didn't send any . . ." Then a possibility clicked in her head, and she snapped, "Noel! Stop eating that stuff! I didn't send it."

"Of course you did — your name is on the label."

"No, I didn't! Stop eating it! Spit it out!"

"I already swallowed it," he said in a small voice. "Why would —" Tilda heard a retching noise, like a frat boy after a three-day weekend.

"Noel!" she yelled.

The only answer was more retching.

"Damn it!" she yelled in frustration. Still hanging on to her cell phone, Tilda grabbed the phone for the land line and dialed 9-1-1. It took her what seemed like an eternity to explain to the operator in Massachusetts that the emergency was actually in Burbank. Eventually the woman asked for Noel's address, promised to get somebody there immediately, and hung up. That left Tilda with nothing better to do than to hold onto her cell phone, alternately screaming at Noel that help was on the way and listening for signs of life. Even more retching would have been welcome. Finally she heard Noel's doorbell ring repeatedly, and a minute later, there was shattering glass as somebody broke into the house. There was a confusion of voices, sounds of movement, and radio noises. Finally somebody came on the line.

"This is the police. Is this the woman who called for help?"

"Yes! Is Noel alive?"

"Just barely. Do you know what he took?"

At the time, Tilda thought she was explaining what had happened with amazing lucidity, but afterward, she suspected she'd actually been babbling. Whatever she said, the cop asked only a few questions before telling her which hospital they'd taken Noel to and offering his opinion that he was going to make it. Tilda didn't know if he meant it or if he was only trying to keep her from hysterics. It worked, at least until she hung up the phone. Then she burst into tears, and she was still crying furiously when Heather got home from work.

Heather had her deficits as a roommate, but at least she knew enough to know when she was out of her depth. She took Tilda's cell phone from where Tilda had dropped it on the floor, went through her saved phone numbers until she found June's number, and called to tell her to come over at once. Then she sat next to Tilda, handing her water to drink and fresh tissues, even bringing a wet washcloth to wipe her face. Only when Tilda's sister arrived did she make herself scarce.

By then Tilda had calmed down enough to explain what was going on.

"Is he going to be okay?" June asked. "I didn't realize you knew him that well."

"I don't. I don't even like him that much. I don't know why I'm crying like this!" The waterworks threatened to break loose again, and June quickly handed her the glass Heather had left. A few swallows of water, and Tilda was ready to speak again. "I'm not upset about him getting hurt or dying — I mean, of course I'm upset, but not like this. It was feeling that helpless that was so awful. June, I could hear him! I could hear him dying. And I couldn't do anything, not one damned thing!"

"You did do something," June pointed out. "If you hadn't gotten the cops out there, he would have died. Right?"

"Yeah, maybe."

"So you weren't helpless. You did what you needed to do. I understand why you feel frustrated —"

"Frustrated! I'm not frustrated. I'm pissed. God, I've never been so mad in my life! That bastard put my name on the poison!"

"The cops don't think it was you, do they?"

"What? Oh, I don't know — I didn't do it, and they'll figure that out. Tracking numbers or fingerprints or something. I'm not worried about that."

"Then . . . ?" Clearly June was at a loss.

"That bastard used me! He read my article and found out Noel likes Sky Bars. Then he used my name to send him some, knowing that Noel wouldn't suspect anything that came from me. That's probably how he found out where Holly Kendricks lived too. I may as well have given him the fucking gun to shoot her with! June, I've never pretended that my work is anything but fluff —"

"Hey! It's not fluff!"

"It's fluff! People knowing Noel Clark's

favorite candy or Holly Kendricks's favorite *Kissing Cousins* episode doesn't change the world or help people live their lives or do anything important. I know that! But to have somebody use what I've written to kill people is a fucking nightmare!"

"Noel isn't dead."

"Not yet. This son of a bitch won't give up. He's going to go after the others, using what I've taught him to get at them. If I find Mercy, he'll go after her too! He's using my articles to kill people!"

Tilda waited for her sister to deny it, to talk her out of it.

Instead June said, "Do you really think he got what he needed from your stories?"

"He must have. Sure, there have been other articles about *Kissing Cousins* over the years, and there are fan sites that would have a lot of the same information. But look at the time frame. My article comes out with the name of the town Holly lives in and what Noel's favorite candy is. Two weeks later, Holly is dead and, two weeks after that, Noel is poisoned. Do you think that could be a coincidence?"

"I think the idea of it being a coincidence is harder to swallow than my husband's nuts," June said. Realizing what she'd said, she put one hand over her mouth, but a self-conscious giggle escaped.

Tilda snickered.

June laughed, breaking into the nerdy snort she tried not to use anymore.

That made Tilda laugh even harder.

In seconds, the two of them were laughing as hard as Tilda had been crying before. Tilda knew it was as much a stress reaction as the crying had been, but was just as unable to stop.

At some point, Heather stuck her head into the room, realized they were laughing and not crying, and went away again. Tilda had been trying to pull herself together, but the expression on her roommate's face set her off again, especially when she heard the click that meant Heather had locked her door.

Finally the outburst ran its course, and after using more tissues to wipe their streaming eyes, the two of them were ready to start acting like semirational human beings again.

"Jesus, June, I'm so damned mad. It's crazy. Here I am writing bits of fluff and somebody is using it to kill people!"

"Hey!" June said, socking her on the arm. "I'm telling you, it's not fluff! I'm speaking as a psychologist here, not as your big sister. People need articles like yours. They love those shows, and those characters, and those actors. For you to write about them with respect validates their feelings."

"And that's a good thing?"

"Of course that's a good thing. Learning about their idols gives people a sense of being part of an in-group, a sense of belonging."

"Also a good thing?"

"Definitely. It also creates a connection between them and their idols."

"A good thing?"

"Well, it can go too far," June admitted, "if the fan thinks there's more of a relationship than there really is, but generally it's a good thing. It's empowering to link oneself to a powerful person, even if it's a tenuous connection. If somebody reads that their childhood idol is now a real estate agent or a mother, just like they are now, that both humanizes the idol and makes the fan feel special. Which is another good thing."

"Good."

"I could also mention the historical aspects of what you write, which are of interest to aspiring actors and television writers."

"You could."

"And even if it were purely fluff, with no other redeeming value, so what? We need fluff! It's impossible to underestimate the importance of entertainment in our lives, and if fluff entertains us, then I think we could use a lot more of it."

"So what I write isn't fluff, but even if it were, fluff is a good thing."

"Right."

"Okay. Then this bastard is taking my noble efforts and using them to kill people."

"Didn't two of those murders take place before you published that article? You can hardly take the blame for those."

"True. So he'd already targeted Holly and Noel before he read my article. I just made his job easier." Tilda looked at her sister. "That doesn't make me feel much better." She got up and started pacing. "I just wish the cops would find the guy, and —" She stopped.

"What?"

"Hell, why don't I try to find him?"

"Excuse me?"

"Finding people is what I do. Why would it be so different to find a killer?"

"Hmm, let me think. Oh, I know! Because you don't know who the killer is!"

Tilda waved that chunk of logic aside. "According to Vincent, the Weldon cops are looking at Holly's husband and business rivals, and the Burbank cops are going to be thinking the same way, trying to find somebody who knew Noel."

"You really don't think they'll make the connection?"

"Okay, they probably will, but I know the people involved in this better than the cops do."

"So why don't know you know who the killer is?"

"Because I haven't been looking for a killer — I've been looking for Mercy. But I've got ideas."

"Like?"

"It could be a stalker. I've met some of the fans, and they can get pretty intense. You said yourself that fans sometimes carry relationships too far."

"I did say that," June conceded.

"Or Irv Munch could be trying to get publicity for a new show."

"Kind of drastic."

"The twins could be bitter because the other cast members never took them seriously."

"At least it's not a hidden twin theory," June said. "Those are such clichés."

"Kat Owen may not be as tolerant as she pretends to be. She could be killing off heathens."

June just gave her a look.

"Okay, that one is lame. But there could be a reason from back when the show was being filmed that I don't know about. Or maybe the killer just wanted to kill Noel, and killed the others first for camouflage. Or Noel could be doing it himself, and either tried to commit suicide or faked the poisoning to draw attention away from himself."

"What about Mercy? Do you still suspect her?"

Tilda stopped pacing, still hating the idea, but said, "If she was killing people, it would certainly explain why I haven't been able to find her."

"Tilda, tell me you're not going to make like Angela Lansbury."

"You mean like Jessica Fletcher. Lansbury is an actress; Fletcher is the character in *Murder, She Wrote*."

"Whatever. I'm back to being your big sister now, and I want to know you're not going to go off playing detective."

Tilda threw herself into her chair. "You're right, you're right. I'm a reporter, not a detective. I wouldn't know how to investigate a crime anyway."

"I'm glad you said that, or else I was going to have to do something drastic."

"What would you do? Ground me?"

"Worse. I'd have called Mom."

"Shit! You minivan-driving suburban moms play hardball."

"Damned straight! You don't survive lunchroom duty if you don't have the balls to do what it takes. Speaking of being a mom —" She looked at her watch. "Are you going to be okay, because I left in the middle of laundry, and if I don't get your niece's soccer uniform washed, she'll have to sit out of tomorrow's game and —"

"Go, go! I wouldn't want to be the cause of that."

"Are you sure?"

"I'm sure. Thank you for coming running."

"That's what big sisters are for. And don't forget to thank your roommate for calling me."

"That's next on my list," Tilda assured her.

She walked June down to her minivan, then walked to Dunkin' Donuts to pick up half a dozen muffins to leave in the kitchen for Heather to find. As soon as she got to the apartment, she called in an order to Town Pizza House for a large pepperoni with extra cheese. There was more than one way to thank a person.

CHAPTER 23

"Episode 40: Sherri-lock Holmes
When Pops's bowling ball disappears, Sherri decides it's been stolen and, using her favorite teen detective books as a guide, searches everybody's rooms. When she finds it in Mercy's closet and drags in Pops to confront the 'thief,' she finds out that Mercy was only getting the finger sizes from the ball to buy him a new one for his birthday. Pops gently reminds Sherri that being nosy is never a good thing."

— Fanboy's Online *Kissing Cousins*
Episode Guide, by Vincent Peters

By the time she and Heather had gorged on pizza and muffins, Tilda was ready for bed — she'd never realized that having hysterics was so exhausting — but she knew that if she didn't let Vincent know what had happened, he'd never forgive her. He answered the phone on the first ring.

"Tilda! Isn't it terrible?"

"You've already heard?"

"Rhonda called me an hour ago, and I've been online ever since, spreading the word."

"Rhonda? How did she find out?"

"What do you mean, 'How did she find out?' Who else could have arranged it?"

"Vincent, what are we talking about?"

"I don't know about you, but I'm talking about Rhonda selling off her *Kissing Cousins* collection. She's already made a deal with the guy who's running the Beantown Collectibles Extravaganza — she's going to sell it all!"

"That's a shame, but she's been out of work a while now, right? She probably needs the money."

"Yeah, I guess," Vincent said with the nonchalance of somebody who'd never missed a paycheck. "But she's abandoning the work of a lifetime. There's no way any one collector will be able to buy the whole collection, so it will be broken up forever. History will not thank her for this!"

As she listened to Vincent's view of historical importance, Tilda started to give more credence to her earlier idea of a crazed fan killing the Cousins. Anybody who thought the way Vincent did clearly wasn't living on the same planet as she was. Though she'd long known about his occasional visits to Vincentland, before she'd always assumed it to be a peaceful place. Now she wasn't so sure.

Come to think of it, what about Rhonda? Her collection had to be worth a lot more than it had been a few weeks before. She'd bragged that many of her items were autographed, and with three of the cast members dead, those things had become irreplaceable. Hadn't she mentioned going both to California and Connecticut for job interviews? Tilda was sure the collector knew about Noel's fondness for Sky Bars, and since Tilda had mentioned seeing Noel during the memorial service chat, Rhonda could have gotten the idea to use her name on the package.

Tilda pushed the thoughts away, mindful of her decision not to remake *Murder, She Wrote.* "Vincent," she said, "I'm afraid I've got more bad news. Somebody poisoned Noel Clark." When he gasped, she quickly added, "He's still alive," and told him what had happened.

"Oh my God!" Vincent squeaked when she was done. "I had the right date, but the wrong person."

"What?"

"All day long I've been afraid to answer the phone or look at e-mail because today was the day Mercy was going to die — it never occurred to me that the killer might go after Noel." Then, almost indignantly, he said, "He broke the pattern. It was Mercy's turn."

Tilda had forgotten about Vincent's timeline. "Maybe there never was a pattern in the first place — the timing could just be coincidences."

"Maybe," he said, not at all convinced. "No, wait!" Tilda heard the sound of Vincent tapping at the keyboard. "That's it! The character of Mercy was older than the character of Elbert, but the actress Mercy is a month younger than Noel. The killer is going in order of the actors' ages, not the characters'! How could I have been so stupid?"

Tilda wanted to respond, but she honestly didn't know what to say. On one hand, the whole timeline still sounded like donkey dung to her. On the other, Vincent had successfully predicted the date of the killer's next attempt, even if he had had the target wrong.

Vincent went on. "I almost got Elbert killed."

"Don't be ridiculous. The only one who

nearly got Elbert — I mean Noel killed was the person who sent the poisoned candy. You didn't have anything to do with that, did you?"

"Of course not!"

"Then stop shitting on yourself." She realized she was echoing June's comments to her earlier, in substance, if not in style.

"You're right," he said. "I can't fall to pieces now. The Cousins need me. You've already warned the rest of them, right?"

"I was about to," she lied, "but I wanted to get you up to speed first."

"How can I help?"

She paused, but realized there was something he could do. "Let me give you the name of the hospital where Noel was admitted. I couldn't get any information on his condition, but maybe you'll have better luck."

"Consider it done."

She had no doubt that within an hour he'd have dug up some connection by which he could get the man's status, including blood pressure, temperature, and bladder output.

After hanging up the phone, she started looking up phone numbers. At first she was only planning to call Kat Owen, but decided she better call Gabrielle and Gwendolyn as well. She'd quoted them in her article, so the killer might well consider them legitimate targets. She added Irv Munch to the list too.

If she'd hoped to startle one of them into a telephone confession, she was disappointed. Nobody answered their phones. Instead she had to try to leave coherent voice mail messages, which admittedly she had down pat by the last call.

Next she sent an e-mail to Jillian, since she was going to include what had happened to Noel in her story. She'd have felt guilty about it if she hadn't known the man. If he survived, he would appreciate the extra publicity. If he didn't, he'd probably still appreciate it.

That done, she'd intended to go to bed, but found herself opening a file to type in the names of all the people involved with *Kissing Cousins,* past and present. Then she read the names over, realizing that any one of them could be a killer if she stretched her suspension of disbelief far enough. Even more fanciful scenarios than the ones she'd presented to June suggested themselves.

No, she wasn't going to play that game. Even without June's threat to call their formidable mother, she knew it was incredibly stupid even to speculate. It's just that she was still so angry. The killer had used information from her article — he'd gone so far as to use her name! How could she let that go? She wasn't going to start pretending to be a detective, but maybe, as she continued to research her story, she'd find out something that would help the police catch the rat bastard.

Idly she considered how the killer would react to the news about Noel. Surely he or she would be disappointed that the attempt had failed. Assuming that he hadn't found Mercy, would he go after Noel again, or would he set his sites on Kat Owen or the twins? Was Irv Munch included on his hit list? How would it affect his timeline? If he followed his previous pattern, the next murder would take place in a week.

What was the point of that damned timeline anyway? She could come up with plenty of motives for the killings, thought admittedly some were ludicrous, but she couldn't imagine a reason why anybody would use accelerating deadlines. She'd never have realized there was a pattern at all if Vincent hadn't figured it out, and she really hadn't believed it even then. None of it made sense to her — maybe she should get June to play psychologist again and explain it to her.

As Tilda shut down her technology and got ready for bed, she realized that she was going to be the center of a lot of attention the next day: the cops, the fans, the people from *Kissing Cousins* were all going to want to talk to her. It might be her best chance yet to shake information out of them. All because she'd foiled the killer's plan. Okay, the killer had been using her — now she was going to use him.

It gave her a feeling of deep satisfaction.

CHAPTER 24

"Episode 20: Damon's Collection
When Damon discovers a box of baseball
cards in the attic and learns that they're
valuable, he gets caught up in collecting
mania. Before long, he's wheeling and
dealing with other boys, even cheating
younger boys out of their collections. Only
when Mercy tells him the original collection was their late uncle's does he realize
that sentiment outweighs dollars, and he
returns all of the cards except the ones he
started with."
— Fanboy's Online *Kissing Cousins*
Episode Guide, by Vincent Peters

As she'd halfway expected, Tilda was woken
the next morning by the telephone. But it
wasn't Vincent hungry for more details, or
the police who had a right to those details,
or even June, checking up on her. It was
Nicole.

"Are you still in bed?" she said waspishly. "Must be nice!"

Tilda started to explain why she'd been up late, but stopped. Nicole wasn't her boss, no matter what she might think. "You're right — it is nice."

Nicole sputtered a second before continuing. "Jillian forwarded me your note about that newest victim of the curse. We want your piece for next week's issue, so I need your copy by the end of the day today."

"Today? Jillian gave me until next Thursday, and I still haven't found the actress who played Mercy."

"Jillian says you don't need her — just give me what you've got. We want the latest on the poisoning while it's still fresh."

"It's not going to be all that fresh by the time the issue comes out," Tilda pointed out, "so why not wait another week?"

"I want it now. If you can't deliver, I'll find a writer who can."

Meaning herself, no doubt. "Can you forward me to Jillian? I want to talk to her about this."

"Sorry," Nicole said, sounding anything but. "Jillian flew out this morning for the editors' meeting. She'll be gone through the weekend, and she left me in charge."

Shit! Tilda knew from previous years

that short of an entertainment emergency on the level of Steven Spielberg dying or the Rolling Stones breaking up, Jillian was not to be interrupted during the biannual meeting.

"One other thing," Nicole said, sounding smug. "I hear that some big time collector is going to be selling her *Kissing Cousins* collection."

"Rhonda Hodgkiss?"

"That's the one. I want a sidebar about it. With pictures."

Many responses occurred to Tilda, most of them colorfully profane, but she bit her tongue. Nicole was only doing this to pay her back for showing her up at the cocktail party the other night. They both knew the sidebar would probably get spiked or cut down to nothing — it wasn't an *Entertain Me!* kind of story. But if she wanted to keep the *Kissing Cousins* assignment, she would have to swallow it. "Fine, but I'll have to make sure I can set up a time to interview Hodgkiss. I'll call her and get back to you."

Nicole hung up without saying good-bye, a habit she'd adopted after hearing that Anna Wintour of *Vogue* ended her phone calls that way.

Still not getting out of bed, Tilda dialed

Cooper's extension. "Cooper, this is Tilda."

"Hey, Jean-Paul. What's up?"

There was no way Cooper could have mistaken her voice for Jean-Paul's, even if he'd misheard her. "Shit! Then Jillian really is out of the office."

"Uh huh."

"Nicole is throwing her weight around, making me rush the story."

"There's a lot of that going on around here today."

"There's a surprise. Anyway, I need to know the absolute drop-dead last second I could get my story in for the next issue."

"Lunch Monday would be great, if you're going to be downtown anyway, but it would have to be early. All the copy for the next issue will be in by one o'clock sharp, so I'll have to start copyediting at 1:01."

"One o'clock on Monday. Got it."

"Oh, well. Sorry the timing won't work. See you tonight. Love you!"

"Love you too," she trilled, and added, "Thanks, Cooper."

As soon as she hung up from that call, she dug up Rhonda's phone number to call her and explained that she wanted to see her collection for the article. Rhonda was all for it and said she could come at four-thirty that afternoon. Then on a hunch, she dialed

Jillian's extension, and, sure enough, Nicole answered. The bitch was sitting at Jillian's desk!

"Nicole Webber, acting editor in chief," she said grandly.

"Nicole, this is Tilda. Look, I did my best, but I cannot get face time with Rhonda until Sunday. Today she's got a plumber coming and a doctor's appointment, and she's booked all day tomorrow for some sort of family thing. You're going to have to let me have until Monday. Say by five?"

Nicole paused, and Tilda knew she was dying to push her harder, but she wasn't willing to lose the article completely. "It's got to be on my desk by one, or forget it."

"Jeez, that's cutting it tight. . . . Okay, one o'clock it is," Tilda said. This time she hung up first, just because she could.

The glow of that small triumph didn't last long. The time she'd bought wasn't going to make any difference if she couldn't somehow become inspired to find Mercy. She got out of bed, showered, and ate breakfast, so as to be ready for inspiration to strike.

It didn't.

So she checked e-mail on the off chance that either the killer had sent his confession or Mercy had sent an invitation to lunch, including directions to her house. They hadn't.

Next she once again skimmed all her notes for the article to see if inspiration was hiding there.

It wasn't. Or, if it was, it was continuing to hide. She sighed. It was useless. She really had given it her best shot, but time was running out. The only rational thing she could do was to go ahead and write the story with the data she had, and since she didn't live in Vincentland, that's what she was going to do.

She started writing, and worked steadily until the phone rang an hour later.

This time it was the Burbank cops, or rather, a Burbank homicide detective, and he asked her to again describe what had happened when she called Noel the day before. It was odd to be on the receiving end of an interview. If asked, she'd have given the detective a solid B for his style — he was thorough, but he was weak on developing rapport. Then again, maybe cops weren't big on developing rapport with potential poisoners.

Tilda told him everything she knew about the poisoned Sky Bars, which wasn't much. Then she asked questions of her own, and was pleasantly surprised when he answered.

Apparently the police had traced the package. It had been shipped from Washington, DC, on Wednesday morning, and thanks to Nick and Cooper, she had an alibi for that whole time. The detective was nice enough not to sneer when she suggested that he might be able to find out how the package was paid for; he just patiently told her that the shipper had used cash, which helped nobody.

Even though she'd answered all of his questions, and he seemed to believe her, he still asked if she'd mind if a pair of Boston detectives came to see her in person, and she lied and said that she wouldn't mind at all. Then she hung up and got back to work.

The Boston detectives — a man and a woman — arrived promptly at eleven, and Tilda told the whole tale again. She'd once heard that witnesses tend to remember more details every time they repeat a story, but the only one she added was the fact that Noel's doorbell sounded like the chimes of Big Ben. This startling revelation might have surfaced because the pair was better than the Burbank cop at developing rapport. She'd have given them a B+ in interviewing, and if the one who was taking notes had written a little faster, she'd have bumped them to an A−. Then they took

344

her fingerprints and asked for handwriting samples to do whatever it was they did with such things.

After they left, Tilda wondered if she should have had a lawyer present while they questioned her — if she'd gotten more of an impression that they really suspected her, maybe she would have. As it was, she thought they accepted her innocence, if for no other reason than because she'd saved Noel's life. Moreover, they were somewhat willing to entertain the possibility that Holly's killer had tried to kill Noel, even though they thought her contradicting theories that Mercy was either a killer or in danger of becoming a victim were something for the circular file. She didn't blame them — when she said it out loud, it sounded about as believable as the average *Kissing Cousins* script.

Tilda grabbed a sandwich for lunch and went back to her article, finishing a draft by late afternoon. When she read it over, she knew she'd done a decent job, but she also knew she'd never produced a piece of writing she detested more. Even if every word had sparkled, she'd have hated the damned thing because it didn't include anything about Mercy's whereabouts.

Feeling wildly dissatisfied, she got ready

to go to Rhonda's place to see the much-vaunted *Kissing Cousins* collection. Despite her annoyance with Nicole for pushing the sidebar, Tilda felt that she owed it to Rhonda to do a good job. First, it had bought her more time, even if she hadn't been able to do anything with that time so far. Second, even under the circumstances, she was going to enjoy rummaging through the collection.

Since Rhonda lived in Waltham, not easily accessible by T, Tilda took her life in her hands to drive up I-93 and then switch to Route 128, the road that was sometimes called America's Technology Highway in honor of all the high-tech firms located off its exits. One would presume that people in such jobs would have higher than average intelligence, but Tilda saw no sign of it in their driving styles. The mix of tailgaters and incessant lane-changers, plus slow-downs at popular exits, made for a frustrating drive. Tilda was relieved finally to arrive at the Gardencrest Apartments, a sprawling complex designed when people thought such developments should look like neighborhoods instead of warrens.

When Rhonda came to her door, the first thing she said was, "You're not going to take pictures, are you? I'm a mess, and the apartment is even worse."

Looking around at the stacks of papers, piles of magazines, and small mountains of boxes that filled the room, Tilda said, "I'll only use close-ups of items. Neither you nor your apartment will show."

"Thank goodness," Rhonda said. "It's been crazy ever since I decided to go through with this. I've got to catalog everything and give estimated values for the insurance company at the collectibles show, and it's got to be done by the middle of next week. There's all kinds of regulations for things being displayed."

"Then you're not selling after all?"

"Oh, I'm still selling, but not at the expo. They're paying me an honorarium for the display, but only if I keep it intact until the show ends. I'll take names and offers, and work out deals afterward. Anything that doesn't sell that way will go on eBay. That's unless I get lucky and sell it as a collection."

"Is that likely?"

"Not really. Only a collector with really deep pockets would be able to afford it, and serious collectors already have enough of the items that they're not going to want duplicates. I don't think Vincent will ever forgive me."

"Why is he so bothered? He's not even

that much of a collector." It was true —
other than a few signed cast photos and a
set of dolls, Vincent didn't have that much
Kissing Cousins memorabilia. He had too
many passions to indulge completely in any
one of them.

"He's treating this like it's a museum collection and I'm the curator, but curators get
paid, and I haven't been for a long time
now. I don't want to give the stuff up, but I
don't want to give up eating either."

"Maybe the article will get you some attention too. Human resource people read
Entertain Me!"

"I never thought of that," Rhonda said,
cheering. "Beats putting up a billboard,
which I had seriously considered. 'Will work
for rent money.' So where do we start?"

"I've got some questions, and then I'd like
to look at the collection and see what would
photograph well."

"Good enough." While Tilda got situated
— not an easy task considering the clutter
— Rhonda went to get them something to
drink and then had to find her own place to
sit. For about half an hour, Tilda asked
questions about how Rhonda had gotten
into collecting and how she went about
finding things from a long-defunct television
series. Then she asked which item was

Rhonda's first (one of the *Kissing Cousins* jigsaw puzzles), her favorite (the *Kissing Cousins* play set), the most rare (a copy of one of the third-season scripts signed by the cast), the most valuable (a full set of *Kissing Cousins* dolls, mint in box), and the most unusual (*Kissing Cousins* panties for girls, thankfully still in the wrapper).

Then Tilda saw the price list Rhonda was working on. "Are these things really worth this much?"

"To a collector? Absolutely. I'm embarrassed to admit how much money I've got tied up in some of it, and I've been at it for years. Prices have been rising steadily, and every time Nick@Nite does a *Kissing Cousins* marathon, there's a jump." She sheepishly added, "And honestly, the recent publicity hasn't hurt prices any either."

Tilda shrugged. "If people will spend big bucks on lousy clown paintings by John Wayne Gacy, why not buy cursed board games?" To herself she noted that her own modest collection might provide a decent nest egg too, should the need arise.

Once she had enough information for the written part of the sidebar, Tilda gathered up some of the items to photograph, using a dark-blue sheet she'd brought along for a backdrop. Though she knew that two or three photos at most would be used, she also knew that her photography skills were basic and that the best way to get one good shot was to take many, many iffy shots. With a digital camera, she didn't have to be shy about film, so she told Rhonda to go back to cataloging while she experimented with angles and such. If nothing else, Rhonda could use the photos when posting on eBay.

Tilda was trying to figure out how to get rid of the glare from the plastic wrappings on the panties when Rhonda said, "Now this is different — take a look."

"What?"

Rhonda handed her what looked like a leather-covered photo album, the kind people put their wedding photos in. But instead of being imprinted with "Bob & Mary, Together Forever," it had the *Kissing Cousins* logo carved into the cover.

"Tell me you didn't have this made," Tilda said.

"Not guilty," Rhonda said, holding her hands up in surrender. "I bought it last year. The original owner was a stone *Kissing Cousins* fan."

"No, I'm a stone fan. Vincent is a bit more than that. This guy was a whole level of magnitude beyond." Tilda flipped through the pages where the unknown fan had carefully pasted in original magazine and newspaper clippings, laminated for preservation; eight-by-ten glossies of the cast, all of them signed and one of them personalized; and even *TV Guide* listings with summaries of every episode. The whole thing was in precise chronological order. "I'm surprised he sold it."

"He died," Rhonda said, "so his partner was selling a whole lot of stuff. He had other albums for other shows."

"That's scary."

"I mainly bought it for curiosity value. Full magazines are more collectible than clippings, even if he did label them so thoroughly. The glossies are good, but I can't get them out of the album without damaging them. Still, it's interesting." She went back to sorting while Tilda kept looking at the album.

The original owner must have been a *Teen Fave* reader — Tilda recognized many of the clippings. Plus there were articles from *16, Tiger Beat,* and magazines whose titles she didn't recognize. She even found a copy of the photo of Mercy with Nick and wondered if she should try to buy the thing as a present for him. That led her to speculate whether or not he and she were on gift-giving terms yet, and she almost missed one newspaper clipping she hadn't seen before.

It was a shot of four couples at some kind of social function — the men were in suits and the women were wearing what Tilda thought would be called cocktail dresses, or perhaps party frocks. Mercy was at the end of the line, and though the other couples were identified as Mr. and Mrs. or Mr. Whoever and Miss Whichever, Mercy and her date were only "Wallace Lambert Jr. and Friend." The accompanying article described the party they were attending in loving detail, and the label underneath identified it as being from *The Desert Sun* in Palm Springs. If the date given was correct, it had been printed in June of 1979.

"This is odd," she said.

"What's that?" Rhonda said. "Oh yeah, I remember that one. Funny that the guy who made the book recognized Mercy, isn't it? It's not a very good shot, and she's dressed so strangely."

Tilda admitted, "I don't know that I'd have recognized her from this myself." Instead of wearing black lace, Mercy was wearing pastel blue, with matching pumps and white gloves. Her hair was pulled back, in a French twist or something similar. Of course, Sophia had told her Mercy didn't always wear black when she was away from the camera, but pastels? It just looked wrong.

She looked through the rest of the album, but ended up back at that one picture. By rights she should pack up and go. It was nearly six o'clock, and she had to write up her notes for the sidebar about Rhonda, and make sure her story was ready to deliver on Monday. It would be ridiculous to try to track down some dude who went to one party with Mercy just to see if he knew where she was now. That was assuming that it really was Mercy in the picture. Absolutely fucking ridiculous.

"Rhonda," she said, "Can I borrow this? I'd love to reread some of these old articles — I might find some quotes for my piece." Just because she'd decided to be ridiculous, that didn't mean she was going to tell Rhonda. "I promise to get it back to you in plenty of time for the collectibles show."

"Sure, as long as you're careful with it."

"Thanks." She quickly finished with her photos, thanked Rhonda for the interview and the loan, and left. Once in the car, she did some rapid calculations. Six o'clock in Waltham meant three o'clock in Sacramento, so she had a good chance of reaching somebody at *The Desert Sun.* Of course, six o'clock on Friday also meant a hellish drive back to Malden. Rather than risk missing her chance, she stayed parked and pulled out her cell phone to take one more stab at finding Mercy.

CHAPTER 25

"I was never crazy about the title *Kissing Cousins,* but it could have been worse. The network wanted *Kissin' Cousins,* which sounded like a *Beverly Hillbillies* rip-off. I had to fight for that 'g.' "
— Irv Munch, quoted in "Curse of the *Kissing Cousins,*" *Entertain Me!*

A call to information got her the number of *The Desert Sun,* but when she asked for Cecily Flax, the author of the article, the operator said nobody by that name worked there. Of course, the article was nearly thirty years old, and the reporter had probably retired or changed jobs. So Tilda asked for the lifestyles department instead. She'd halfway expected that the lifestyles editor would be as lost as the operator, but he recognized Flax's name immediately. She'd been a longtime society reporter and still lived in the area. Once Tilda explained who she worked for, the editor gave her the woman's phone number, but warned her that Flax was always Miss Flax, not Mrs. Flax or Cecily, and particularly never Ms. Flax.

Feeling unreasonably excited, Tilda dialed the woman's number, and she answered on the second ring.

"This is Cecily Flax. To whom do I have the honor of speaking?"

Tilda told herself not to use the f-word, the s-word, or even the d-word. She had a hunch that somebody who answered the phone that formally would hang up if she did. "Miss Flax? This is Miss Tilda Harper calling from Massachusetts. I'm researching for an article for *Entertain Me!,* and I was hoping you might have a few minutes to speak with me."

"I always have time for a fellow journalist," Miss Flax replied.

"This is going back a few years. I've got an article you wrote about a Junior League party back in June of 1979. It includes a picture of four couples, and one of the women isn't identified by name. She's just 'and Friend.' Do you suppose you could consult your files and see if you remember that photo?"

"I don't have to, Miss Harper. I remember

that picture quite well — it's the only time I ever wrote a caption like that. You see, Wallace Lambert Senior came up to me after I took the picture and told me in no uncertain terms that he didn't want the young lady's name linked to his son's in the paper. Wallace Junior was furious, and the lady was horribly embarrassed, but Mr. Lambert was a personal friend of the editor so I didn't dare cross him. I should have used a different photo, but I was quite the rebel in those days, so I ran it with her unidentified." She giggled, or perhaps it was a titter. "My, what a stir it caused!"

Tilda was starting to like the older woman. "I don't suppose you remember the young lady's name."

"Let me think. It was an unusual name. Hope? Charity? Some kind of virtue."

"Mercy? Mercy Ashford?"

"That's it! For Wallace Junior to bring her to the cotillion was quite a scandal. Don't misunderstand me, she was perfectly well behaved, but it was common knowledge that she was an actress. The cats were all whispering NQOTD in the powder room."

"NQOTD?"

" 'Not quite our type, dear.' Such snobs! If they'd known half the tales I know about people of 'their type,' they'd have been delighted to have an actress with nice manners around. Unfortunately Mr. Lambert agreed with them, and I heard that he forbade Wallace Junior from seeing her again. Mr. Lambert controlled his son with an iron hand — a most unpleasant man. His wife had passed away young and the story was that she'd died to get away from him."

"Did Wallace Junior obey his father or did he continue dating Mercy?"

"The rumor was that he snuck around and went to Los Angeles to see her, but nobody ever caught him at it. All I know is that something happened nine or ten months later — I never could find out what — and Mr. Lambert sent the boy to Europe. No farewell dinners, no explanation, no forwarding address. Wallace Junior was just gone, and word came down not to ask questions."

Tilda hesitated, but then risked it. "Surely a strong-willed journalist like yourself wouldn't stand for that."

This time it was definitely a giggle, a surprisingly sweet sound. "We do think alike, my dear. I did do my best to ferret out the story, as a matter of fact, but I didn't have much success. There were so many rumors flitting about — that Wallace Junior had killed somebody in a duel, or that he wanted to become an actor. Somebody swore he'd been seen dressed as a woman in some disreputable bar! Those are just the theories I remember — there were many more."

"Did you have a favorite?"

"Well, you wouldn't expect it from a hard-bitten reporter like myself, but I'm quite the romantic at heart. I wondered if he'd proposed to Miss Ashford, and perhaps planned to elope with her." She sighed. "He was quite a charming young man."

"What happened to him? Where is he now?"

"I don't know. He only came back to Palm Springs once, when his father died four or five years later. Wallace Junior attended the funeral, collected his inheritance, put the family home up for sale, and went away. I never heard anything else about him. Does this help you any?"

"You know, it just might." Maybe Tilda was a romantic at heart too, because she couldn't help wondering if he'd gone looking for Mercy to rekindle their romance. Even better, since she'd disappeared from sight around the same time as he'd been sent to Europe, could she have followed him? Could they be there now, living happily ever after? "I may take a shot at tracking down Wallace Junior to see what he can tell me. Do you have any background on the family you could send me? By fax if you don't have Internet access."

"Of course I have Internet access — I just upgraded from DSL to a cable modem, as a matter of fact, and the increase in speed is positively invigorating."

"That would be perfect," Tilda said, and gave the woman her e-mail address. "Thank you so much, Miss Flax. You've been an enormous help."

"My pleasure, dear. I'd love to know what you find out about Wallace Junior. I think all reporters just hate it when they don't hear the end of a story, don't you?"

"Miss Flax, I agree completely."

Rush hour was still going strong, but Tilda just didn't care. Though she was eager to get the e-mail from Miss Flax, for the moment she was content to imagine happy endings for Mercy and Wallace Junior and their bevy of children while she drove. Of course she didn't necessarily approve of a woman giving up her career for a man, but she was sure Mercy had found some outlet for her talent. Maybe she'd assumed a new name to perform quirky roles in foreign films or avant-garde theater. The couple could have forged such a happy life for themselves that they felt no need to return to the old one, even after Lambert Senior was safely in his grave.

She finally made it back to Malden, gave Heather a cheery greeting on the way to her room, and booted up her computer to see what Miss Flax had sent her. It was an embarrassment of riches. She had upwards of thirty items waiting in her mailbox. Tilda made a note to herself to send a thank-you note to Miss Flax, the old-fashioned hand-written kind. Then she opened the first file.

She quickly learned that the Lamberts had been extremely socially active, despite Wallace Senior's unpleasantness. At first there was no mention of Wallace Junior, just the mister and missus, who attended any number of cotillions, debutante balls, charity fund-raisers, mixers, and other varieties of soiree. The only slow spot in the couple's social career was when Wallace Junior was born. According to the birth announcement, he was a year older than Mercy. There was a few months' gap, presumably until little Wallace — Tilda felt sure that they'd never called him Wally — started sleeping through the night, but then the merry antics started up again. Then came the last mention of Mrs. Lambert: her obituary. She'd fallen down a flight of stairs at her house and had broken her neck. Tilda suspected she'd slipped because she was worn out from all those parties, but after all her thoughts about murder, she briefly speculated about a more sinister explanation.

After a year's worth of mourning, Mr. Lambert started showing up at parties again, and the first mention of Wallace Junior joining the fun came a few years after that. He followed the family tradition of never staying home a night that he didn't have to, and escorted any number of debutantes, heiresses, and suitable young ladies. The last articles Miss Flax had sent were Lambert Senior's obituary and coverage of his funeral.

Now that she had the background, Tilda hit the Web to find more mentions of Wallace Junior. There were a few, but all from his sojourn in Europe, which was mostly spent in Paris. If he'd been mourning his forced separation from Mercy, it didn't show — he attended just as many parties as he had in Palm Springs, and went back to escorting suitable young ladies. There were, however, no permanent attachments. When his father died, the Paris papers took note of Wallace Junior's return home for the funeral, but that was the last mention of him. Just as Miss Flax had said, once he got his hands on his father's estate, he disappeared.

Tilda continued working the Web for all she was worth, but found nothing later than Wallace Junior's appearance at his father's funeral. She even hunted for "Mercy Lambert," but found nothing that could be her Mercy. She rubbed her eyes from frustration and not a little eyestrain. Mercy dated this guy, then disappeared. He went away, then came back and disappeared. Could it be a coincidence that both of them had disappeared? Could they be living together somewhere? Could Mercy have completely abandoned acting, and could Wallace Junior have abandoned all the parties he was apparently addicted to? It didn't make sense.

Tilda had told Nick how she would take the same set of facts and slant it to match the audience. When Jim Bonnier died in an overdose, it could become a cautionary tale about drugs, a warning about the costs of fame, or a character assassination of Bonnier for being weak. With Holly Kendricks's shooting, she could slant it as an indictment of crime in suburban areas, or a warning to working women, or even imply she'd brought it on herself by not staying at home with her children. But she had to have facts to work with. This time she didn't have enough facts — all she could come up with were fantasies.

What if Lambert Senior had had Mercy killed? Then, when Wallace Junior came back, he found evidence of the murder in his father's safe deposit box and killed himself so he could rejoin his love in the afterlife? And what color straightjacket would they give Tilda to wear if she tried to print that?

Okay, what if Mercy followed Wallace Junior to Europe, and all those European heiresses he squired around were actually Mercy in disguise? She was an actress, after all. How hard could it be to come up with alternate identities and wardrobe, and then infiltrate society without anybody noticing? About as hard as it would be to swallow that shit.

Then there was the paranoid version. A crazed fan saw Mercy with Wallace Junior, just before Mr. Lambert separated them. As Mercy cried her eyes out, the doorbell rang, and she rushed to answer it, hoping without hope that her love had returned. Instead the crazed fan came in to profess his undying love, and when she refused him, killed her in a jealous rage. Still raging jealously, he hid the body someplace where it would never be found. Flash forward to Wallace Junior's return to the US, and the killer decides to kill him for being the man Mercy had loved instead of him. He'd have done it sooner, but couldn't afford the plane ticket to Paris. Flash forward many years, and for no rational reason, he starts striking out at the other people in Mercy's life, starting with her former costars.

Tilda decided that even Vincent couldn't have come up with that tangle of bad movie plots.

That was when she realized it was after midnight and she had yet to polish off the article and sidebar that were due on Monday. After all that effort, she still hadn't found Mercy, and it was time to put the quest aside. Maybe later on she'd get Vincent to do some Web hunting — he had sources she didn't. Maybe she'd come up with some more ideas. Of course, she had a lot of articles to work on, so it might be a while. She sighed, knowing that, realistically, it would probably be ages before she tried again.

She was about to shut down when her computer sounded the alert that she had more e-mail. Miss Flax, bless her heart, had tracked down some photos of the Lamberts, and thought Tilda might like to see them.

Tilda decided that a gift to accompany the thank-you note would not be amiss. Then she pretended that she hadn't already decided that this was a waste of time and looked at the first photo. Mr. Lambert might have been a tyrant, but he was an attractive one, and Mrs. Lambert was even more so.

There were later shots, with Mr. Lambert getting more distinguished over the years and Mrs. Lambert starting to look worn, probably from all the parties. Then she got plump, and a few months later, there was the baby picture from Wallace Junior's birth announcement. Tilda thought most newborns looked like Winston Churchill, and the appearance of the little Lambert did nothing to convince her otherwise.

More parties for the parents, then a shot of Mrs. Lambert's funeral, with the mourning father and son. Next came Wallace Junior's entree into society, standing next to his father in what was probably his very first tuxedo — a proud moment for any parent.

He was a good-looking kid, Tilda decided. He reminded her of somebody, somebody who had that clean-cut look. Tom Cruise? Brad Pitt? She opened the next file and looked at a shot of Wallace Junior alone. He looked even more familiar. She barely glanced at the next few, of the young heir with various candidates of the apparently endless supply of suitable young ladies, going past the fuzzy shot that had included Mercy and finally getting to the last picture — a clear shot of the mourners at Wallace Senior's funeral.

Tilda stared at the screen for what seemed like an hour. She finally had her fact, but she didn't know how the hell she was going to slant it.

CHAPTER 26

"Jumping the Shark: It's a moment. A defining moment when you know that your favorite television program has reached its peak. That instant that you know from now on . . . it's all downhill. Some call it the climax. We call it jumping the shark."
— Jon Hein, creator of jumptheshark.com

Tilda knew she wasn't going to be able to sleep, so she went to the kitchen and brewed a pot of coffee and gathered cheese and crackers to keep herself going. Then she used every bit of willpower she had to ignore the implications of that picture long enough to finish her *Kissing Cousins* article, including the sidebar about Rhonda's collection. Once she had the article out of the way, she focused her attentions elsewhere.

By that time it was nearly three, and maybe parts of Boston were still hopping, but it was deathly silent in Malden. Tilda purposely moved away from her keyboard so she could sit and think through what she knew and what she thought she knew and how she was going to be able to use it. By five o'clock she thought she had a way to pull it all together, but before she could get started, she needed sleep. She fell into bed.

She jerked awake as soon as the alarm went off at eight and, moving much more quietly than Heather ever did, she showered and put on fresh clothes. Then she headed for the subway, stopping briefly at Dunkin' Donuts for a fresh coffee transfusion and a bag of bribes.

Though she had a plan, or at least the bare outline of one, for it to work she was going to need help and lots of it. So her first step was to enlist Cooper. Since the situation wasn't something she wanted to discuss on the phone, at nine-thirty she rang his bell, fresh doughnuts in hand.

After administering CPR to help him recover from his heart attack at seeing her so early on a Saturday morning, she started explaining the whole mess to him. He wasn't easy to convince and had to have some points made more than once, but Tilda didn't mind. Every time she went through her reasoning, she became more and more convinced that she was right.

Finally he was willing to say, "Okay, I think what you've got is solid. But you don't have it all."

"I know that, but I've got as much as I'm going to get without doing something drastic."

"Entertainment reporters don't do things — you report things."

"Yeah? Then why did *Entertain Me!* have a cocktail party? Are you saying they weren't hoping some of the guests would have too much to drink and do something reportable? Why do we have the phrase 'media event' if we don't make our own news?"

"You're saying this is a media event?"

"Absolutely."

He thought about it, then said, "I see your point. If you really can't get any further without doing this —"

"I can't. I've tried to come up with another way, believe me."

"Then I'm in."

"I won't even bother to tote up how many I'm going to owe you — can we just assume that I'll owe you forever?"

"That should be about right."

They spent the rest of the weekend making detailed plans, calling around to see if what Tilda had in mind could be arranged in time, getting price estimates, and talking to the other people she needed. Tilda never went home — there was too much to do to waste time going back and forth — she just sacked out on the couch and borrowed T-shirts from Cooper as needed. Afterward she wasn't sure when or if she'd slept but was sure that she'd gone through a towering amount of takeout food and gallons of coffee.

On Monday morning they faced their last and most important hurdle. Tilda walked Cooper most of the way to the *Entertain Me!* office but ducked into the closest Dunkin' Donuts to sit and wait to hear from him. Never had she been so grateful for the chain's relentless market penetration — by that point there was considerably more coffee than blood in her veins.

Cooper was hoping to get to Jillian without Nicole being there to interfere — Jillian was due back from the editors' meeting, and since she usually came in early, his chances were good. Tilda almost wished she'd stayed where she could watch the front door, but she didn't want to risk being spotted.

By a few minutes after nine, when Tilda had read both *The Boston Globe* and *The Boston Herald,* completed both papers' Sudoku puzzles, and was trying to remember how to fold the sports section into an origami swan, her cell phone rang.

"Tilda? It's Cooper."

"Well?" she asked breathlessly.

"It's in the bag."

"You rock! How did you manage it?"

"Simple. When it looked like Jillian might turn us down, I told her that I'd talked to Bryce first, and that he hated the idea. Naturally she decided that she loves it."

"What about Nicole?"

"She's late! She called in with car trouble — she's still not here."

"There is a God."

"Jillian wants to talk to you, and I said you'd be here as soon as you finished your article for this week's issue."

"My article!"

"Tell me you didn't forget to write it."

"No, it's written — I just forgot to send it."

"Then bring your laptop and yourself over here."

"I'll be there in a few!"

When she walked into the *Entertain Me!* office, she swept past Nicole, who had apparently just arrived, to go to Jillian's desk.

"You look like shit," Jillian said.

"I know," Tilda said cheerfully. "But I got the story done."

Jillian nodded, acknowledging the fact,

but not wasting any words on congratulation or thanks. "Cooper told me about this promo idea you two cooked up. I think it's a winner."

"Great."

"What promo idea?" Nicole said, hopping up to hover over them. "Tilda didn't tell me about any promo idea."

"We didn't come up with it until this weekend," Tilda said truthfully, "so of course it only made sense to wait until Jillian got back to put it through channels." She smiled at Nicole. Or perhaps it was more of a smirk. To Jillian she said, "Are the numbers I sent you about right?"

Jillian pulled out a printout. "They look doable. I see you included a fudge factor."

Tilda nodded.

"Don't use it."

"Understood. Will Cooper be available this week to help me pull it all together?"

"As long as it doesn't get in the way of his regular work."

"What is this all about?" Nicole asked again. "Do you need me to help? I've got time this week."

"Is that right?" Jillian said frostily.

"I mean, if it's okay with you," she said hurriedly.

"I'm sure Tilda and Cooper will tell you if

they need you," Jillian said with an edge in her voice. Tilda had never been sure if Jillian truly trusted Nicole or if she was just giving her enough rope to hang herself, and she still wasn't sure. But since the conflict benefited her, she wasn't going to complain.

"Thanks for the offer, Nicole," Tilda said. "We'll let you know." She yawned. "As soon as I get my article handed in, I'm going to go home to catch a few z's before hitting the phones. I've been short on sleep all weekend."

"It shows," Nicole muttered.

It took only a few minutes to link into the magazine's network to e-mail her article. Tilda felt a little more kindly toward it now that she'd added a sidebar of her own. As she headed for the door, she saw Nicole making a beeline for Cooper to start picking his brain. She felt a little sorry for him, but not enough to delay her. As it was, she nearly conked out on the subway and was sound asleep precisely four minutes after she got back to her apartment.

The next few days were probably the busiest of Tilda's life, and she wondered why it was she thought being a freelancer was easier than having a real job. First she had to get in touch with the folks she needed for her plan and let them know it was definitely going to happen. Then she had to make plane and hotel reservations, arrange for limousines and security, and round up costumes and an endless variety of props and incidentals. Everybody involved had to be kept up to date, but different people needed different information, and it gave Tilda no end of problems keeping it all straight.

She also had to deal with Vincent's panic as the week went by. He was convinced that somebody was doomed to die on Thursday, though he couldn't make up his mind about who it would be, and though Tilda was sure everybody was safe, after a while she got nervous too. Finally she got Nick involved. He made a few calls and arranged for full-fledged security details to protect the surviving cast members. Still, Tilda guessed that Vincent didn't sleep all day Thursday — she didn't get to bed until well after midnight herself.

Finally it was Friday night, and Cooper insisted that she spend the night at his place. His stated reason was to make sure she drank enough wine to get a decent night's sleep, instead of being up all night worrying over details it was too late to change, but not so much as to give her a hangover the next morning. She knew the real reason was that he wanted to make sure she stayed alive until their plan came to fruition, but since she was in favor of the concept, she didn't argue.

CHAPTER 27

"A lot of teen shows like *Kissing Cousins* were forgotten on award night, but I used to tell the actors not to worry about awards. Awards are great to hang on your wall or put on your mantle, but they don't mean squat to a career. If you want a career, respect the fans. Take care of your fans, and they'll take care of you."
— Sophia Vaughn, quoted in "Curse of the *Kissing Cousins*," *Entertain Me!*

At eleven o'clock Saturday morning, Tilda was standing outside the Bayside Expo Center. The Beantown Collectibles Extravaganza had opened at ten, but while a few of the attendees had gone inside to start stocking up on must-have collectibles like McDonald's Happy Meal toys, pirated videos from British television shows, collector cereal boxes, and Neopets trading cards, the majority were waiting outside to see the arrival of the surviving members of the cast of *Kissing Cousins,* who were going to be reuniting for the first time since the show was canceled.

Had it been before the advent of the Web, Tilda doubted she could have gotten the word out in time. Or rather, she doubted Vincent, Rhonda, and Javier would have been able to — they'd been burning up the Internet ever since she'd called them on Monday to let them know that *Entertain Me!* was sponsoring the event. They were so excited that she'd hardly needed the bribes she'd offered them. Except for Javier of course.

Tilda had considered arriving with the Cousins, but had decided she'd rather be there to watch and, if necessary, direct the photographer and videographer Jillian had sent. More importantly, she wanted to watch the crowd. So far she hadn't spotted the face she was looking for, but she could easily have missed it in the mass of fans. And what an enthusiastic mass they were.

They were armed with cameras, autograph books, and memorabilia to be signed; and carrying posters professing their love for whichever Cousin they favored or just "*Kissing Cousins* 4-Ever!" The were dressed in *Kissing Cousins* T-shirts — the one Tilda liked best said "Cousin Kisser" — and surprisingly elaborate costumes from the show. She saw three blondes in cheerleader costumes more or less identical to Sherri's, two biker dudes, a lab-coated scientist drinking something green from a beaker, and at least a dozen Mercy look-alikes in various guises, including three in the lacy black dress and veiled hat from the homecoming dance episode.

Somewhere in the crowd, Tilda was sure, was a killer.

Just after eleven, the first black limo pulled into the parking lot. There were cheers until the limo turned so the crowd could see the banner on the door that said "Gabby & Gwen." Tilda knew the twins would have been awfully unhappy if they'd heard the disappointed murmurs, including the start of a chant of "shark jumpers." Then the limo driver and a tuxedo-clad Vincent hopped out to open the two doors simultaneously, and, in unison, out stepped the twins. The fans gasped.

No Barbie outfits, no hair ribbons on bouncy pony tails. Their hair hung down, though Gwendolyn's looked shorter because she'd curled it into ringlets while Gabrielle had left her straight. Both of their dresses had corset bodices with long filmy skirts, and they were wearing ridiculously high heels. But Gwendolyn's outfit was pastel pink, with white stockings and pumps, while Gabrielle was in black, and the fishnet stockings she wore with black ankle boots were red. The two posed for photos, Gwendolyn looking sweet but flirtatious, and Gabrielle looking not at all sweet and even more flirtatious. The crowd broke out into applause.

Cooper, who'd been the twins' stylist and was now acting as emcee, stepped up to them with a portable microphone and said, "Welcome to Boston, Gabby and Gwen. Is there anything you'd like to say to the fans?"

Gwen said, "We're both so happy to be here with all of you. Working on *Kissing Cousins* was such an awesome experience, and you fans are the best." Then she looked sad. "Though I guess some people think our joining the cast was when the show jumped the shark."

There were shouted denials, including one from a guy who was surreptitiously stuffing a poster of a shark eating the twins into a trash can.

Then Gabrielle said, "Jump the shark? I thought we were supposed to hump the shark. And I say, bring on that bad boy."

This time, the applause was thunderous.

With that as an exit line, Vincent offered one arm to each to escort them inside, looking as if he were caught betwixt heaven and hell and loving every minute of it. A phalanx of security guards, some in the uniforms of the expo center and some in black T-shirts with "SECURITY" emblazoned on the back, opened a corridor through the crowd and inside the center.

The fans were so busy watching the twins strut away that they hardly noticed when the next limo pulled up. This one was labeled "Felicia," and there were scattered hisses in the crowd as well as a new chant: "Tattletale." When the limo driver opened the door, Kat Owen stepped out, dressed in a striking plum pantsuit with an Hermès scarf around her neck and wearing the kind of gold earrings fashion writers call important. She beamed confidently at the crowd.

Cooper offered his welcome and the microphone, which she accepted with a smile. "I'm so glad to be here to meet up with my old friends. Now some people say I was a Goody Two-shoes on *Kissing Cousins,* and it's true that Felicia didn't drink and didn't smoke. I'm still that way myself. Don't drink, don't smoke." She paused while Cooper surreptitiously turned on a backup tape, then ripped into a cover of

"Goody Two Shoes" by Adam Ant.

The crowd went crazy. They sang along, they bopped in place, a few even danced across the parking lot. Some of them had decent moves too, Tilda was pleased to see. The *Entertain Me!* photographer and videographer were even more pleased.

When Kat finished, there were shouts of "Encore, encore!" but the singer only smiled and handed the microphone back to Cooper before letting Javier walk her into the expo center, escorted by more security people.

The next limo, bannered "Elbert," drove up. The chauffeur came around, opened the door, and stood at attention. Nothing happened. A minute passed. The crowd grew restless. Finally the chauffeur reached into the limo and came out with a white lab coat in one hand. The man shrugged his shoulders, then reached into his pocket, produced a packet of powder, and threw it down onto the parking lot. There was a flash and smoke and more than a few yelps of surprise. As the smoke cleared, Tilda saw that the chauffeur had shed his cap and livery, and had pulled on the lab coat. As everybody watched, he produced goggles from a pocket, put them on, and in his trademark squeaky voice gave Elbert's trademark line: "Time to go back to the lab." Noel Clark, sitcom scientist and soap opera chauffeur, had arrived, showing no ill effects from his recent poisoning.

There was a pause and Tilda was afraid the joke had fallen flat — it had been a gamble, but the man couldn't sing and he couldn't very well dress like the twins. Then she heard a chuckle, and another, and soon laughter was running through the crowd. Noel bowed, nodded at Cooper's welcome speech, and repeated his line for the mike. The fans said it with him, and went on to chant it as his security people got him inside. Rhonda had been the only actual passenger in the limo, and she emerged with a big grin on her face to walk in with Noel.

There was one limo left, and the crowd grew quiet as it pulled up. This banner said "Mercy." The driver came around to hand out a figure in yet another version of Mercy's homecoming dress, but this one was — though not the actual dress — almost indistinguishable from the original. Even Cooper seemed daunted by the presence and barely remembered to give his welcome spiel. The veiled figure didn't reach for the microphone, only raised one gloved hand to the crowd in greeting before taking Cooper's arm. They swept inside to the sound of cheers.

The *Kissing Cousins* had arrived.

CHAPTER 28

"Episode 15: Cousins Detective Agency
When Brad is accused of stealing a wallet from a fellow team member's locker and gets suspended from the football team, the Cousins join forces to find the real thief. They stage a denouement involving Sherri and Mercy dressing to distract, Elbert and Felicia booby-trapping other lockers, and Damon intimidating witnesses, but it's Brad himself who catches the supposed victim retrieving the wallet from a hiding place. He'd faked the theft to get Brad off the team so he could be quarterback."
— Fanboy's Online *Kissing Cousins*
Episode Guide, by Vincent Peters

Once Mercy disappeared inside, the throng on the sidewalk started making its own way into the expo center. The cast was scheduled to appear on stage in an hour and a half, but in the meantime there was plenty of memorabilia to look at and buy. Tilda passed the intriguing displays to go through to the back of the hall, where the celebrity guests had been stashed in private rooms just off the exhibit hall. A cluster of reporters, photographers, and cameramen were waiting at the door to the secured area, but the security guard kept waving them back, saying, "Give us a few minutes to get them settled, and you'll have your chance." Tilda sailed right past them, quite enjoying the grumbles she left in her wake.

The door opened onto a long corridor lined with more doors. Though each of the cast members had been assigned a private room for downtime and interviews, as Tilda walked past the twins' room, she saw Kat and Noel were crowded in with Gabrielle and Gwendolyn, all of them chattering like . . . like former stars who'd just been given the kind of attention they hadn't received in years. Cooper was pouring champagne provided by *Entertain Me!* as the performers congratulated one another on their entrances. They hadn't been able to rehearse, and the performers were clearly stoked from having nailed it. Vincent, Rhonda, and Javier were in there too, looking as happy as only fans getting personal time with celebrities can be.

Cooper caught sight of Tilda and called for her to join them, but she only waved and kept going. The door on the very end was labeled for Mercy, and she tapped on the door and let herself in. The room's one inhabitant was sitting on a battered vinyl sofa, still wearing the veil.

"Are you okay?" Tilda asked.

A nod was the only response.

"Do you need anything?"

A shake of the head.

"I'm sorry you missed everybody else's entrances — they were spectacular! Even better than we'd hoped." She went on to give more details, but after a few minutes, she realized she was babbling. "You can watch the video later, if you want to." She paused. "Are you nervous?"

Another head shake.

"Good," she said. "There's no reason to be nervous."

A gesture for Tilda to come sit on the couch. She did, but found it somehow disturbing to have only a veil to look at.

As if sensing her discomfort, her companion reached for Tilda's hand and squeezed, then pulled the hand up under the veil and kissed her palm.

Tilda knew it was the absolute wrong time

to be aroused, but it was impossible not to be, especially when a greedy mouth sucked in one of her fingers. Tilda's heart, already beating fast from nervousness, went even faster.

She was wondering how much further they were going to go when the door to the room opened and a man stepped inside and quietly closed the door behind him. He didn't bother to lock it — the nasty-looking pistol aimed at them was plenty enough to keep them in place.

"Bitches!" he hissed. "Disgusting, perverted bitches!" His normally handsome face, with the tan Tilda had so admired, was blotchy red with fury.

"Hello, Lawrence," Tilda said as calmly as she could. "Or should I call you Wallace?" Without making any sudden moves, she scooted far enough away on the couch to leave room to maneuver. "Are you here for an exclusive?"

"I'm here to end this once and for all," he said, looking directly at the veiled figure. "I'm just sorry it's going to be quick — I'd like to drag it out to make you pay for all the years it's taken me to find you. If I could, I'd make you tell me where you've been hiding." He barked a kind of laugh. "Hell, it doesn't matter. I found you. I win."

Tilda said, "Found her? Dude, her appearance here was in the *Globe,* on TV, and all over the Internet. A cockroach could have found her."

"Shut up! You're dead too."

A gloved hand lifted to warn Tilda to be quiet, but it wasn't something she needed to be told. Her intent was to distract the man, not make him act faster.

Lawrence barked, "Take off that damned hat. I want to see your face before I blow it off."

Slowly, deliberately, the black-clad figure reached up and lifted the veil and then the hat. Knowing what had been hidden, Tilda was watching Lawrence, and she saw his face go slack with shock when he realized it wasn't Mercy after all. It was Nick Tolomeo.

Lawrence's hand shook just for a second, but that was long enough for Nick to fling the hat into the other man's face. Then he shoved Tilda to the floor and flung himself at Lawrence. Tilda threw her arms over her head, waiting for a gunshot, but instead there was the sound of men bursting into the room and tackling Lawrence. Dom, who'd led the way, was the one to wrest the gun out of Lawrence's hand, and he stepped back with it as the other security guards handcuffed the killer's arms behind his back, despite his kicking, spitting, and truly impressive cursing. It took four men to drag him off, and Tilda couldn't help but wince when she saw his head bouncing off the floor. She already knew where they were taking him. Out in the loading area, where the fans couldn't see, a van was waiting to deliver Lawrence to the nearest police station.

Tilda heard worried voices coming from the twins' room, but she also heard a security guard assuring them that everything was okay.

Nick helped her up off of the floor. "Are you okay?"

"Peachy. You?"

He grinned. "I'm stoked! We got the bastard!"

"You got the bastard. And we didn't get shot. That's a plus."

"Hey, I'm wearing my vest. You wore the one I gave you too, right?"

"Do I look like an idiot? I'm not the hero around here."

"You are to me. You're the one who figured it all out."

"And you're the one who wore the outfit that might as well have had a bull's-eye painted on it." She inspected the right sleeve of the dress. "And tore it. Vincent will be very distressed." She hadn't asked Vincent why he had just happened to have an ersatz Mercy dress big enough for a man, and didn't intend to.

"It's not my color anyway," Nick said. "I think I'm more of an autumn."

Dom said, "Hey, Nicky, you coming with us? The cops are going to want to talk to you."

"Sure thing, Pop, there's just two things I've got to do first." He took hold of Tilda's shoulders and kissed her thoroughly. "That's to remind you that I'm secure in my masculinity, dress or no dress."

"I wouldn't dream of arguing with you," she said, a little out of breath. "What's the other thing?"

"I've got to take off this getup. If the cops see me in it, I'll never live it down."

After making sure Nick and his father were on their way and agreeing to meet them at the police station, Tilda stopped to check on the other Cousins. Noel hugged her to thank her for catching the man who'd nearly killed him, and Cooper hugged her because they'd brought their scheme off successfully. Then Kat offered a quick prayer that everybody was safe, to which Tilda added a heartfelt amen. She even crossed herself for the first time in ages. The twins were more subdued, and Tilda suspected Lawrence had managed to bed at least one of them, if not both. It was another question she didn't intend to ask.

As for Vincent, Javier, and Rhonda, they were happily using their pocket electronics to get the word out to the fan world, so she didn't bother them.

When she got back to the security checkpoint, it was obvious that the reporters who'd hung on had scented blood in the water, but they didn't know what had happened, and it was driving them crazy. Fortunately nobody recognized Tilda, so she walked on by.

CHAPTER 29

"Episode 72: The Happiest of Endings
(One-hour series finale.) When the two
older boys graduate from high school,
they're surprised to see Brad's father and
Damon's mother at the ceremony. The
parents clash instantly, and both decide to
take their kids away. The kids, now that
they're to be separated, realize they've
become a family. Meanwhile, Pops "accidentally" locks the feuding parents in the
garage, and by the time they're found,
they've fallen in love. Dad decides to leave
the Army, and Mom announces that what
she really wants is a husband and family.
The Cousins are going to be step-siblings."
— Fanboy's Online *Kissing Cousins*
Episode Guide, by Vincent Peters

That night Tilda enjoyed a festive dinner
with Nick, Dom, Cooper, the Kissing Cousins, and the triumvirate of fans, followed by

a more private, mutually satisfying affirmation of life with Nick. The next morning she finished up another story for *Entertain Me!* bowing to its inevitable title, "Reversing the Curse of the *Kissing Cousins*." As soon as it was done and e-mailed to Jillian, she hopped onto a train to New York.

In a near repeat performance of her last visit, Tilda arrived at Penn Station, directed the cab to The Palm, picked up two orders of prime rib with the appropriate sides, and arrived at Sophia's condo, where Bill walked her up and picked out his tip from the cookie jar while Juan took the food and disappeared into the kitchen. At least Tilda was fairly sure it was the same Juan.

Sophia, this time wearing glorious yellow-gold, smiled widely when she saw her. "Tilda, you're exactly who I've been wanting to talk to. Tell me everything! How did you know that Lawrence White was the killer? What did he do when you caught him?"

Tilda didn't bother to ask how the older woman had gotten wind of it all. It had been over twenty-four hours, so there'd been plenty of time for the news to reach her by whatever mysterious methods she used. "I'll give you every detail," she promised, "but first I want to ask you a question."

Sophia arched one eyebrow, but said, "Ask away."

"Are you a lesbian or bisexual?"

Tilda had expected shock, denial, or at least some small loss of composure. What she got was a belly laugh.

"I knew you'd figure it out!" Sophia said with one last chortle. "Juan!" she called out, "I win! You owe me a week without pay." If Juan was concerned about his loss, he kept it to himself. Her attention back on Tilda, Sophia said, "Bi, of course. I'm more of a gourmand than a gourmet when it comes to the bedroom. Why limit myself to pretty boys when there are so many pretty girls around?"

"Was Mercy one of your conquests?"

Sophia's smile didn't exactly fade, but it somehow became sadder. "No, not a conquest. I may actually have loved Mercy."

"Are you still together?"

"No, that's long since over." The smile was definitely a sad one.

"But you did help her disappear, didn't you?"

"How did you figure that out?"

"An educated guess. Lawrence was a little bit quicker than we expected, and he caught our faux Mercy giving me a kiss. Just on the hand, but from the way he freaked, you'd have thought we were dancing with a double-headed dildo. That's when I started wondering if the person Mercy had left him for had been a woman, not a man."

"Whoa there, partner! Start at the beginning. How did you put the two of them together in the first place?"

Tilda sat down and reached for the glass of Dr Pepper Juan was handing to her. "I found a photo of Mercy and a very young Lawrence in a Palm Springs newspaper. It wasn't a good shot, so I didn't recognize him, especially since the caption said his name was Wallace Lambert, Junior."

"That's the name I knew him under. I wondered if he might have changed it."

"My first thought was that Lambert might know where Mercy was, and I tracked down the society columnist who published the picture and got the lowdown on him. I was doing my best to glue on some fairy-tale ending until the society writer sent me a better picture from his father's funeral. That's when I realized that Wallace Lambert and Lawrence White were one and the same." Tilda put down the Dr Pepper, reached into her satchel for copies she'd made of both pictures, and handed them to Sophia.

Sophia held the pictures at arm's length,

then ruefully opened a drawer in the table next to her to pull out a pair of reading glasses to take a better look. "You've got a good eye," she said. "I don't know that I'd have realized it was the same man."

"I've made a career of comparing stars' younger selves to their older versions — I think he's had some work done, and of course he dyes his hair, but I knew it was him. Anyway, I was told that Wallace — or Lawrence — had been dating Mercy, but his father didn't approve, so Daddy sent him to Europe to separate them. But there was more to it than that, wasn't there?"

"God, yes. Mercy met Lambert between the second and third seasons of the show, and she fell for him hard. He was cultured, educated, and from a good family — everything Mercy thought she wasn't. Lawrence seemed to be just as in love with her as she was with him."

"So why didn't this make the gossip columns?"

"They worked hard to keep it secret. On her side, she knew the studio wouldn't approve of her dating somebody who looked so much older, even though they were close to the same age. As for Lawrence, the one time they did go out publicly, his father threw a major tantrum. The snobby bastard didn't approve of his son and heir dating a woman with no family connections, so he forbade him from seeing her again. Naturally, being young and in love, they took the relationship underground. Secrecy probably only added to the romance of it all, at least for a while."

"Then what happened?"

"Despite Lawrence's claims that he liked Mercy just the way she was, he started trying to remake her into his own image. Or maybe into an image of which his father would approve. Mercy was smitten, but she wasn't smitten enough to let that happen. They argued, and one day he got physical."

"He hit her?"

"He gave her a black eye you wouldn't believe."

"Jesus," Tilda said. The black eye Jasmine the makeup artist had had to conceal hadn't been caused by a fall, after all.

"Mercy was no fool — she knew a black eye one day meant broken bones the next. So she told him she didn't want to see him again. Between that and Lambert Senior keeping him on a tight leash, that worked for a few months. Then he showed up at her apartment one night, drunk and demanding that she start seeing him again. Mercy called the cops to chase him off.

Even though she didn't press charges, I heard about it through a snitch at the police department — I was still living in LA at the time, God only knows why. I went snooping to see if there was anything I could print, and found her terrified that he'd come back."

"But you didn't print anything about it?"

Sophia looked affronted. "I've passed up plenty of stories, missy!"

"Even when you weren't hot for the subject?"

Sophia allowed a small grin. "Not as many, but even then. Anyway, I took her in and . . . and comforted her."

"Was she bi?"

"I was her first woman," Sophia said with a hint of pride, but then admitted, "Honestly, I don't think she would have wanted to be with me under other circumstances. I didn't mean to take advantage of her — I don't think I did, anyway — but she turned to me. It didn't last long, just a couple of months. I wish it had lasted longer, for her sake."

"What do you mean? What happened?"

"It was after she started work on that movie. She hadn't heard anything from Lambert in such a long time that she decided it was safe to move back to her own place. That second weekend after she started filming — when she was so happy about working on an honest-to-God movie — she came home and found Lambert in her house, waiting for her. He was enraged. He said no cheap slut actress was going to turn him down. He'd heard about us too — I don't think he knew it was me, but he knew Mercy had been seeing a woman, and it made him crazy."

The older woman took a swallow of her own drink, and Tilda was sure it wasn't Dr Pepper. She both wanted to know, and didn't want to know, what came next.

"He beat her. Then he raped her. And beat her some more. He may have raped her again — she wasn't sure what was happening by that point. Only that it hurt."

"Jesus," Tilda whispered.

"But she never stopped fighting," Sophia said proudly. "She never stopped screaming. And finally, thank God, somebody heard her. A yardman was doing the grass next door, and when nobody answered the bell, he looked through the window and saw what that animal was doing. He broke down the front door and pulled him off of her. Lambert wasn't armed and the yardman had pruning shears, so Lambert ran away.

"The yardman called the police and an

ambulance, and Mercy called me. I met her at the hospital, and once I was sure she was going to live, I went out into the hall and called the best doctors in town and made them come out immediately. Then I went out into the parking lot, crawled into my car, locked the doors, and cried." Her voice broke. "She was so . . . She looked so . . . God, I'd never seen anybody hurt like that."

"What did he do to her?"

"Broken arm, cracked cheekbone, and I don't know how many broken ribs. Bruises everywhere, cigarette burns, tears in . . . She was torn. Her chin was split open, but at least he didn't use a knife."

"Then he never went to Europe. He was in prison."

"The bastard never saw the inside of a cell!" Sophia snapped. "By the time Mercy's ambulance arrived, Lambert's daddy had him lawyered up. They spun an alibi for him and spent enough money to make sure that the cops didn't poke too many holes in it."

"But Mercy could have testified against him."

"Her word against his. Who would they believe? An actress, or the ultrarespectable heir to a fortune?"

"What about the yardman?"

"He was willing to be a witness, but he

was illegal. He nearly got deported."

"What happened to him?"

To Tilda's bemusement, Juan answered, having just come in with fresh drinks. "Miss Sophia got him a green card," he said. "He is my uncle." He replaced their glasses with full ones, and left again.

Tilda turned to Sophia, and realized the woman looked almost embarrassed. "It was the least I could do," she muttered. "He saved her life."

"You've been getting green cards for his family ever since, haven't you?"

Sophia ignored her. "Anyway, I wanted to see that bastard in prison for the rest of his natural life — I called in every outstanding favor I had — but I couldn't make it happen. Finally I realized that there was no way Lambert Junior was ever going to trial. The best I could manage was to insist that Lambert Senior send him away and keep him away. I told him that unless he did, I'd spread the real story to every gossip columnist in the country. If he wanted to try to sue me, he could go ahead and try, but that would only make it a bigger story. Lambert Senior was desperate to keep the lid on, so he agreed. Junior was on his way to Europe days later, and I transferred Mercy to a private hospital under an assumed name for the next two months. Of course, she had to give up the movie role."

"Why didn't she go back to work after she recovered? I know her reputation must have suffered, but with your connections, she could have started over."

"She thought about it," Sophia said, "but how long would it be before Lambert Junior came back? We knew his father couldn't keep him in Europe forever. Besides, there was nothing to stop him from hiring somebody else to finish the job he'd started. We even caught a guy snooping around the hospital and knew he had to be hired muscle. That's when we got full-time security and when Mercy realized that Lambert was never going to give up on her. She decided that the only way to escape him was to disappear. I had the money and the friends to help her."

"You saved her life," Tilda said.

"I have no doubt of that," Sophia said. "I kept an eye on Lambert Junior as best I could, but I had to be careful to make sure I didn't draw attention to myself."

"I don't blame you — I wouldn't want him coming after me, either."

"That, and I was afraid he'd beat Mercy's

location out of me. I'd seen what he could do, and I had no illusions that I could stand up to that."

Tilda wasn't so sure — she thought Sophia was one of the toughest women she'd ever met, and she'd learned nothing so far to change her mind.

Sophia went on. "After Lambert Senior died and Junior got his hands on the family money, I lost track of him."

"That's where I picked him up," Tilda said. "When I realized that Lawrence White was Wallace Lambert, I knew he was the killer. Why else would he have lied about knowing Mercy? So I did some research. He must have bought himself a new identity, because he showed up as Lawrence White in Los Angeles a few months after his father's funeral. I suspect he pulled the old trick of using a dead infant's name to get a birth certificate and social security number." Actually it had been Nick who speculated that, and Vincent who helped her find the man's tracks on the Web, but like Sophia, she preferred not to give up all her secrets. "With his privileged upbringing, and a veneer of European styling, he had no trouble getting himself invited to the right parties to start covering the industry. But he never gave up searching for Mercy — in fact, that may be why he got into the business in the first place." For a moment, Tilda considered the idea that Lawrence's and her motivations hadn't been all that different — her affection for Mercy's character had been why she'd started writing entertainment features too. The difference, of course, was that she hadn't wanted to kill her idol. "Anyway, once I made the connection between Lawrence and Wallace Junior, I decided to lay a trap for him."

"Why the play-acting? Why not just set the police on him?"

"One, it made for better copy." Tilda knew that Sophia wouldn't question that. "And two, we did get the cops. Dom Tolomeo had a connection on the Weldon police force, and they tried to find evidence that Lawrence had been in town the day Holly Kendricks was killed. There was none. Maybe they could have found some eventually, but our way was quicker, and safer for the rest of the Kissing Cousins. We didn't want to risk Lawrence finally finding Mercy, or going after Noel again, or Kat, or the twins."

"What set him off anyway?" Sophia asked. "Why did he strike at the other Cousins now? Tilda, I swear I'd have said something if I'd thought it was him. Sure, I knew he was capable of murder, but I didn't see what

405

his motive could be."

"He didn't have a motive," Tilda said. "At least, not at first. It's all about slanting stories."

"Excuse me?"

"You know that reporters can slant the same story for multiple markets because different people read different things into the same set of facts."

"Freelancer's 101. So?"

"Apparently Lawrence read something into "Curse of the *Kissing Cousins*" that I never put there. He was a killer, in his fantasies if not yet in reality, and when he read about the two deaths, his first thought was that there was a killer at work. Or rather, another killer."

"Another killer? Then the first two Cousins were killed by somebody else?"

"Nope. Both deaths were accidents, just like the cops said. Lawrence only interpreted the deaths as murders."

"I read that article — you don't even hint that those men were murdered."

"I don't say anything about a curse, either, but that's what my editor saw when she read it, and that's why she came up with that title. People read in what they want to, or what they're sensitive to, or whatever."

"And what Lawrence read was that there

was a killer going after the Cousins?"

"I think so. Remember that he'd been hunting Mercy for years, but he'd run out of leads long ago. He followed all the news about the cast members, and even lurked on the *Kissing Cousins* Listserv, just in case something gave him a clue. The man was obsessed. Who knows how many fantasy scenarios he's whacked off to."

"There's a vivid image."

"I am a writer. Anyway, he was afraid that this imaginary killer would get to Mercy before he did, and he just couldn't stand the idea of somebody else killing her instead of him."

"That's sick."

"He's one twisted son of a bitch," Tilda agreed. "He may also have seen it as an opportunity. He could kill Mercy and let the other killer take the blame."

"Assuming he could find her before the other killer, that is."

"Right. Since he was getting desperate, he did the same thing I did — he went to the other cast members, starting with Holly. Only he wasn't content to just ask questions, not when he could beat the information out of her. Of course, she didn't know where Mercy was, but he wouldn't believe her. Either he killed her while trying to make her talk, or he realized she didn't know anything and killed her to cover his tracks. Then he came to her funeral, hoping Mercy would show."

"She wanted to," Sophia said. "I talked her out of it."

"And saved her life again. That's where he met me, and became convinced that I was onto something." Tilda cleared her throat. "I may have implied that I knew more than I actually did."

"Again, Freelancer's 101," Sophia said. "Never let the competition know what's really going on."

"He was getting more and more desperate, so he started keeping an eye on me. It was no accident that he showed up here in New York when I was here."

"He was here?" Sophia said.

"I let him take me to dinner, but passed on his offer of dessert." Remembering that she'd actually been tempted sickened her. "I don't know if he was trying to pick my brain or my laptop when he tried to sweet-talk his way into my hotel room, but he didn't get a chance at either. The next day, when he found out I was on my way back to Boston but would be busy for a good while, he hopped onto a plane so he could go to Malden and break into my apartment."

"I didn't know you'd had a break-in."

"At first, I didn't realize it myself. I saw traces of somebody snooping, but I thought it was my roommate's latest boy toy. Fortunately, I hadn't left any paper notes to be found and Lawrence couldn't get into my computer. So he couldn't find out what I was up to." Tilda ruefully added, "Not that I was up to anything useful at that point."

"But he didn't know that."

"No, because I'd exaggerated my progress. So he was starting to panic. On one hand, he hoped I'd smoke out Mercy so he could get to her, but on the other hand, he wanted to get to her first. He hung around Boston, dogging my steps, trying to find out what I knew. When that wasn't working, he decided to go after more of the cast members to try to smoke Mercy out, going by the timeline a fan came up with to predict the killer's next move so he could preserve the illusion of a serial killer. Since he was still trying to stay reasonably close to me, he mailed the poisoned candy to Noel Clark instead of going after him directly. The son of a bitch even used my name on the package!"

"That may have been his biggest mistake," Sophia said. "That's what put you on his trail, isn't it?"

"Probably. I might have given up if it hadn't been for my being so damned mad. Anyway, it was obvious that the one thing that could bring him out into the open was Mercy, so I announced that she was going to be appearing at the collectibles show, knowing that he'd hear about it. The rest was just window dressing. I wasn't planning to go Jessica Fletcher on him, but events overcame me."

"Sounds more like *Scooby-Doo* than *Murder, She Wrote.*"

"Yeah, the trap and pulling off the disguise is more *Scooby-Doo.* Jinkies. Just tell me I'm Velma, and not Daphne."

"How about Velma's brains with Daphne's looks?"

"I'll accept that."

Juan came in to let them know that their dinner was laid out.

"Maybe I should pay for dinner this time," Sophia said as they sat down.

Though Tilda was tempted to accept, for the historical value if nothing else, she shook her head. "This is on *Entertain Me!*"

"You mean you haven't written the story yet?"

"Of course I have. But the trip is going to get folded into my expenses somewhere — Nicole will take care of it."

"Nicole? The one who hates you."

"More importantly, the one who's been feeding information to Lawrence. When the cops checked the history on his cell phone, they found a number of calls to and from her extension, so they pulled her in for questioning."

"She was helping him?" Sophia said, shocked.

"Yes and no. She didn't know about the murder. She just thought he was trying to steal the story out from under me."

Sophia sounded even more shocked when she said, "She was helping him steal a story?" As a former editor, she probably found that idea even more appalling.

Tilda nodded. "He mentioned her name when I met him — they'd met at some party or another. I don't know if she was a notch on his bedpost or not, but he knew her well enough to know how to manipulate her. He said if she helped him get this story, he'd use his connections to get her a better job at a bigger magazine — I think he was dangling *Entertainment Weekly* or *People* in front of her."

"And she fell for that?"

"She may or may not have believed him, but the temptation of scooping me was more than she could pass up."

"That's outrageous. I mean, helping some-body steal a story from her own magazine. And putting you in danger, of course."

"A double helping of sin, to be sure."

"Did you get her ass fired?"

"Where's the fun in that? No, I'm keeping her dirty little secrets, just as long as she behaves herself."

Sophia cackled, but asked, "Won't her role come out at the trial?"

"It might, but that could be a year or more, and she might come up with a better excuse by then. In the meantime, I'll keep milking it."

Sophia cackled again, and Tilda couldn't resist a cackle or two herself.

They took their time over dinner, with Sophia asking for more details. It wasn't until dessert was over and they were back in the living room that Tilda asked the other question she'd come to New York to ask.

"You know where Mercy is, don't you?"

"Yes, I do. I've known all along." Sophia hesitated. "I didn't like lying to you, Tilda, but I gave her my word."

"You mean you put her safety above the needs of a fangirl reporter? For shame!" Tilda said mockingly. "Hell, you know I'd do the same thing in your position. It's just that . . ."

"What?"

"Is she happy?"

Sophia smiled. "Yes, she's happy. She has a very nice life. Not in the industry, of course, but she's loved and she's safe. That's more than a lot of us ever get."

"But it's over now, right? She can come out of hiding."

"Not yet," Sophia said. "The bastard could make bail, or even manage to get off. He's still got money, which means he can still afford the best lawyers. She's waited this long — she can wait a little longer, to be sure."

Tilda thought about it. Now that she knew that Sophia had been in recent contact with Mercy, she was reasonably sure she could find her if she tried hard enough. She could even use a bit of emotional blackmail — if Mercy had spoken out about Lawrence years back, Holly Kendricks wouldn't have been killed. *Entertain Me!* would pay handsomely for the story, or she could pitch it elsewhere as a cautionary tale about how even the famous can be abused.

Nick had once asked if she'd ever found anybody who didn't want to be found, and she'd told him there was no such animal. Now she knew different, and the question she had to ask herself was would she try to find somebody who had a good reason not to be found.

The answer was no.

So she sighed and looked disgusted with the situation. "Fine, but if she ever decides to come in out of the cold, I get the first crack at her. Deal?"

"Deal," Sophia said.

They rehashed events for most of the rest of the night, but there was one part of the story Tilda didn't tell Sophia, and didn't intend to.

CHAPTER 30

" 'It's always sad to see a show end,' our beloved Mercy admitted, 'but nothing can take away the joy of having touched people's lives in some small way.' When asked about her plans, the sable-haired star would only say, 'The world is full of challenges — I don't know what's next, but I do know that I'll never forget my fans.' "

— "The Cousins' Good-bye Kisses,"
Teen Fave

It happened when Tilda was on her way out of the expo center. Though she knew that Nick and Dom would be waiting for her, she couldn't resist taking a few minutes to check out the exhibit of *Kissing Cousins* memorabilia, including Rhonda's collection, minus two pieces. First, Tilda had bought the issue of *Teen Fave* with Nick's picture to give to him. And second, Tilda had bought the album with the photo that had led Tilda to Lawrence — it was in her car, ready to take to the police, along with printouts of the photos Miss Flax had sent. The cops could keep the printouts, but the album was only on loan. Tilda was keeping it for herself.

Before she left, she went to take a look at the stage that had been dressed for the Kissing Cousins' upcoming appearance. Vincent, Rhonda, and Javier had worked for hours to create a reproduction of the Cousins' rec room — half in school pennants and cute puppy posters and half in Goth trappings and a Harley calendar — and they'd done an amazing job. The security guards were letting fans walk through, one or two at a time, to look more closely and even take photos of themselves in front of Elbert's lab equipment or holding Brad's football.

Tilda hated to miss the moment when the Cousins came on stage, but the *Entertain Me!* photographer would be there to capture it, so she wasn't needed. She already had her story. Besides, she was just as glad she wasn't going to be there when Cooper had to announce that Mercy wasn't there after all. People were going to be disappointed. She was disappointed herself, but wherever the woman was, at least now she was safe from Lawrence.

As if in answer to her thoughts, one of the many Mercy clones stepped onto the stage and sat in the black velvet-covered womb chair that Mercy had favored. Tilda wished the *Entertain Me!* photographer were handy. The woman's dress was perfect, so she lifted her cell phone camera to take a shot herself. It wouldn't be good enough for the magazine, but Vincent would like it.

She was trying to focus when the woman lifted her veil. Tilda was impressed. Other than a scar on her chin, the woman strongly resembled Mercy, though she was too old for the part. She was closer to Mercy's current age than to the actress's age when the show was filmed.

The woman caught Tilda's eye and smiled a crooked Mona Lisa smile. Just like Mercy.

Exactly like Mercy.

For a moment Tilda couldn't breathe, and though the room had been too noisy a second before, suddenly she couldn't hear a thing. The camera was still in her hand, aimed and ready, but she didn't even push the button. She just stared at the woman, knowing that it was really her. After all those years, it was really Mercy.

Tilda didn't know how long they'd have stayed like that if the exhibit guard hadn't

417

come up and gestured for the woman — for Mercy — to leave and let somebody else have a chance.

Mercy lowered her veil and stepped off the stage and into the crowd. Freelance reporter Tilda Harper should have been right on her heels, demanding to know where she'd been and why she was there, but Matilda Harper, the gawky teenager who'd idolized the character, just stood there with her mouth half open until somebody elbowed her aside to get at a bin of posters. By then it was too late to go after Mercy, even if she'd wanted to.

She hadn't told anybody yet — someday she might tell Nick, or June, or Vincent, or Sophia — but, for now, she wanted to keep it to herself that she'd finally found Mercy.

ABOUT THE AUTHOR

Award-winning author **Toni L. P. Kelner** has spent far too many hours watching old TV shows, and admits that seeing one rerun of *The Brady Bunch* too many inspired this novel. She is the author of the eight Laura Fleming mysteries and has published a number of short stories. *Many Bloody Returns,* a vampire anthology coedited with Charlaine Harris, is her most recent release. Kelner has won an Agatha Award for Best Short Story and an *RT BOOKclub* Career Achievement Award, and has been nominated for the Anthony, the Macavity, and the *RT BOOKclub* Reviewers' Choice Award. She lives in Massachusetts with her husband, fellow author Stephen P. Kelner, and their two daughters.